THE ROVING TREE

THE ROVING TREE

BY ELSIE AUGUSTAVE

AKASHIC BOOKS

OPEN LENS

Published by Akashic Books/Open Lens
©2013 Elsie Augustave

ISBN-13: 978-1-61775-165-3
Library of Congress Control Number: 2012954507

Akashic Books/Open Lens
PO Box 1456
New York, NY 10009
info@akashicbooks.com
www.akashicbooks.com

To wander through this living world
And leave uncut the roses
Is to remember fragrance where
The flower no scent encloses.
—Langston Hughes

For Sébastien

PROLOGUE

From whatever place I write,
you will expect that part of my "Travels"
will consist of the excursions in my own mind.
—Samuel Taylor Coleridge

As I approached death hours after giving birth to Zati, my hospital bed floated above blue water. My body felt weightless, my head light and airy. The salty freshness of the sea penetrated my nostrils; foamy waves swallowed the pains in my womb. A woman stood above the sea, her smile as bright as the colors that crowned her.

"Iris," she said, leaning toward my bed, "I am here to grant you your last wish."

"Who are you?" I whispered, blinded by a surge of intertwining colors.

"I am Aïda Wedo," she said while tenderly stroking my hair. "Your great-great-great-grandmother was a good African who lived by the laws of her ancestors," she went on. "To reward her for all she has done to keep our traditions alive, I am here to grant her last wish. All that she wanted was for me to come to those who carry her blood and grant them *their* last wish."

In a skeptical voice, I asked, "Can you grant me life?"

"Only God, our Granmèt, can decide who should live or die."

I thought for a moment and decided that I wanted my daughter to know how I came into the world that I believed

I was about to leave. I did not want her to feel rootless, trapped in a world of darkness. Although I doubted her power to grant my wish, I told Aïda Wedo I wanted my daughter to know my life story so that she could understand who she is.

"That will be no problem," she promised.

"How will Zati know my story after I'm gone?" I asked, looking into her glowing eyes.

"When you reach your destination, all you must do is write it. I'll take care of the rest."

"I . . . I don't understand," I stammered.

Aïda Wedo shook her head as if she pitied me. "You may be a daughter of Guinen, but you are unfamiliar with our ways. Everything will become clear when you leave this world." She flashed a mocking smile. "I guess that is what happens to Haitian children raised in foreign lands, away from their ancestors' wisdom. Perhaps one day, when the spirits of great men like Toussaint Louverture return to Haiti, our children will not have to cross the waters to find a better life." She became pensive and then said, "You will reach a gate at the end of your journey. Knock three times. If your time has come, it will open for you. If God, our Granmèt, is not ready for you, He will send you back to resume your life."

Stories of my great-grandmother coming back from death invaded my mind, and I thought in a flicker of hope that perhaps the same miracle could happen to me. A dimmer, more subdued hue that seemed like dawn replaced Aïda Wedo's presence, and she vanished as suddenly as she had appeared. Just as immediately, I left behind the weary body that had housed my soul.

I have no idea how long it took to reach the end of the journey, but when I came to a door and knocked three times, as Aïda Wedo had suggested, it opened to a landscape of trees. Colorful daisies, lilies, roses, and hyacinths surrounded a cascade of the clearest water. A cushioned chair, along with a desk with a pen and paper, had been placed in the center of a grassy field.

"Welcome," said a deep male voice.

I looked around but saw no one.

"Greetings to you, Miss Odys," said the same voice. "I was told your last wish is to write your life story. You have everything you need."

As I sat on the chair, I contemplated the surroundings with its blend of colors that reminded me of a Monet painting. The gurgling sound of water was as enchanting as Debussy's fluid and soothing melodies. I held my head in my hands, watched the steady flow of water, and thought of the newborn daughter I had left behind.

"You may begin now," urged the voice. "Write the first word and the Holy Spirit will inspire you along the way. One more thing: Should you feel the need to know about someone close to you, just look into the water. You will see and hear that person."

The Holy Spirit then opened the window of my soul. Thoughts and words poured forth; past events gushed and multiplied. The story I had to tell seized me and flooded my mind with vivid memories.

PART ONE

CHAPTER 1

Who would have known of Hector, if Troy had been happy?
The road to valor is built by adversity.
—Ovid

When I left my native village in July 1961, the lightbulbs that hung from ceilings and the vehicles that went up and down the paved streets of Port-au-Prince reminded me that I was away from Monn Nèg's narrow dirt roads, where cars seldom passed and torches and gas lamps brightened dark nights. Indeed, my way of life had changed. I no longer slept on the floor with my cousins nor ate each meal holding an enamel plate on my lap. Now I slept alone in a bed and sat in a hotel dining room at a table covered with a white tablecloth; I learned to use a knife and fork. A man in black pants and a white shirt came to ask what I would like to eat and always there was a choice of meat, fish, or chicken at lunch and dinner. I found it hard to believe that I could have chicken because, at home in Monn Nèg, it was a special treat reserved for Christmas, New Year's Day, or Easter.

When John and Margaret visited our home in Monn Nèg, I was far from imagining that they would mold the rest of my life. I remember being intrigued and fascinated by their appearance. I could not stop staring at their skin that was even lighter than the shop owner in town who everyone called the Syrian. They both had long, slender legs and hands that felt so soft. The color of their hair reminded me of the straw that women weaved to make hats and baskets to sell in the market. Their lips were thin and pink; their noses long. As far as I knew, they fit the descriptions of the master and mistress of the waters that I had heard about in the folk tales that adults told every evening. Everyone called them *blan*. What I liked most was their soft-spoken voices and the way they showed interest in whatever little things I did or said.

The real change in my life happened when Margaret held me by the hand as we said goodbye to John at the Port-au-Prince hotel and watched the taxi disappear down the elegant street, taking him to the airport. A few days later we boarded a Pan American jet to New York, to meet him and the big sister who I was told would be waiting for me.

Fascinated, I thought that the airplane was a house in the air above the clouds that even had toilets inside, like those in the Port-au-Prince hotel. Women with Margaret's complexion placed food on small tables attached to the backs of the seats in front of us. As soon as I finished my meal, I fell asleep and woke up to a woman's voice announcing, in English and in French, that we should prepare for landing. I remember that the airplane dropped and rose back up, causing my stomach to curl.

"That's just a bit of turbulence," Margaret said, in her usual soft voice.

Although I had no idea what she meant, I no longer felt safe. The airplane bounced and tipped to the side and felt like someone was shaking it. I looked out of the window but all I could see were thick, dark clouds.

My breathing quickened and my heart raced. Margaret placed her arm around my shoulders and drew me close.

"Take a deep breath," she said. "Slowly, let the air out through your nose." She held my hand until we touched ground.

We joined a line of people and waited our turn to be directed to a man in a booth, who examined the little books that Margaret handed to him. After a brief conversation, she showed him some papers and he stamped our books and waved us through.

Margaret recovered our suitcases from a moving black rubber belt, then we walked to a place where people stood searching for exiting passengers. Some called out names, while others hugged. As voices echoed around us, I could not understand what they were saying. I had never seen so many people in one place, not even in the Monn Nèg market. We followed a man in a blue cap who pushed our suitcases on a cart, and all I could think of was how quickly my life had changed.

"There they are," Margaret said, pointing to John who was waving to us and holding a young girl by the hand. She looked older than I was and she was holding the biggest doll I had ever seen.

Margaret smiled and hugged her tight. "Iris, this is Cynthia; Cynthia, this is Iris."

Cynthia looked like John and Margaret and like most of the people in the airport, even though her hair was the bright orange color of the sun when it is about to go behind the mountains. There were brownish spots on her nose, and her smile made her eyes sparkle.

"How old are you?" she asked me in French.

"Five," I answered.

She studied me briefly, then handed me the doll with hair that looked like corn bread and eyes that were the indigo color that women in Monn Nèg used to rinse white clothes. I took the doll and smiled at it smiling back at me. I had seen dolls in the store in town where I had gone with my mother a few times, but none as big or as beautiful as the one Cynthia gave me. I held it in my arms, recalling that my cousins and I used to make clothes out of rags to dress up mango seeds that we pretended were babies.

Breathing the fresh scent in the car, I shivered feeling a

chill similar to what I had felt in the hotel room in Port-au-Prince and inside the airplane. I wrapped my arms around my body and looked out the window at the cars speeding by in the opposite direction.

"How can people cross the street with cars driving by so fast?" I asked in the Creole-flavored French that my mother had taught me so that I could achieve her dream of succeeding in life. The little French she knew she had learned in school and later working as a maid for a rich family.

"This is a highway," Margaret commented, and explained that people did not walk across highways.

After what seemed like a very long ride, John pulled into the garage of a redbrick house with brown-trimmed Tudor windows. I admired the slender drooping branches of a tree and the cut grass that was so unlike the wild weeds behind our mud-plastered house in Monn Nèg.

"This is your new home. We live in Westchester, New York," he said.

Holding my hand, Margaret showed me around the house. Going from room to room, I wondered why there was so much space for only three people. In the kitchen, I inhaled an aroma that reminded me of the tea my great-grandmother used to make with cinnamon sticks and brown sugar.

At this point, I don't remember every detail of the house when I first saw it, but later this is the way I came to know it. Built on a slope, the main entrance opened onto a foyer that divided the lower and upper levels. The spacious kitchen had a center island and a breakfast nook that led to an outside deck. Adjacent to the kitchen was a large formal dining room, living room, and a guest bathroom. The master bedroom suite was upstairs along with two other rooms: one was Margaret's study, the other was John's. A family room, three bedrooms, and two full baths were on the lower level.

A world of magic opened to me. Everything seemed so

vast, open, and clean. There were no clothes hanging from lines outside, no pots and pans and calabash bowls stashed inside wicker baskets. I had to get used to a kitchen with appliances and food that I never knew existed. The days I spent in the Port-au-Prince hotel hardly prepared me for this new life.

About a month later, when the novelty of it all wore off, I began to think about my family in Monn Nèg and missed the aroma of smoke from my great-grandmother's pipe. I missed the warmth of my mother's dark, watery eyes, the sounds of my cousins' laughter, and the taste of mangos that had fallen from the trees. This left me with a yearning for a familiar world. Sobs often rocked me to sleep when there were no tears left. One night, holding my doll, my sobs became so violent that I woke up Cynthia, who ran out of our room to get John and Margaret.

"What's the matter?" Margaret asked, as she turned on the light.

"I want my mother!"

Margaret sat me on her lap and said with fondness in her voice, "I'm also your mom. John is your dad, and Cynthia is your sister."

As he took Cynthia out of the room, John whispered to Margaret, "I think you'd better stay with her until she falls asleep." Feeling secure with the doll close to my chest, I fell asleep as my new mom sang a lullaby.

The next evening when John came home, he smiled and with excitement in his eyes, said, "I have a surprise for you." I rushed toward him to accept the framed photograph that he handed me. Seeing my mother brought a gradual smile to my face. There she was, stiffly sitting on a wooden stool, eyes fixed on the camera. Large, black, timid, scared eyes. Head tied with a scarf, her limp arms hung at her sides. John placed the picture on the nightstand next to my bed.

After that, whenever I was alone I would tell her about the important and unimportant things that happened to me.

Eventually I got used to life without my Haitian mother. Within a few months, I had adjusted to eating new foods and speaking French and English. I even learned to accept the way people stared when I was out with my new family. The only thing I couldn't get used to was the anguish my hair caused. I hated the daily morning ritual of Margaret combing out my matted hair. All she could manage to do was tie it with a ponytail holder that made it look like a pig's tail. Usually I ended up in tears, wishing I had Cynthia's soft hair flowing down my back.

What I disliked most was the way people found an excuse to touch my hair like a woman did one Sunday when Mom, Dad, Cynthia, and I went to brunch. While we waited for a table in the restaurant's lobby, my sister and I went to the restroom, and when we returned we found Mom and Dad engaged in a conversation with an older couple.

"This is my daughter Cynthia, and my younger daughter Iris," Mom said, wrapping an arm around each of us.

The man raised his eyebrows. His wife stared at me, then at Mom and Dad and Cynthia, before moving closer to me. With a frown on her face, she said, "I always wondered what these people's hair felt like," and without the slightest hesitation, she patted my head.

Flushed with irritation, I took a step back. "Stop petting me. I'm not a dog," I said.

She quickly removed her hand from my hair. I noticed Mom and Dad smile when the couple moved away.

Still, I have a clear memory of another incident that seriously disturbed the peaceful and agreeable life that I was living with the Winstons. On the day before the start of Easter vacation, as I walked into the student cafeteria in our small bilingual school, I waved to Cynthia, picked up a tray, and joined the food line, where women dressed in white uniforms behind a counter served sandwiches, vegetables, salad, and spaghetti and meatballs. I heard a boy ahead of me ask if he could take another carton of milk. I saw his disappointment when he was told that he had to pay extra and returned the carton. By then I had been in the United States for three years and still had not adjusted to drinking cold milk, so I told him he could have mine. Instead of being grateful, he gazed at me with his icy light-brown eyes, causing me to think I had done something terribly wrong. With my head lowered and holding onto my tray, I looked for Cynthia, wondering why the boy had acted the way he did.

"That nigger better not sit here," the boy said to a girl who was sitting next to him and across from Cynthia. "They're loud, lazy, and stupid."

I raised my eyebrows and set my tray on the table. "Are you talking to me?"

The girl snickered. "There's no other nigger here, is there?"

I didn't know what the word "nigger" meant but suspected they were talking about my skin color. Back in Monn Nèg, people talked about my complexion with admiration and envy because its reddish-brown color was different, but I never detected contempt in their voices.

"If you don't want to sit with me, you and your friend should move," I told him, holding my head up high and pulling back a chair.

"Why should we move? Go back to Africa!" the girl snapped, fixing me with a cold gaze. She and the boy then burst into laughter.

"What does Africa have to do with this?" I asked.

"Isn't that where you people came from?" the boy questioned, pulling back his lips.

Cynthia's face turned red. "Leave my sister alone!" she screamed, hitting the table with a fist.

"Your sister? Which one of your parents is the nigger lover?"

Cynthia reached across the table like a thunderbolt and slapped the girl, who was about two years older. Seconds later, they were on the floor tearing each other's clothes and pulling each other's hair.

"Fight! Fight! Fight!" the other students screamed.

The girl was on top of Cynthia, throwing punches. A hollow sensation sped inside my stomach, prompting me to jump on her back. I bit her shoulder as hard as I could. Several teachers rushed to the scene.

All afternoon the words "nigger" and "Africa" echoed in my mind. Later that day, sitting in the family room at home with Cynthia, I couldn't concentrate on the book I was trying to read. I needed to talk. "How do you feel about being adopted?" I asked, breaking the silence, happy to have a common issue we could discuss.

"Sometimes I wonder who my real parents are. But I don't really care." Cynthia shrugged and buried her head in her Nancy Drew book.

It now occurs to me that she probably didn't care about being adopted as much as I did because she had our parents' skin color. Besides, she had no recollection of a life without the Winstons. And I did.

"Why did you fight that girl?" I asked, determined to hold her attention.

"Didn't you hear what she called you?"

"What's a nigger?"

"I'll answer that question," Mom said, walking into the room with Dad.

The headmistress had contacted Dad about the fight, and he had picked us up from school after calling Mom at work.

"Racists in this country use this name to insult black people," she said, taking a seat next to me.

"I don't understand."

"Those kids didn't want you to sit with them because

they don't like people who are different." Mom leaned back and crossed her legs. "They have a disease called racism. A lot of people in this country are infected with it. Dr. Martin Luther King is trying to cure them." She touched my hand gently as she spoke.

"Are they in a hospital?"

Mom and Dad looked at each other, smiling at my confusion.

"Dr. King is not a medical doctor," Dad explained. "It's just like people call Margaret 'doctor' because of the degree of education she has earned."

"How is Dr. King going to cure them?"

"With his ideas," Mom answered. "He wants to make them understand we can live together no matter how different we are. But he doesn't believe we can achieve that through violence."

That evening, I overheard Mom and Dad's whispering in the living room on my way to the kitchen to get a drink of water. I stopped to listen when I heard my name.

"I wonder if adopting Iris was the best thing for her," Dad said.

"Why do you say that?"

"I don't know if this country is ready for a black child living with a white family. I'm afraid she may suffer from more racist acts." He took a deep breath and went on: "Maybe we're taking this dream of little black and white children living happily together a bit too literally."

"I still think she's better off here than in Haiti."

"What happened on the phone?"

"The father said he didn't owe me any explanation, that liberals like us are ruining this country, and that life would be better here if we would leave Negroes where they belong."

I didn't want to hear anymore. Tears filled my eyes as I wondered where people like me belonged. The girl in the cafeteria said Africa.

CHAPTER 2

For the black man there is only one destiny.
—Frantz Fanon

I sat in the waiting room with Mom and Dad, trying to figure out why I had to see Dr. Connelly. Mom had said he was a different kind of doctor who was just going to talk to me.

"Is he going to give me shots?"

"No, no shots."

"What is he going to do then?"

"He's going to help you understand the things that bother you."

"Nothing's bothering me."

"It's good to have somebody to talk to," Dad insisted.

"Why can't I talk to you and Mom and Cynthia?"

"It's not the same."

Dr. Connelly looked like some of the professors at the university where Mom taught. He wore brown corduroy pants, a plaid shirt, and a brown tweed jacket with patches on the elbows. His gray hair matched his beard; his eyeglasses were perched on the tip of his nose. He sat in a black leather chair behind a desk, and held a pad and pen in his hand.

"You told me over the phone you adopted Iris when she was five. Is that right?"

"Yes," answered Mom.

"Where is she from again?"

"Haiti," Dad answered this time.

Dr. Connelly wrote on a yellow pad. "That's where Papa Doc is, right?" He raised his head.

"Correct," Dad said, nodding.

"Iris," Dr. Connelly turned to me, "tell me how it feels to have a white family."

I wondered why he needed to know, and I didn't think it should be of any concern to him. So I offered no answer.

Turning to Mom and Dad, Dr. Connelly said, "It should be expected that a child would be traumatized when she's taken away from her rudimentary living environment, put on an airplane, and brought to live with people who are different from her in every way."

Mom straightened her back and pushed her hair behind her ear. "Iris has adjusted to her new life here," she said, "and as you can see, she is fully Americanized."

"Separation and loss may still be an issue," Dr. Connelly explained. "I would like to speak with Iris alone. Please wait for her outside." On their way out of the room, Mom smiled at me, and Dad touched my shoulder.

"Are you happy living with the Winstons?" Dr. Connelly asked.

"Yes."

"What is it like to live with them?"

"Nice."

"How old are you?"

"Eight."

"Do you miss your Haitian mother?"

I swallowed hard to get rid of the lump in my throat that wouldn't go away. I had been separated from my natural mother for three years and had learned to adjust to life without her. I didn't like to think about her because I became sad whenever I did. I shrugged and looked away from Dr. Connelly, who raised his eyebrows and wrote again on his yellow pad.

"Can you draw a picture of your family for me?" he

asked, handing me a piece of paper, a pencil, and a box of crayons.

A few minutes later, he examined the picture of the red house with four people standing in front of it. I had colored in all the faces.

"Who are these people?"

"Mom, Dad, Cynthia, and me."

"Why does everyone have a beige face?"

I shrugged again.

"Think about it," he said in a soft voice, leaning forward. Seconds went by, and I remained silent. "Tell me why," he coaxed in an even softer voice.

"Because . . ." I uttered, thinking how I could get him to stop asking me questions.

"What's that behind the house?"

"I don't know."

"It looks like a moon."

"It is."

"Why does it have two eyes, a nose, and a mouth?"

No answer.

"Do people in Haiti think the moon is a person?"

Annoyed and close to tears, I mumbled that I didn't know.

Dr. Connelly looked at his watch. "That's all for today. Think about what you want to tell me about Haiti on your next visit, okay?"

I walked out of his office relieved, wishing never to go back.

On the way home, I tried to understand why I had painted everyone's face beige and figured it was probably because of an incident that occurred two weeks after the fight in the cafeteria. Determined not to be different from my new family, I was willing to do anything not to stand out.

Lighten up your skin!
Lighten up your life!
Be beautiful!

My heart jumped with joy when I read those words in a copy of *Beautiful Black Teens* magazine that I had picked up at the library. Thinking that I had found my salvation, I tore out the advertisement and carefully folded it before hiding it in my book bag. When I reached home, I looked at the ad again and again. Whatever it took, I decided, I had to look like the woman in the magazine. It was hard to tell whether she was white or black, and that was how I wanted to be. If people could not tell that my skin was dark, they would not reject me or single me out. After comparing the woman's features to mine, I decided that I also needed to work on my nose.

Later that evening, as I helped Mom take the laundry out of the washing machine, an idea came to mind. Once I was sure Cynthia was asleep, I took out the clothespin I was hiding under my pillow. I clipped it on my nose, and though I could hardly breathe, I endured the pain and concentrated on breathing through my mouth. I woke up several times during the night, not only to breathe, but to rub my swollen nose and put the clothespin back on.

The following morning, when after a soft knock Mom entered the bedroom, I heard her say, "Jesus!" when she noticed the clothespin. "What are you doing?" Her voice was higher than usual and her widened eyes were gray. They seemed to change color depending on her mood. At times they were blue, and at other times green.

"I . . . I want a nose like yours," I struggled to say. "Please buy this for me." I handed her the ad that had been under my pillow.

Mom cocked her head. "Do you know what this is?"

"It will make my skin white. Buy it for me, please!"

Mom rested her apprehensive eyes on me. "No cream

will ever change who you are." She studied me for a few seconds, then asked why I needed to be white.

"To be like you, Dad, and Cynthia."

At that moment Cynthia woke up, probably because she had heard her name. "What's going on?" she asked, rubbing sleep from her eyes.

"This doesn't concern you," Mom snapped, and turned back to me. "You are beautiful the way you are." She ran the back of her hand across my face. "Put the clothespin back where it belongs. That ad goes in the garbage." She shook her head as though she refused to believe what I had done. "Listen to me, Iris," she said, sitting on the edge of my bed. "You need to look at yourself differently. Your smooth, tamarind-colored skin is beautiful. The warmth of your loving smile brings me happiness, and the hair on your head is a regal crown. Do you understand?"

I nodded yes so she would leave me alone.

"Anyway, it's time for ballet class," she announced, walking out of the room.

I couldn't go to dance class that day. My nose hurt too much. I was also tired from trying to sleep with the clothespin squeezing my nostrils. So I stayed in my room, contemplating the print of a black girl jumping rope on the wall across from my bed. She looked happy and carefree, and I wondered if she, too, ever wanted to be white.

I dreaded going to my next appointment with Dr. Connelly. As I was getting ready, I walked aimlessly around the house and wiped my sweaty palms on my jeans. I tried to think of an excuse to stay home, but I could not come up with one. Reluctantly I followed Dad to the doctor's office. Once we arrived, he stayed in the waiting room.

"How are you?" Dr. Connelly asked.

"Fine." I took a seat across from him.

"Are you ready to talk to me?"

"Yes."

"The last time you were here, I asked you to think about why everyone in the family picture you drew had a beige face."

"Yes."

"Did you think about it?"

"No."

"Why not?"

"I don't know."

"Is there a reason why you didn't want to think about it?"

"I don't know," I said with a shrug, unable to hide my annoyance.

"Tell me about the dreams you had."

"What dreams?"

"When your mother called for your first appointment, she said you had nightmares."

"I saw a snake with the head of a man."

"What happened then?"

"He stared at me and went like this." I made an inviting gesture with my fingers.

"Then what?"

"I ran away from him and woke up screaming."

"What happened when you woke up?"

"Mom and Dad came into the room when they heard me scream."

Dr. Connelly then said something I didn't hear because I was trying to recapture the effect of the dream. His voice suddenly reminding me I was still in his office.

"Excuse me?"

"Tell me about the other dream."

"There was another man with fire on his body. He wanted me to come to him too."

"Tell me about Haiti."

"What about Haiti?"

"Whatever you remember."

Images of Monn Nèg were engraved in my mind. But I had no idea how to explain them to a stranger. He kept his expressionless eyes on me, waiting for me to say something. The absolute silence in the room and his blank stare persisted until he cleared his throat and spoke again. "I was thinking," he said, "the dreams you had are probably because of your exposure to *vaudou*. Did your family in Haiti practice *vaudou*?" He tilted his head and waited for an answer.

But I had no idea what he was talking about. "I don't know what *vaudou* is."

"I'm reading a book now about *vaudou*," he said, sounding proud of himself. "I think it may have something to do with those dreams."

I stared at my feet, wishing to be anywhere but in that office.

"The author of the book compares *vaudou* adepts to devil worshippers. But I'm not so sure of that. What do you think?"

The pressure from his questions confused me and brought tears to my eyes.

Looking back at the incident, I find it odd that Dr. Connelly would ask me to comment on the subject, when I had told him I knew nothing about it. Did he forget how old I was? I suppose he was hoping I might react in a way that would give him the opportunity to better analyze me. Whatever the reason, I decided, at that moment, that I was not coming back.

"How about drawing another picture," he suggested, after a moment of silence.

I drew another picture of Mom, Dad, Cynthia, and me without adding any color to their faces.

"What color are these people?"

"They have no color."

"Why not?"

I shrugged.

"Where do they live?"

"Nowhere."

He gazed at me with intense eyes, forcing me to lower mine. Finally, he looked at the clock and announced that our time was up. I quickly rose to my feet and rushed out of the office to meet Dad in the lobby.

"I don't want to go back there again," I told Dad, crossing my arms over my chest, fighting tears that were ready to burst from my eyes.

Dad turned on the ignition and shifted his head toward me. "What happened?"

"He said bad things about Haiti," I declared, bending the truth to my advantage.

Dad looked at me and narrowed his eyes. "What did he say?"

I stared at the snow on the tree branches. "Something about *vaudou* and Haitians being devil worshippers."

"What exactly did he say?"

"I don't remember."

"Most people have a misconception about the *vaudou* religion. That's why your mom is writing a book about it." He turned a button on the dashboard. The windshield wiper swayed back and forth, making a soft, swishing sound. "It seems like there is no sense in your going back."

I had won a battle. But there was one more thing I needed to do. Once I reached home, I threw the picture of my biological mother in a large black plastic bag that the garbage truck would pick up the next day. Rather than being the person I used to talk to for comfort, she had become responsible for my confusion and I no longer wanted her in my memory. The mother I once loved eventually vanished into oblivion and became a mythical figure beyond reach.

CHAPTER 3

That a lie which is all a lie may be met and
fought with outright,
But a lie which is part a truth is a harder
matter to fight.
—Lord Alfred Tennyson

ris!"

Whenever I heard that tone in Mom's voice, I knew she meant business. I rushed up the stairs and tried to think why I was being summoned. Maybe Madame Glissant told her I didn't turn in my book report on time, or she may have found out I ate a slice of cake before dinner, or that I went to bed last night without brushing my teeth.

"I called Dr. Connelly today," she said as soon as I entered the dining room. "What exactly did he say about Haiti that upset you?" She sat down at the head of the table, across from Dad and next to my godfather Latham, who had come over for dinner. I stood there with my arms hanging loosely, unable to move or to speak, feeling like I was in front of a jury. Dad pulled back a chair next to him and invited me to sit.

My heartbeat accelerated as I realized the seriousness of the situation. I was unsure of why I had accused Dr. Connelly of saying Haitians were devil worshipers, other than the fact that I didn't want to go back to his office. I had thought a simple twist of the truth would go unnoticed and would allow me to have my way, just because I despised how his questions made me feel. I dreaded the soul-searching process that meant thinking about a past that I wanted to forget. My eyes traveled from Mom to Dad, then to Latham, trying to decide which of the three could be a possible ally. Their impassive faces revealed nothing.

I heard Mom say, "We're concerned about what you told us that Dr. Connelly said."

"I don't know what you mean," I responded, as I tried to think of a way to get out of this situation.

"Let's begin with your telling me again what Dr. Connelly said that offended you," Dad suggested.

"I don't remember his exact words. Something about Haitians being devil worshippers," I blurted out for the sake of consistency, though I was aware it wasn't all true.

"What exactly did he say?" Mom insisted. She leaned back and peered at me with a dubious gaze, and waited for an answer.

"I don't remember," I said in a faint voice, having noticed the tension showing on her face.

"When your Dad told me what you said happened in his office yesterday, I called Dr. Connelly for clarification. Apparently you have taken his words out of context."

"I didn't mean to." My voice trembled and echoed guilt.

The room grew so quiet I could hear myself breathing. The questioning gaze persisted on their faces until Latham, who had not said a word thus far, spoke.

"Maybe Iris didn't understand Dr. Connelly's words."

"Let's hope that's what it was," Mom said without conviction. Anger suddenly covered her gentle face as she let out a moan of anguish and reached for the coffee pot on the table. Sadness had replaced the usual softness in her eyes. A pearl of tear found its way to the corner of her eye. She got up and left the room without drinking her coffee.

Latham's eyes sent a message of sympathy. Though maybe it was pity. I'm not sure. Nonetheless, I was grateful that he had come to my aid, as he had so often done in many ways since the day after I arrived in the United States, when he showed up with his arms filled with clothes and toys, announcing that he was my godfather. I vaguely recalled seeing him with the Winstons when they came to Monn Nèg. What I did remember about him was that although he had the same skin color as the people of Monn Nèg, he couldn't speak Creole. I had smiled broadly when I saw him again, happy to have someone who reminded me of the familiar faces I had left behind.

The conversation we had that night left a hollow feeling in my heart that grew deeper and larger as the days went by. Thinking I had betrayed Mom and Dad, I was embarrassed and tried to avoid them as much as possible. I spent more time in my room, grateful that only two weeks earlier they had given Cynthia and me separate bedrooms. This went on until they summoned me one Saturday afternoon after ballet class.

"We need to talk." Mom crossed her legs and asked me to sit next to her on the sofa.

"What did I do now?" I asked grumpily.

"I don't like the tone of your voice, young lady," Dad cautioned.

I relaxed a bit, hoping the conversation that had not yet begun would soon be over. The fearful, gnawing feeling inside me quickly melted, and I told them I was sorry.

"We would like to know why you've been avoiding us," Mom said.

I wiped my moist hands on my skirt, and felt a throbbing sensation in my heart. I blurted out that I did not want to go back to Dr. Connelly. "I don't like the way he makes me feel," I explained.

"That's still no reason to stain someone's reputation," Mom scolded.

Dad leaned toward the coffee table. "That wasn't very nice of you," he said, resting reproachful eyes on me.

Tears of redemption rolled down my cheeks; waves of regret grew. A gush of sun penetrated the living room through the sliding windows, and Dad reclined in his seat. "The reason we took you to Dr. Connelly," he said, "was so that you could understand your frustrations."

Two weeks later, Dad accompanied Mom to an out-of-town conference, and Latham stayed with Cynthia and me. He picked me up from ballet class and dropped Cynthia at her music school before taking me for a snack.

"I heard Dr. Connelly is disappointed that you wouldn't go back to see him," he said, backing up onto the road.

"Mom told me."

He looked over his shoulder. "I suppose you don't want to reconsider."

I turned to face the window. "Talking about these things makes me nervous," I said in a soft voice.

"What things?"

"Things like my mother and about Haiti."

"Why should talking about them make you nervous?" He stopped the car at a traffic light and searched my eyes. The light turned green; Latham shifted gears. He drove off the main road and then pulled into the parking lot of a stainless steel and porcelain enamel place with a red neon sign that read, *Good Food Diner*. We walked into the long and narrow room where customers were seated on stools mounted into the floor; at the end of the blue Formica service counter there were apple pies and cherry pies, chocolate cakes and pound cakes displayed in clear rotating cases. Hamburgers and hot dogs sizzled on a grill; french fries in a basket were lowered into hot boiling oil on a stove against the wall. Latham led me to a booth opposite the counter. I studied the menu, even though I knew I wanted a strawberry ice-cream soda.

"What are you and your daughter having today?" asked a blond waitress with a forced smile. I thought at the time that one of the things I enjoyed about being with Latham was that people didn't stare at us as they did with my family.

"I heard about a Haitian dance class in the city that you might want to try," he said, bringing a steaming cup of coffee toward his lips. "Margaret told me you used to love to dance to the sounds of Haitian drums," he added, as he set the cup on the table. "The class is for adults but I spoke with the instructor, who has agreed to enroll you."

"When is the class?"

"On Saturdays."

"What about my ballet class?"

"What about it?"

"I guess I can go to the Wednesday class. Mom doesn't teach on Wednesdays."

The sounds of drums played in my mind; adrenaline flushed in my veins. Something beyond the physical occurred, pressing me to reconnect with the culture that only weeks ago had made me feel so ashamed that I had gotten rid of my mother's picture, the only physical thing that connected me to my past. The thought of hearing sounds from my childhood in rural Haiti was suddenly like seeing and feeling the sun in the middle of a winter day.

On the following Saturday, Latham accompanied me to the dance class, a few blocks away from Times Square. As I climbed the wooden stairs leading to the studio that, later I found out, used to be a cosmetics factory. I imagined making Haitian friends who would tell me about Haiti and who would perhaps help bring back memories of a life I once knew.

Latham introduced me to the instructor, a short, dark-skinned man with a thick mustache, who wore a black tank top and a black leotard. "You go stretch now. Class begins in five minutes," he said with a heavy accent. He then moved on to speak to the drummers. Latham waved goodbye and left me to my fate.

The only Haitians in the dance studio were the three drummers and the instructor, but they offered me no special treatment. As the drums rolled, I timidly began to imitate the instructor's movements; but when the syncopated rhythm grew louder, a greater force prompted me to dance with surprising confidence. My body moved in an undulating motion, my back moved toward and then away from the unpolished wooden floor. When the drums reached a feverish beat, I entered a state of ecstasy.

I regularly attended the classes and continued to hope to make Haitian friends. Dancers came and went over the years, but no other Haitian person ever visited the studio. Eager to learn about the Haitian culture that I often heard described as exotic, the dancers who took the class were almost always white women in their twenties and thirties. For me, however, the classes became valuable to my understanding of my heritage, as the instructor introduced me to the richness of Haitian folklore and brought to life the circumstances of the survival of the Ibo, Nago, Congo, and Mandinga traditions on the island. I enjoyed hearing about the important role those dances played in major historical movements such as the slave revolts. I listened to the instructor talk about African spirits, like Ogoun Badagris and Damballah Wedo, who would descend into the soul of their Haitian children all the way from Africa, the magical place that had been an enigma ever since the girl in the cafeteria had said that was where people like me belonged. I began to feel closer to Africa, the place where most Haitian culture originated. When I danced to the rhythms of Africa, my soul found healing in a holistic manner that took me, each time, deeper into a level of consciousness and self-realization. The dance classes triggered an emotional and physical release that uplifted and energized me and allowed me to explore and accept the essence of my being.

One Saturday, something unusual occurred. Something that became vital to bringing me closer to my journey, toward discovering and accepting my past, as it opened doors and connected me to the culture that suddenly seemed more accessible.

"Mademoiselle Iris," said the dance instructor. It was the first time he addressed me after class, and I was surprised.

"Yes?"

"How old you now?"

"Seventeen."

"I been watching you dance since you a young girl. I like your energy," he drawled.

Happy that he had noticed me, I offered a broad smile and thanked him.

"How long have you been dancing with me now?"

"Nine years."

"You master Dunham's techniques." He scratched his head and turned to say goodbye to the drummers who were leaving the studio with their instruments secure in army duffel bags over their shoulders. He turned to me. "Yes, you a good dancer now, old enough to join the company. We rehearse three times a week in Brooklyn. Is that okay?"

Although it sounded like a great opportunity to dance with professionals, I knew my parents would never allow me to join. They always made it clear that dance should just be a hobby and that I needed to focus on my schoolwork, especially since I was in my junior year in high school.

"It sounds really good, but I live in Westchester and I have a lot of homework."

"Too bad." He shook his head. "You coming to the meeting?" he asked, as I was about to push open the door to the dressing room.

"What meeting?" I took a few steps toward him.

"You didn't get the flier I mailed you?"

"No, I didn't." I then remembered that Latham had used his address and telephone number when he registered me for the class years ago.

"There are some left in lobby. Try to come, okay?"

I looked through the piles of fliers and advertisements until I found the right one.

The double-glass door of Dad's gallery opened to a vast room with a glossy wooden floor. Original paintings by contemporary African-American abstract expressionists Charles Alston, Romare Bearden, and William Johnson hung on the walls alongside works by Haitian artists, who represented a magical, colorful world in the folk art tradition. My attention was drawn to a bronze sculpture by Augusta Savage in the center of the gallery. On the pedestal was the bust of a young black girl with soft and curious eyes.

When he heard me, Latham, wearing a French beret, Levi's, and a white starched long-sleeve cotton shirt, lifted his head from a Jacob Lawrence print of Toussaint Louverture that he had just framed.

"How was class?"

"We had a visiting master drummer today."

"That sounds exciting."

"Can you come to a meeting with me this evening?" I asked, watching him spraying and wiping the foam off the glass frame.

"What meeting?"

"A meeting about Haitian refugees." I showed him the flier and told him about my conversation with the dance instructor.

"The flier may be in my mailbox. I haven't opened it in almost a week."

"Why not?"

"All I ever get is bills."

We took the number 4 train to Utica Avenue in Brooklyn. Approaching an old Gothic church, we saw hundreds of Haitians gathered on Eastern Parkway. A sea of black faces carried the original red and blue flag of Haiti in the chilly autumn air. "Hey, hey, USA! Stop supporting Duvalier!" they shouted. Drummers from my dance class joined by others were in the front row. They nodded and smiled when they saw me. The electricity of the booming sounds of their instruments intensified.

A Jewish lawyer for the Haitian refugees read a quote from Emma Lazarus's poem "The New Colossus" carved at the foot of the Statue of Liberty: *"Give me your tired, your poor, your huddled masses yearning to breathe free, the wretched refuse of your teeming shore . . ."*

A brown-skinned Haitian priest with curly hair moved to the pulpit and began to speak. "Fellow Haitians and citizens of the United States, we welcome and thank you for being here tonight. To support the Haitian refugees is to support the ideology of justice this country represents." With a white handkerchief, he wiped sweat from his forehead. "The American government has extended a welcoming hand to Cuban refugees. But Haitians, who took that same perilous trip across the sea, are imprisoned because they're black, poor, and uneducated." He paused. "Let us remind the politicians in Washington that if Haitians are poor and uneducated, it is because of the political system they fled." The priest's voice rose. "Doesn't that make them political refugees, ladies and gentlemen?" Applause exploded, and the priest paused, waiting for calm to return. "We must inform the national and the international communities that Mother Liberty has denied Haitians their natural right to freedom in this land of opportunity." Again, waves of applause roared across the church's sanctuary as the priest stepped off the podium. Sweat glistened on his face.

The women, many of whom wore gold earrings, neck-
laces, and bracelets, served thick espresso coffee and meat,
chicken, and codfish patties in a dark hallway seriously
in need of a paint job. They talked with their hands, often breaking into laughter. As I watched them, I wished
that I could talk to them about Monn Nèg. My mother's
black-and-white picture came to mind and a knot of regret
tightened in my throat. I wished that I could reverse the
irredeemable act. How I would have loved to have that picture to compare my mother's features to the women at the
church.

The religious and political personalities were no longer present, but many Haitian businesspeople and cultural
leaders mingled and spoke about their dreams to return to
Haiti without the Duvaliers.

Latham and I were preparing to leave when the dance
instructor called my name. "Iris, let me introduce you to
some people," he said.

On a quest to connect with more Haitians I visited the Haitian book and record shop in Manhattan on Amsterdam Avenue near 85th Street. The owner, a bald, round-bellied man
who had given Latham and me business cards at the meeting in Brooklyn, introduced me to his friends as a long-lost
daughter of Haiti. He remembered I had told him I couldn't
speak Creole anymore and that I didn't know any Haitians
other than my dance instructor and the drummers. The
men looked at me with pity, as though they thought I was
deprived.

I listened to the men discuss Haiti's latest political development. They spoke Creole laced with English. It vaguely
reminded me of Monn Nèg and forced me to summon memories of the little girl I once was. Even though her presence in
me was undeniable, a body of more recent experiences overshadowed her. I lingered in the store and browsed through

books by Haitian writers. The owner recommended the novel *Gouverneurs de la rosée* by Jacques Roumain and recordings that introduced me to Ti Roro's *vaudou* drums, Martha Jean-Claude's lamenting voice, and the rhythms of Tabou Combo.

Months later, *The Haitian Peasant Family and Spirits*, the book Mom had researched in Haiti, was published. Although she had completed the manuscript years earlier, she waited for nearly a decade to find a publisher. Soon after its publication, Dad and I attended her lecture at Yale University. Cynthia was a sophomore at Princeton University and, as usual, she was buried in her books. Determined to make it to medical school, she didn't want to take any time away from her studies. In fact, she almost never came home, except on major holidays.

Nearly one hundred people had gathered in the lecture hall to hear Mom speak. They were mostly from the anthropology department, the divinity school, and the Africana studies department.

She read from her notes. "*Vaudou* spirits share the life of a family that shows reverence to them, and they, in return, provide guidance and protection against evil intentions. Like Roman, Greek, and Egyptian gods, they have human flaws. They visit when summoned but can arrive unexpectedly to deliver messages. They may also appear in a person's dreams, taking on a human or an animal form, or they may occupy the body of a person who becomes a horse that the spirit mounts." Mom talked about my family in Monn Nèg as a case study, then took questions from the audience.

"Can one actually see the spirit ride the horse?" a white male student asked. His question prompted laughter from the audience.

"The spirit rides the horse's mind and dictates the steed's words and movements," Mom explained.

"How do Haitians reconcile their Christian beliefs with pagan practices?" the same student asked in a more serious tone.

An older man commented that it would have been helpful to read the book before the lecture. The young man turned red; another man, who was sitting next to me, said to one of his colleagues, "Richard is a theology student. He has conservative views about non-Western religious concepts."

More questions followed. Listening to the people in the audience discuss the culture of my birth made me want to remember my life in Monn Nèg even more, but my recollections remained vague. I wondered how the mind decided what to remember and what to forget.

Later that night in the hotel room, Mom stood in front of the dresser removing her eye makeup, while Dad laid on their double bed. I kept thinking about Mom's lecture and what Dr. Connelly had said. "So, Mom, you actually believe in this stuff?"

"What stuff?"

"You know, the *vaudou* stuff."

Dad put down the book he was reading. "Well, do you?" he asked her with a smirk.

"My job, as an anthropologist, is not to believe or to practice. It is to understand in a nonjudgmental manner those whose belief it is. The *vaudou* religion is, to me, as fascinating as Greek or Roman mythology . . ."

"Okay. We get the point," Dad teased.

"Yeah, Mom. One lecture a day is enough."

The three of us laughed, and I left to change into my nightclothes. I hated sharing a room with them, but I had joined them at the last minute. There was a big Yale-Princeton football game scheduled for the next day and there were no available rooms in the same hotel.

"What is my birth mother like?" I asked, while watching Mom brush her hair.

"Hagathe is a dignified and humble woman," she answered. "We haven't talked about her much since we noticed that her picture disappeared from your room."

I sat down on the other double bed and thought aloud, "I wonder what it would be like to see her again." I recalled the shame and resentment I felt the day I threw her picture away.

"We'll visit her after you graduate college," Dad said.

"Hagathe asked us to wait until you were an adult before bringing you back to Monn Nèg, but if you miss her, we can arrange a trip sooner."

"It's okay. I'll wait," I said, realizing I wasn't so sure I wanted her back in my life. What if she wasn't the warm and loving woman I wanted to believe she was?

Drifting off to sleep, I summoned images of *vaudou* spirits visiting family members, as Mom had mentioned in her book. But none came to my mind, even though she had told me on our way to the hotel that I was present when a spirit came to visit my family. That night I dreamed I was kneeling in front of a body of calm, crystal-clear water. As I was about to dip my cupped hands in it, a woman dressed in white emerged from the bottom of the spring and rose to a standing position; a colorful arc of light reflected above her.

I awoke from the dream drenched in sweat, thinking that I had been the woman in white. I quickly dismissed the thought. How could it have been me when I was the one looking into the water?

Mom placed her book on her lap, peered at me, and quietly asked, "Are you okay?"

"Yes," I nodded.

"You were asleep for less than an hour. What happened?" Dad asked.

"I don't know. I'm all wet."

"But it's not hot in here," Mom said.

Afraid they might take me to some other Dr. Connelly,

I said nothing about the dream that left me with fear, yet coupled with serenity. It seemed odd that I would have those unusual dreams when I thought about my mother. It occurred to me that it was time to find out why I was with the Winstons.

Questions I had forced myself to dismiss suddenly began to haunt me.

"Why did my birth mother give me up?" I asked, pulling the cover up to my neck.

"There is no limit to a mother's sacrifice to protect her child," Dad said.

"Why did you adopt me?"

Mom abruptly sat up, her kind eyes focused on me as she spoke. Her eyes were wet with sadness and nostalgia, or maybe it was joy. I don't know.

CHAPTER 4

What we call our future is the shadow
that our past throws in front of us.
—Marcel Proust

Inspired by the American scholar Melville Herskovits, who wrote Life in a Haitian Valley, Margaret decided to study traditional Haitian beliefs. To help her with her field research, Latham wrote to his friend on her behalf. When Margaret, her husband, and Latham arrived in Haiti, Brahami, Latham's friend, took them on short trips to nearby villages, mostly to Kenscoff and Furcy, where his family had properties. But Margaret soon faced the difficulty of finding peasants who were willing to contribute to the study. People were reluctant to talk to strangers because their comments could be misinterpreted and could be the cause of trouble with the authorities. The air was infected with fear.

Brahami and his guests were talking after dinner one evening, when Margaret expressed her disappointment. Granted, her husband had enriched his collection of paintings with primitive, abstract, and religious art that were expressions of the Haitian soul, but she hadn't even begun her fieldwork. "I really need to meet peasants with traditional lifestyles," Margaret insisted. "I've been here a week, and still there are no prospects."

Brahami remembered a family that might be of help to Latham's friend. "They don't live close by and the roads are bad," he said. "Besides, you won't have any comforts there."

"That's no problem," Margaret reassured Brahami. "Doing fieldwork means eating anything and sleeping anywhere."

"I'll drive you there early tomorrow morning. But I'm not sure how easy it will be for you to communicate with them."

Margaret seemed worried. "Do they only speak Creole?"

"Someone there speaks French; not the most fluent French, but you'll be able to communicate somewhat."

Days later, Margaret and Hagathe sat under the shade of a mango tree, enjoying the afternoon breeze and the smell of ripe fruit. Margaret, who was anxious to move her research forward, asked Hagathe if she believed in vaudou.

Hagathe looked away. "We're Catholics. We believe in God, our Granmèt."

"Does being a Catholic mean a person cannot believe in vaudou?" Margaret asked, frowning, the thought of syncretism in the back of her mind.

"I don't know, Madan Winston," Hagathe replied and looked away again.

Margaret stared at the three-foot wooden cross in the yard and the bottle wrapped in black cloth that leaned against it. She would have to be patient, she thought.

Later that day, Margaret began another conversation with Hagathe, still hopeful to engage in talks about vaudou.

Not far away from where they sat, the son of one of Hagathe's cousins held an old pot upside down between his legs and rhythmically beat on it with sticks. His younger brother, also holding a stick, beat on a bottle to the same rhythm. Young Iris danced. Margaret watched, and then turned to Hagathe. "Your daughter is a natural dancer," she said.

Hagathe smiled faintly. "She's a good child."

"If you ever want her to visit the United States, she can always stay with us. My daughter Cynthia would enjoy her company."

"That would be nice," Hagathe said, "but I will never be able to come up with that kind of money."

"Don't worry. We can arrange that."

"How many children do you have?" Hagathe asked, after a brief silence.

"I can't have children. I adopted Cynthia when she was six weeks old," Margaret said, as she applied lotion on her bare arms to protect her pale skin from the Caribbean sun.

"Does she know she's adopted?"

"Of course," Margaret replied. "We're thinking about adopting another child soon."

"You really like children?" The question sounded more like an observation.

"I do. I didn't give birth to Cynthia, but I'm totally devoted to her." Margaret spoke in a voice just above a whisper. "There's the argument about heredity and environment. In some cases, heredity is more important, but it's not always true," she proffered.

"I don't know what those words mean."

"Let's see." Margaret paused. "Heredity refers to genes passed down through family lineage; environment implies conditions that surround a person."

Hagathe nodded, but Margaret thought she looked as confused as before.

"I worry so much about my daughter," Hagathe suddenly said. "I can't sleep at night. Sometimes I walk around like a zombie, worrying about what might happen to her."

"Why?"

Hagathe let out a moan of anguish mixed with fear and exasperation. "Vilanus, the Tonton Macoute," she said, "you know, the village militia, he can't stand my daughter." Alarm and sadness covered her face as she spoke. She moved closer to Margaret and lowered her voice. "He thinks it's because of her that I don't want him. God only knows what that evil man will do to my daughter!"

That evening, Margaret lay next to John on the oak queen-sized bed in their room in town. She put down the Alfred Métraux book she had been reading and sighed deeply.

"What's the matter?" John asked, turning down the light from the kerosene lamp on his side of the bed. "Are you still thinking about how to get Hagathe to talk?"

"She spoke about Iris today." Margaret related the conversation she'd had with Hagathe about a Tonton Macoute and her fear for her daughter. Margaret couldn't help noticing the horror on her husband's face. She wiped her face with a wet towel to cool off from the heat and humidity of the late evening and waited for his reaction.

"Poor woman!" John exclaimed. "I wish there was something we could do to help."

Long after the light had gone out, Margaret thought about Hagathe's fear and apprehension. An idea slowly emerged. She had to figure out how to present it to her husband and, most importantly, to Hagathe. Although she assumed she could persuade John, she knew enough about the strength of motherhood to think Hagathe might not go along with the plan.

"Are you okay?" John asked, waking up from a light sleep. "You're still awake." He struck a match, lit the gas lamp, and wrapped an arm around Margaret's shoulders.

"Since we've been thinking about adopting another child . . ."

John moved his arm away from her shoulders, raised his eyebrows. "You're not thinking about adopting Iris, are you?"

"You said you wanted to help."

"That doesn't mean we have to adopt the child!"

"But we're thinking about adopting another child."

"A lot of thinking must go into adopting a five-year-old of a different race who doesn't even speak English."

"We could become her guardians and then put her through school. She's bright enough to catch up with what she missed in preschool."

"We'll see."

"John," Margaret said in an exasperated voice, "We enjoy being parents and have already bonded with Iris. If you ask me, I'd say that's a tremendous advantage. At least we know who we're getting."

"But Margaret, you do realize that whites who adopt black children are viewed with suspicion."

"And you think we should care? Didn't we already agree that what really matters is to find a child in need of a loving home?"

"All I'm saying is that Iris may suffer from lack of cultural identity."

"Come on, John. We may be the only opportunity she has!"

John blew out the lamp. In the sheer darkness, with his eyes opened or closed, he could see the young Iris's mesmerizing, tear-filled eyes with an indefinable sparkle to them. No matter how much he tried to erase them from his memory, they were there, forcing their way to the depth of his soul. As minutes and hours went by, his heart softened and he imagined the guilt he would live with if something irreparable were to happen to Iris. By early morning, he had begun to envision himself holding her hand and escorting her to school.

John was tired the next morning after only a few hours of sleep. Yawning and stretching, he watched Margaret brush her hair in front of the distorted mirror. "I've been thinking," he said, "perhaps taking Iris back with us might be a good idea after all."

Margaret put down the brush and moved toward John. As she wrapped her arms around his neck, she looked into his eyes. "You are truly the best. That's why I love you so much."

Hours later, John and Margaret found Hagathe seated on a low chair with her head bent toward a large straw tray. She was cleaning the rice that was to be cooked that day. "My husband and I have something to ask you," Margaret said, taking a seat next to her. "I told John about your concerns for Iris and we thought that, if you agree, we could take her with us to the United States. I promise she will be in safe hands and we will make sure she receives a good education."

"I know it would be hard for you," John added. "But Iris can spend summer vacations with you. And if you're not happy with the job we're doing, you can always take her back."

"We would treat her like our own." Margaret spoke slowly, making an effort to enunciate every word even more than she usually did.

John shifted in his seat. "If you want, we can adopt her to get her legal status," he said, ending a brief silence that had fallen between them.

"I need to talk to my grandmother about it," was all that Hagathe said.

Days later, John sat on the porch while Margaret paced the verandah, waiting for Hagathe, who was supposed to pick them up on her way back from buying wholesale merchandise that she would later sell in the market. For the third time, Margaret glanced at her watch and said that maybe Hagathe couldn't come to town after all. "We should go there now," she suggested.

Walking along the sugarcane field, they saw a figure lying on the ground. As they came closer, they recognized Hagathe with her panties hanging loosely around an ankle. Margaret gasped, and John shook his head in disbelief before realizing he needed to act quickly. The nerves at his temples pounded, as he felt Hagathe's pulse. He tied his handkerchief around her head to stop the blood that was flowing from above her neck, then carried her to a nearby stream to dab cool water on her face. "I'm taking her to the main road," he told his wife. "She's got to get to a hospital." He left Margaret with Hagathe while he ran to the church around the corner so he could borrow the Jeep from the priest.

When Margaret told the women in the village that Hagathe had been attacked and that John had taken her to the nearest hospital, they became hysterical. After they calmed down, Hagathe's aunt Jésula swept the dirt floor and sprinkled water to keep the dust down. She put dried red beans in a pot to boil. Standing erect, she sighed heavily and shook her head before returning to the kitchen, which was a tent covered with dried palm leaves to shelter it from rain and sun. She fanned the wood fire with a torn straw hat, darkened by smoke and time, until the flames grew taller under the cooking pot.

"Goddamnit!" said a nasal voice that took possession of Jésula's body.

"Papa Guede is here!" Jésula's daughter, Marie Ange, announced with excitement. She removed the pot of beans that was balanced on three stones, and rushed to welcome the spirit who had come to visit the family through Jésula, a favorite steed.

Papa Guede tied Jésula's faded black dress around his waist, exposing a seven-colored slip; each color was cut in a square. He walked to the wooden cross, took a drink from the bottle wrapped in black cloth, and entered the peristyle, the place where the people worshipped spirits. The women followed.

Margaret had finally found material for her study. And, though it was true that they sometimes chatted with her freely, whenever she mentioned vaudou, all lips were sealed. But she hung around, hopeful that one day they would expose her to the secrecy of their religion. Looking around the peristyle, she took mental notes of the religious icons and objects that she later recorded in a notebook.

"Everyone says I'm an indecent, gossipy good-for-nothing who speaks in a foul language," the spirit boasted through Jésula's lips, as he surveyed the room. "But you must admit, I speak the truth."

"Papa Guede, we know you don't keep anything to yourself," said Lamercie, Hagathe's grandmother. She laughed.

"Didn't I tell you misfortune was on its way?"

"You did, Papa Guede," Lamercie admitted.

"Se byen, very well. Hagathe will be fine. That lowlife Tonton Macoute is furious with her because she rejected him. But Granmèt will render justice." Papa Guede suddenly noticed Margaret for the first time. "Oh! I'm honored to have a guest here," he said, shaking her hand. "So you're here to learn about the spirits of Guinen."

Margaret smiled and nodded. "I'm happy to meet you." She spoke to the spirit in French.

"I'm a nèg of Ayiti Toma. I don't speak fancy like those people from the city," Papa Guede said. "These women here, including my horse, were trying to hide us spirits from you. They thought we would not know how to behave around white people. That's why I came uninvited." Papa Guede broke into boisterous laughter, inviting everyone to do the same.

"Papa Guede, you are too much!" Lamercie said with a chuckle.

Papa Guede ignored Lamercie and turned to Margaret. "Bèl famm, beautiful woman, they show me no respect. They would never talk to Papa Ogoun that way," he said and rolled his eyes. "O-revoi-la-société." He then dismissed himself as abruptly as he had come.

A day later, Margaret touched Hagathe's shoulder, leaned close to her, and asked, "How are you feeling?"

"I'm here at the Lord's mercy," Hagathe said with a faint smile. "Thank you for everything you and your husband have done. I wouldn't be alive without you. Doctors in this country don't even look at you if you cannot pay in advance. Mèsi anpil, *thank you very much. I've decided to let you take Iris with you,*" Hagathe mumbled as tears filled her eyes.

"*I will take good care of her.*"

"*Wait until she's an adult before bringing her back here; wait long enough for that Tonton Macoute to forget her,*" Hagathe said, as she turned her head away and closed her eyes.

"*Get some rest,*" Margaret advised and started to leave the room.

Hagathe opened her eyes. "*I would like for Iris to keep her name,*" she uttered in a feeble voice.

Margaret turned to face Hagathe again. "*I will do as you wish.*"

A young marine in his early twenties led John and Margaret to an austere room where the official flag of the United States of America hung high on a rod in a corner. A picture of the first Catholic to occupy the Oval Office decorated the otherwise bear walls. The consul, a tall middle-aged man with a full head of curly black hair and a mustache, informed them that they had to file papers with local authorities because François "Papa Doc" Duvalier wanted the names of all Haitians who wished to travel outside the country to go through a special screening process. The Winstons reluctantly left the air-conditioned room to brave the heat as they went from one office to another before coming to the desk of Dieudonné, who looked vaguely familiar, probably because of his resemblance to Jésula.

He invited John and Margaret to sit on folding chairs across from his desk, where they had a full view of a black-and-white photograph of Papa Doc in a black suit and a tall black hat, hiding behind thick glasses. Dieudonné asked his secretary to read the papers out loud because he did not have his reading glasses. His mask of indifference disappeared when he heard Hagathe's name.

"What are your plans for the girl?" he asked in a throaty voice, keeping his eyes fixed on the couple.

"We promised her mother to give her a good education," John said.

"Why are you doing this?" Dieudonné's resonant voice filled the room.

"We love children, but we can't have any of our own. We have already adopted a girl in the United States and we would also like to adopt

Iris. We have become fond of her and her mother wants her to have a better life," Margaret told him.

Dieudonné leaned forward on his chair. "What do you do for a living?"

"I'm an art collector and gallery owner. My wife is an anthropologist."

"I see," said Dieudonné, even though Margaret believed that he had no idea what their work entailed. All the same, he looked impressed.

"I'm here to study Haitian culture," Margaret added. "A friend of ours introduced us to a loving family in Monn Nèg. That's how we got to know the child and her mother."

Dieudonné remained silent with a frown on his face. His features gradually relaxed before giving way to a smile. He summoned his secretary back to the office. "Make sure all the necessary papers are on my desk no later than tomorrow."

CHAPTER 5

We have not passed that subtle line between childhood
and adulthood until we have moved from the
passive voice to the active voice . . .
—Sydney J. Harris

On my way to visit Wayberry, the college that I had chosen, I thought about the story that Mom had shared about my birth mother, Hagathe Odys. I imagined her being proud of my achievements and, for the first time ever, I wondered what my life would have been in Monn Nèg.

At this point, I was anxious to begin a new life. My past suddenly became an insignificant parenthesis and I realized I was now in a totally different frame of mind.

A valley of green foliage sheltered the institution from the outside world. Hours after we met, I followed my roommate to the student cafeteria for dinner. She was from West Hartford. Her family background was no different from that of the kids at the private bilingual school I had attended in Westchester. As soon as I entered the large room, I spotted two tables where the black students sat and spent the rest of the evening thinking about my plan to sit with them.

The next morning, I told my roommate that it was okay to leave for breakfast without me. Later, filled with anticipation, I entered the cafeteria and walked to where the black students were sitting. Standing behind an empty chair, I asked the students, who were chatting and laughing, if I could join them. The looks on their faces made me feel like

I had said something foolish. As I was thinking about walking away, welcoming voices uttered "Of course" and "Sure."

"So, how does it feel to be a college freshman?" one of the girls asked.

Again I became nervous, thinking that because of my awkwardness, she knew I was a freshman. I mumbled something that I don't recall. Felicia Thompson introduced herself and the other students at the table. She must have sensed my uneasiness because she went on to say, "There are just a handful of us here and we all know each other. You look too young to be a transfer student, so you've got to be a freshman." Her unpainted lips were well-lined, and the roundness of her cheeks suggested kindness.

I relaxed a bit and was trying to think of something to say when Felicia told me I should get my breakfast because they would stop serving soon. When I returned to the table, she engaged me in conversation. I learned that she was from California and majoring in anthropology.

"No kidding," I said. "That's my major."

"Is that right? I'll have to tell you who's who in that department. But right now I've got to run. Be sure to come to the Black Students League party this evening."

On my way back to my room, I thought about the few dances I had attended in middle school. The girls usually danced together and the boys ran around playing games that we thought were silly. When Cynthia and the girls I hung around with in high school started dating, I stopped going. A few times they had tried to find a date for me, but that never worked; not even with the boy I liked who was in most of my classes.

Walking to the Frederick Douglass lounge, where the Black Students League held its social events, I thought about the dance steps I had learned while watching *Soul Train*. I was eager to practice them at a real party, instead of at home in front of the television. The song, "Play That Funky Music" was blasting. No one was dancing. A handful of people sat or stood in the corners of the room under neon lights. When Felicia waved, I walked over to her. She was talking to a guy who was about six feet tall. A huge Afro crowned his head, and he wore an African-print dashiki over faded jeans and a silver bracelet.

"This is Jamal, the BSL president."

"How you doing, sistah?"

"Fine," I said. He had a nice smile.

"I'll catch up with you later," he said. "I got to get this party started."

The room soon filled up, and it seemed that people had arrived all at once. The Ohio Players' new hit "Fire" blared through the speakers. Everyone moved to the center of the room as if under a spell of urgency.

Two hours later, the energy died out and most people left. On my way out Jamal came up to me and asked if I'd had a good time.

"Better than I expected."

A girl with a pierced nose and a gypsy skirt crept up behind him, wrapped her arm around his waist, and whispered, "Ready to go, baby?"

Weeks later, after a committee meeting for the upcoming Black Parents Weekend, Jamal said to me, "Sistah, I can't wait to see you dance. I know it's going to be good."

"How do you know that?" I replied, staring at the raised black fist on his white T-shirt that read, *Power to the People*.

"I just have a feeling!"

That evening, I thought about Mom and Dad coming to the Black Parents Weekend and called home, hoping to find a way to ask them to send Latham instead.

"How are things?" greeted Mom.

"I'm fine."

"Keeping up with your classes?"

"Of course."

"I'm glad. Did Cynthia call you?"

"Not today. I just got back to my room."

"She was admitted to Johns Hopkins medical school."

"That's great. I'll call her later."

"Your dad and I received our invitation to Parents Weekend."

"Actually, it's *Black* Parents Weekend."

"I see. Anyway, your dad and I will be there."

Silence.

"You do want us to come, don't you?"

"Sure," I lied.

"I love you."

"I love you too."

As I placed the phone back in its cradle, it occurred to me that I shouldn't care what the black students and their black parents thought about my white parents.

I was getting out of my leotard and tights while chatting with the other dancers after the piece I had choreographed when Wanda, Jamal's girlfriend, stormed into the dressing room. She stood arms akimbo, demanding to know what those white people were doing in *our* lounge.

"You must be talking about my parents," I said in a calm voice.

An uncomfortable silence fell over the room, and I walked toward Mom and Dad, holding my head high, ignoring the stares and indiscreet whispers.

That night when darkness and silence covered my room, I thought of Jamal's militancy, his leadership, and his artistic talent. Hours ago, listening to him read his poem about black solidarity and the greatness of men like Marcus Garvey, Toussaint Louverture, Malcolm X, Martin Luther King Jr., Shaka Zulu, Kwame Nkrumah, and Frederick Douglass was inspiring and uplifting. His soft-spoken voice had the cadence of a conch shell that had gathered the lamented voices of Haitian revolutionary slaves. The poem ended with a plea to our generation to carry on the dreams of Pan-Africanism and to valorize the greatness of our race.

I thought about it hard and long, and decided if I were a poet, I would write a poem about my adopted parents. The incident with Wanda prompted me to realize they had always accepted me for who I was and never had an issue with my race. I considered myself lucky to have had them in my life and concluded that my love for them would not have been any different if they, too, were black.

During late hours the library was a desolate place. It was just minutes before closing, and I was trying to finish a paper that was due the next morning. In spite of the numerous promises I had made to myself not to wait until the last minute to complete my assignments, the old habit lived on. As I wrote the last sentence I let out a deep sigh of relief. While I was gathering my books, someone tapped my shoulder.

"Jamal!"

"Burning the midnight oil?"

"I just finished a paper and have to go to my room to type it," I said, glancing at the titles of the books he was holding.

"I'm doing research on postcolonial Africa," he told me. "I hope to make it to the motherland someday."

"Felicia is planning on going there after graduation. Every once in a while I have a feeling it is where I belong," I responded, thinking about the fight in the cafeteria all those years ago.

"As children of the African diaspora," he said, "our salvation is our African roots and our cultural heritage."

I stared at the colorful dashiki and the red, black, and green cap he wore, and began to understand the sentimentality and reverence that he had for the ancestral homeland.

* * *

Late during a cold, windy winter night, Felicia knocked on my door. Immediately I knew that there had to be an important reason for her to be there, because hours earlier we'd had dinner together and I had not expected to see her until the next day.

"What's up?" I asked, watching her hang her jacket on the back of a chair.

She sat down on the antique rocking chair Latham had given to me the day I graduated from high school. "Have you heard what Wanda's up to?"

I sat on the edge of my bed and gazed at her. "I haven't heard a thing. What's happening?"

"Wanda and her friends are saying you have no business running for chairperson of cultural affairs because you grew up white."

"Meaning what?"

Felicia shrugged. "I guess they don't think you're black enough."

"What makes them think they know more about being black than I do?"

For about a week, I had tried to write my electoral statement but couldn't decide what to talk about. Wanda's comments motivated me. As soon as Felicia left, I sat at my desk to write before the ideas escaped me.

The day of the election, I walked up to the lectern, ready to deliver my statement. I cast a glance at Felicia, who smiled and nodded.

"I was born in the first black republic of the world," I began, "a place where slaves defeated Napoleon's undefeated army. Raised in the true spirit of white liberals who, in good conscience, believed in Martin Luther King's dream, I grew up in a home that advocated the utmost respect for cultures from around the world. Being a dance and anthropology major is a clear indication of my interest in culture." Even though Wanda sat next to him, Jamal smiled at me, encouraging me to go on. "As the cultural chairperson of the Black Students League, my goal would be to share our common African heritage with the college community so everyone can better understand the souls of black folks, as W.E.B. Du Bois would have put it." Loud applause erupted.

"Congratulations!" Jamal exclaimed afterward, hugging me. "It's so beautiful that even though you grew up with a white family, you are so together in the head."

I didn't get a chance to ask him what he meant by being "together in the head" because, as expected, Wanda was right there, pulling him away.

I won three-fourths of the votes.

CHAPTER 6

We cannot erase the sad records from our past.
—A. Maclaren

S
he sat slouched on the steps of the student hall terrace, eating a strawberry ice-cream cone; seemingly enjoying the New England Indian summer. She reminded me of a little girl the way she licked the ice cream dripping down the cone.

I had just returned to campus that day, ready to begin my junior year. I walked over to her, eager to welcome a new black face.

"So, you're the new Haitian on campus. I have wanted to meet you ever since I heard you would be coming here. I even thought of sending you a letter over the summer, but I didn't get around to it."

She looked puzzled. "How did you know there would be a Haitian on campus?"

"Before the start of summer vacation, the president of the Black Student League receives a list from the dean's office of incoming black freshmen. I was born in Haiti. I even went to the admissions office to see a picture of you. Right now I'm going to check my mail. When I come back you can tell me about your first days on campus. Also, we must talk about Haiti."

It didn't take long for that opportunity to present itself. About a week later Pépé came to my room, sat on the floor with her back against the wall, and faced my twin bed that was covered with Indian fabric.

"The way your eyes light up when you smile reminds me of my father," she said. I noticed, at that moment, that the dimples on her cheeks made her face even more pleasant.

"I don't know much about my natural parents," I said sadly. Even though I hated myself for encouraging pity, I felt compelled to tell her my story. "My mother sent me to the United States with my adoptive parents when I was five. She told them I shouldn't return until I'm adult."

"Why not?"

"Something about a Tonton Macoute," I said, flipping through a stack of albums, recalling the story that Mom had told me.

"When you go back to Haiti, you should talk to my father. He can tell you a lot about Haitian politics."

"Is he a politician?"

"An armchair politician," she said, laughing and stretching out her legs. "Are you in touch with your mother?"

"She can barely read and write, and of course she has no phone. No one in Monn Nèg does. But we send her Christmas cards and pictures."

"Do you miss her a lot?"

"I did at first," I said, thinking about her picture that ended up in some unknown location.

"What's your major?"

"I have a double major: anthropology and dance. And you?"

"American literature."

"How did you learn English?"

"I studied at an American school in Haiti."

"How many years?"

"I went to the Union School from first grade on. You have so many books on Haiti," Pépé commented as she read the titles on my bookshelf.

"My godfather gave most of them to me. I bought the others at a Haitian bookstore. I read many of them this past summer."

"I see a lot of books about *vaudou*."

"Knowing about *vaudou* will help me to understand the Haitian culture better." As the Isley Brothers finished a ballad I closed the window. A cool early-evening breeze had replaced the sun's warm rays. "How about listening to some *vaudou* music?" I suggested, while looking through the albums the Haitian dance instructor had recommended.

"I don't usually listen to that kind of music."

"Why not? You're Haitian, aren't you?" As I turned on the hot plate to boil some water, then poured chocolate powder into a cup, I realized, to my dismay, that I sounded like Dr. Connelly.

"I've never been exposed to it," Pépé said in a neutral tone, and shrugged.

Legba an ye o-o-o, a strident voice filled the room with sounds that have entranced Haitians since before they arrived from the coasts of Africa, when Bartolomé de las Casas suggested their importation to replace the disappearing Indian race.

"Do you speak Creole?" she asked.

"I spoke it as a child in Haiti." Drumbeats resounded in the background, and I handed a cup of steaming hot chocolate to Pépé. "That was my first language. When I listened to Haitians at the bookstore, I could understand quite a bit. But I'm not sure I'd be able to speak it if I'm back among Haitians. I speak fluent French, though. I went to a bilingual school."

A shaft of sunlight cut through the window and brightened the room. The drumbeats shifted to a hypnotizing tone. Its fluidity evoked water flowing in a river. I executed the *yanvalou* snake dance that honored Damballah Wedo, the spirit of wisdom that resided in cool springs. Responding to the pulse of the music, my head, shoulders, and torso coiled into a spiral, and I moved around the room with increased abandon.

"You dance so beautifully!" Pépé exclaimed, watching every step with admiration and fascination.

About a week later, after a meeting of the Black Students League, I stopped by Pépé's room. "You should join BSL," I suggested.

As an upperclassman, I felt responsible for guiding her the way that Felicia had guided me. She looked at me with incredulous eyes; then glanced away before speaking. "I don't want to get too involved with black Americans."

I raised my eyebrows. "Why is that?"

"My mother warned me against the Black Panthers and their 'black is beautiful' talk," Pépé said, and smiled faintly before taking a sip from his cup of tea. "Why are you looking at me like that?"

"Like what?"

"I don't know . . . like in a funny way."

"I was trying to understand why your mother would say something like that."

"A couple of years ago, the Haitian government arrested people who wore Afros because they thought it was a sign of rebellion."

"No kidding!" I said, admiring her long brown hair.

"BSL members are not just black Americans. There's a guy from Ethiopia, one from South Africa, and a sister from Kenya," I told her. "Some of us are West Indians or Latinos. Together we celebrate our common African heritage."

Looking out the window, it dawned on me that the splendor of summer had disappeared in a cloud to give way to a withered brown meadow. Crisp leaves moved swiftly along the campus yard as an autumn breeze hinted at the coming of winter. It made me think of Christmas, and I asked Pépé if she was going to Haiti for the holidays.

"My father's friend from his student days in Paris has

invited me to his home in Manhattan," she answered. "He's a painter who manages an art gallery."

"What's his name?"

"Latham Blackstock."

"I don't believe it! That's my godfather."

I called Latham as soon as I returned to my room to tell him the Haitian girl who was coming to visit him for Christmas was my new friend.

"Her father is a longtime friend," he said. "He asked me for a list of good colleges in the United States for his daughter. Wayberry College was one of the names I gave him."

How ironic that it was the college Pépé had selected! I did not think anything of it then. But I should have thought it strange that Latham had never told me about Pépé. I guess he did not want to interfere with destiny.

CHAPTER 7

Or will it mend the road before,
To grieve for that behind?
—Walter C. Smith

Mom wrote a book about Haiti," I told Pépé, who had come to our home with Latham the day after we arrived in New York for the holidays.

"Your father helped me meet the right people to make it happen," Mom said. "You must have been about two or three when we were there."

"I can't remember meeting any of you."

Mom smiled and twirled her glasses. "You were too young."

"I told my father about Iris," Pépé said, "but he didn't know she was Latham's goddaughter."

"I'm meeting two friends at a jazz club," Cynthia butted in. "You two are welcome to join me." She then turned to Latham. "Is it okay if Pépé spends the night? We'll probably come back late."

"It's up to Pépé. Any plans for tomorrow?"

"Shopping in the city," I answered.

"Here's the key to the loft. You can drop Pépé back there whenever you like."

"Pépé should just stay here with the girls. It will probably be more fun for her," Mom suggested.

"That's a good idea," Latham said.

Continuing the tradition that started three years earlier, Cynthia and I were in charge of Christmas dinner. We roasted a turkey with chestnut stuffing and baked broccoli soufflé. Pépé made spicy rice and beans. Latham, who almost always shared our Christmas dinner, brought some of the best French wines. Mom baked a pumpkin pie. Dad's duty was to play Christmas carols on the stereo. When the meal ended, we all retired to the living room to share Nat King Cole's Christmas spirit.

The phone rang and Dad picked up the receiver after the third ring. "Could you leave a number where we can call back in half an hour? I can't talk right now," I heard him say in French.

I grew inquisitive when Dad called Mom and Latham to his study. When the three of them emerged about twenty minutes later, they sat down at the dining table where Cynthia, Pépé, and I were having tea.

"We have some serious news to share," Dad said in a solemn tone that made me nervous. Somehow, I had a feeling the serious news concerned me. He moved his seat closer to mine, wrapped an arm around my shoulders, and gazed at me. "Life is about good moments and bad moments. We should be grateful for the good ones and strong enough to endure the bad ones." He lowered his head.

Unable to think of what this was leading up to, my confusion gave way to irritation and impatience. "Just tell us what happened," I snapped.

He covered me with a kind look and softly said, "Hagathe passed away this morning."

The room started moving and shutting in on me. Feeling suddenly out of breath, I closed my eyes and inhaled deeply as guilt took me by the neck, choking me. I wanted to cry, but no tears came to my eyes. "Why didn't you take me to her?" I shouted, casting accusatory eyes at both of my parents, though unsure of why I was blaming them. They turned red, but offered no explanation. My mind drowned in a body of doubts and suspicions. The wood burning in the fireplace crackled and the humming of the fan above the stove grew louder in the room that had gone silent.

"It was her desire for you to travel to Haiti to pay your last respects," I heard Dad say. "We'll take the first flight out to Port-au-Prince."

Latham, who sat between Pépé and me, reached for our hands and held them in his. "We have something else to say; something that concerns the two of you." His grip tightened. "Everything happens for a reason, and I think it's because of destiny that we are all here in this room with Iris in this time of grief."

"What is it?" I asked, convinced the lengthy prelude was to prepare me for more bad news.

"I tried to bring you and Pépé together," Latham said, turning to me. "I have even prayed the two of you would eventually discover the truth, but now the day has finally come. Brahami just gave me permission to tell you . . . to tell you that you are half sisters."

My vision blurred; my heart fluttered. Speechless, I stared at Pépé with empty eyes. She looked away, wiped her silent tears with a bare hand.

Anger unreasonably stirred inside me again. "What's with all these secrets?" I blurted.

Dad gently put an arm around me, and I buried my head in his chest.

"I'll call the airlines," Mom suddenly announced.

"Please make a reservation for me too," Pépé said in a shy voice, fixing tearful eyes on me.

I wanted to thank her, but no sound came from my mouth. Unrest and resentment seethed inside, challenging me.

"There's an American Airlines flight at nine o'clock tomorrow morning," Mom said, holding her hand over the telephone mouthpiece.

That night, I couldn't fall asleep. Questions whirled in my

head like an endless drum roll. I wanted to know how my natural parents knew each other and, most of all, I wanted to know why my father had never acknowledged me.

"I have a headache," I said, entering Mom and Dad's bedroom.

"Come here." Dad signaled for me to sit. I lay on the bed between them and closed my eyes. Mom left the room and returned with a bottle of aspirin and a glass of water.

"I'm going to try to sleep now," I said, after swallowing the pills.

"Do you want to talk for a while?" Mom asked.

"I don't know what to say," I offered, sitting down again.

"When we get to Haiti, you should talk openly to Brahami," Mom suggested.

"Listen to him with an open mind," Dad added.

I left the room, pondering how it would feel to meet the man who fathered me and how I was supposed to have an open mind when all I felt was animosity.

Just as I was reaching to turn off the lamp, I heard a knock at the door.

"How are you feeling?" Pépé asked, as she stepped in.

"Fine. Just fine," I said, looking into her puffy red eyes.

"May I sit down?" I ignored the question, but she sat at the foot of the bed anyway. "I don't understand why Papa never mentioned you." She paused, as if waiting for a reaction from me. "I wonder if my mother knows about you."

I can still hear the urgency and intensity in her voice.

"What difference does it make? She wasn't the one who screwed my mother," I responded in a flash of malice. I watched her delicate features tense up. Her hazel eyes suddenly seemed deeper and darker. I turned away from her, faced the wall, and heard her say good night before closing the door.

Half an hour later, I was still awake with thoughts of having mistreated Pépé. I eventually fell asleep, wondering how to apologize. I expected to see a reproachful look when I saw her the next morning, but there was only for-giveness. No words were needed, yet a tidal wave of regret still washed over me.

The plane hovered above the Caribbean Sea. The sadness of the circumstances overshadowed the happiness to see the not-so-familiar land of high mountains. After going through customs and immigration, Pépé guided us toward a man in a pastel yellow guayabera and white pants. He stood before me, seemingly anxious. Unsure of what to do, I extended a hand. He flashed a nervous smile, and when he embraced me I could feel his heart race. As he lead us out of the crowded airport, beggars reached out with bare, ashy hands.

Perched on top of a hill in an elegant suburban neigh-borhood, Brahami's villa stood behind a garden of tropical flowers and palm trees. Pépé's mother sat on the veranda, fanning herself with a newspaper. She looked beautiful in a sky-blue, spaghetti-strap dress. Hair pulled back in a pony-tail, her delicate features glowed, and I admired her striking beauty and regal frame.

Pépé and I sat by the pool at the back of the house, under the mild late-afternoon sun. "I'm sorry I talked to you the way I did when you came to my room last night," I told her.

"It's okay. I know you were upset." She smiled gra-ciously, though there was sadness in her eyes. "I'm going to join Cynthia in the pool," she announced, as she stood and walked away.

Left alone, I thought about the fact that in just a few hours I had lost a mother, discovered my friend was my half-sister, and met an estranged father. I gave in to the sun's warm caress and dozed off on the lounge chair, ex-hausted from my emotional upheaval and lack of sleep.

About an hour later, Brahami's footsteps on the gravel woke me. "May I join you?" he asked, taking the seat where

Pépé had sat earlier. We glanced at each other for less than a second, and an awkward silence engulfed us. "I owe you an explanation, but I don't know where to begin," he said.

My eyes roamed over his tall frame, looking for his biological traits that I might have inherited. I suddenly felt self-conscious about staring shamelessly. I continued to silently observe him, and stared into his expressive, deep brown eyes.

The complexity of my feelings took me to an unfamiliar place. "You don't have to explain anything," I told him, assuming a detached tone. Dad's voice rang in my mind, urging me to keep an open mind, reminding me that I needed to engage in a conversation with Brahami, to find out about his relationship with my mother.

"What was she like?" I finally asked, turning away from his stare.

"Your mother was a quiet woman," he said, and mopped his perspiring forehead with a white linen handkerchief. "I knew your grandmother a lot better. She practically raised me. When I came back from Paris, Acéfie had died and your mother had taken her place, working for my parents."

"Who was Acéfie?"

"Hagathe's mother."

"If you hardly knew her, how did she get pregnant?" My voice had risen to a higher pitch, and a cloud of anger that resembled grief settled in my heart. I made an effort to lower my voice. "There must be more to it than you're telling me."

"Try to understand what happened."

As I listened, I tried not to be judgmental.

CHAPTER 8

The rudder of man's best hope
cannot always steer himself from error.
—Martin Farquar Tupper

I n late spring on an exceptionally chilly Paris day, Brahami walked into a café on rue de la Huchette in the Latin Quarter. He stood at the bar that reeked of tobacco and was spanned by pinewood beams and waited for a table with a view of the narrow cobblestone street. Brahami watched the goings-on of the patrons and passersby intently, hoping his memories of the place would stay with him long after his return to Haiti. The headwaiter, an Algerian, came to let him know that Latham called and had been delayed but would meet him as soon as possible. Brahami thought about his imminent return home and wondered why his friend was late.

Moments later, Latham greeted Brahami: "Bonjour. Sorry I'm late. Did you get my message?"

Brahami nodded. "What happened?"

Latham removed his gray tweed jacket. "I was expecting an important call from New York. It looks like I'll be going home too," he announced as he settled into a chair across from Brahami.

"I thought you wanted to make Paris your home." As the waiter took Latham's order, Brahami fixed an inquisitive gaze on his friend. "Why did you change your mind?"

"There's a whole lot happening back home with the civil rights movement," Latham said, stretching his long legs underneath the table. "I'm too excited about it to stay here."

As the waiter returned with their drinks, Brahami took a Gauloise from the pack and studied his friend under half-closed eyelids. "Can we actually make a difference at home?"

"I don't know the answer to that, but I do know that I want to make whatever contribution I can."

They finished their beers and became absorbed in their own private thoughts, enjoying the city's youthful optimism and excitement, dreaming of a world of justice, free of racial and social discrimination.

On a sunny day in June 1954, Brahami left Paris, filled with unlimited hope. The anticipation of being among family and old friends was greater than the sadness he felt about leaving. After all, he had everything that seemed to destine him for a good life, and that included finding his place in Haitian high society. He was ready to take over the family's estate and also had his beautiful childhood sweetheart waiting for him.

As he drove through the gate, his father beeped the horn and guests rushed to welcome the young Bonsang. Instantly Brahami was distracted by the distinct smells of spicy food that mingled with the scent of hibiscus flowers and bougainvillea. Darah waited under one of the palm trees in the courtyard that had been transformed into an outdoor dining area with elegant blue tents that blended with the color of the Caribbean sky.

Brahami remembered that he had not answered her last two letters, but immediately noticed her iridescent eyes radiated love and forgiveness. Her hair was pulled into a chignon adorned with a white hibiscus flower; the white dress she was wearing accentuated her square shoulders and complemented her honey-colored skin. Brahami turned away from the crowd as soon as he could and walked toward Darah who extended her manicured hand to be kissed.

He sat at a table with her and their friends who also belonged to the exclusive Bellevue Club, where the passport for entry was to be a member of an influential mulatto family. The influence had to do with money and pedigree; the more French ancestors one could trace, the better. Madame Bonsang approached the table and embraced Darah. The older woman wore a straight black skirt and a white embroidered linen blouse; her long hair was styled in a French twist.

"Manman, the food is superb. It's been so long since I ate a hearty meal like this."

"The credit goes to Hagathe," she told him.

Brahami stood from his chair. "I haven't had a chance to say hello to her yet." He excused himself from his friends and looked for the maid, who was clearing food from the buffet table. "Bonjour, Hagathe," he said.

"Bonjou, Mesye Brahami." A smile brightened her dark face as she wiped her hands on her apron.

"My parents told me about your mother in one of their letters. I'm so sorry she's gone." Brahami realized he was speaking Creole for the first time since he'd left Haiti seven years ago. He was definitely home, he thought.

"I'm glad you're back, Mesye Brahami. Please excuse me."

He looked up and watched the golden rays of the sun behind the mountains. A patch of cloud covered the sky as he walked away from Hagathe.

Brahami and Darah's engagement lasted only a few months. Despite the short notice, her family prepared a lavish wedding that gathered Haiti's most prominent mulatto families. The bride and groom received many valuable gifts, including Hagathe, the loyal family servant. Shortly after they returned from their honeymoon in Havana, Brahami received a letter from Latham, who wrote about the steady changes in civil rights for Negroes in the United States, which made Brahami consider questions he had not thought of since his return to Haiti.

"Bad news from Latham?" Darah questioned.

"Not at all," Brahami said, folding the letter and putting it in his pocket as he announced that he was going for a drive.

Like Latham, Brahami had considered getting involved in the political struggle when he returned home; so his friend's letter was a reminder of the promise he had made to himself. He drove through the streets of Bois Verna, Canapé Vert, and Champs de Mars, where people lived behind closed gates in houses adorned with red, pink, white hibiscus, and laurel flowers. He then continued through the more popular rue Pavée and rue du Centre, where houses were close to the sidewalks, one right next to the other. Driving along the shabby streets of Bel Air, he observed les misérables of Port-au-Prince with growing interest, eager to learn about their lives, wondering how he could be useful to them.

The streets of Bel Air, with their peeling, crumbling houses, were quite noisy. Brahami was impressed by the shrieks and cries of street peddlers that rose in crescendo, inviting people to purchase food staples such as ground corn, rice, and salted pork. "Min-bel-mayi-moulin-diriblan-mayi-sinmak-min-soupoudre-e-e-e," said the voices that reached the walls of nearby houses. Listening to the musical sound that translated a unique cultural reality, Brahami realized he had never paid attention to those ambulant merchants before he left for Paris and that being away for so long made him more appreciative of them.

Women hurried through rundown gates to make purchases. People sat on porches and carried on with their everyday activities. A young girl sat between the legs of an older one on a low stool, having her hair braided. A woman bent over a sewing machine, and next to her, loose cigarettes, mint candy, coconut cakes, and grilled peanuts were set up to be sold. At other places, men cut each other's hair. Boys played with colorful marbles. Passersby stopped to exchange bits of friendly conversation. Some sat alone with their thoughts; others gossiped.

Brahami parked his jeep next to three women who were carrying empty buckets to a public water fountain. They stopped to talk with another woman, sheltered under a cloth tent, who was selling cooked rice and beans and goat stew. She kept clean enamel plates and spoons in a wicker basket on one side, dirty ones on the other. Brahami listened to their conversation.

"How's business today?" one of the women asked.

The vendor fanned herself with an old straw hat. "Half of the rice is gone. I'm hoping I won't have to take the rest with me tonight."

"Do you know what happened to that girl who lives inside this alley here?" another woman asked, pointing to a chipped metal gate that was open. "We heard her scream a little while ago. What was the beating about this time?"

"Adye!" the vendor cried out in pity. "The poor thing has to clean the place, do the laundry, and wash the feet of the lady of the house for scraps of food." She sucked her teeth and continued to fan herself.

A man walked up to her to buy a plate of food. She served him a small piece of goat meat on a sea of rice and beans. He ate his meal on a wooden crate a few yards from her.

"The poor girl was on her way back from the fountain. She was right there." The vendor pointed to a street corner. "A schoolboy pushed her, and the water fell from the bucket she carried on her head, and she had to return to the fountain. When she came back to the house, the woman beat her with a rigwaz because she took too long. You know how much that dried cow skin hurts!"

"Oh yes," said another woman. "I used to get my share of it when I was a restavèk."

Brahami peered through the opened gate and watched the restavèk, an unkempt, undernourished servant girl, no older than eight or nine. She wore a torn, faded dress that hung limply below her shoulders. He felt even more pity when he saw that her face was badly burned, which made him ponder the question he had often asked himself in Paris when he flirted with Communism: could Marxism be the answer to Haiti's color and class division?

Two years after they were married, Darah went to France to seek medical treatment that she hoped would put an end to her infertility. One evening after supper, Brahami and his high school friend Georges sat on the veranda. After Hagathe had brought the rum punch that he had requested and was no longer in sight, Georges exclaimed, "What a bel nègès! A true black beauty!"

"You're talking about the maid?"

"You mean you haven't noticed?"

"Not really," Brahami lied. Although he had fantasized from time to time about having sex with her, he had, thus far, managed to brush away the desire.

After Georges left he helped himself to another drink. At the sight of Hagathe putting dishes away, he stopped at the doorway of the kitchen. She was startled when she became aware of his presence.

"I didn't mean to frighten you," he said. "I just came for some water."

His eyes searched hers as she filled a glass from a pitcher, then presented the tray to him.

"Tonight's conch was the best," he said, unable to think of anything else to say. Giving in to an impulse, he put his arms around her and pulled her close. As he touched and squeezed her breast, he told himself to stop. The liquor had fogged his better judgment. He held her tightly and continued to fondle her soft breasts. He unbuttoned her skirt and let it fall to the floor. His knees weakened, and when he could no longer stand, he pulled her down to the mosaic-tiled floor and grappled to free himself; he quickly discovered she was a virgin.

Regret covered him when it was over. He gathered his clothes and left the kitchen. After showering, he wrapped a towel around his waist and leaned against the bedroom balcony. Sleep eluded him. His irredeemable act haunted him. He gazed into the night, trying to erase the memory.

By the time he fell asleep, night had fallen. In the morning, he was too distraught to eat the breakfast that awaited him and too embarrassed to face the maid. At ten o'clock Brahami left for his office.

There, he hid behind his closed door, and smoked more than usual. That afternoon, he drove up the northern highway and stopped at a roadside vendor for a lunch of fried plantains and fried fish. He watched the passengers in crowded buses on their way to Cap-Haïtien. They seemed anxious and resigned to the lengthy trip on the bumpy roads that were still greatly in need of repair despite the improvements made by Americans during the fifteen years they had occupied the country.

By nightfall, he found himself roaming aimlessly in the neighborhood of Carrefour. He walked into a bar where Dominican women allowed Haitian men to live out their fantasies of possessing a light-skinned woman. He ordered a rum punch and, alone with his thoughts and the drink, he considered the troubles that he had created. From that day on, Brahami stayed away from Hagathe. Seeing her was an unpleasant reminder of the unforgivable night in the kitchen.

Darah returned from Paris three weeks later, radiant and relaxed. Brahami thought her more beautiful than before. He was delighted to have her home because now he no longer had to discuss expenses or other practical matters with Hagathe.

Months later, when Brahami's mother came for supper along with her husband, she noticed that Hagathe's hips had broadened. Afterward, she went into the kitchen where the maid, wearing a dress that fit her loosely to disguise the roundness of her stomach, was washing the dishes.

"I need to talk to you." The seriousness of the older Madame Bonsang's voice alarmed Hagathe, who lowered her head. "I've known you since you were a young girl. You're like family to me, so what happens to you concerns me. Is there a man in your life? Could it be that you're pregnant?"

Hagathe's heartbeat quickened. "Wi, Madan Bonsang, I'm pregnant, wi. That's one thing I cannot deny, non."

"You're right. Sooner or later you'll have to admit it. Tell me who the father is. I must see to it that he marries you. I owe it to your mother."

"Madan Bonsang, I can't tell you, non."

"What's the matter?" Monsieur Bonsang asked when his wife returned to the veranda.

"Hagathe is pregnant."

"Who is the father?" Darah wanted to know.

Madame Bonsang twirled her thumbs. "She wouldn't say. I'll talk with her again in a few days."

After his parents left, Brahami closeted himself in his study to avoid his wife. Early the next morning when the smell of coffee reached him, he went to the kitchen.

"Good morning, Hagathe."

"Good morning, Mesye Brahami," she answered without looking at him.

"My mother told me you're expecting a child. Could it be mine?" he asked, a stifled smile surfacing across his face.

"Mesye Brahami, you know it couldn't be anybody else's, non."

"I'm sorry," was all he could say.

At that moment, the steady flow of Brahami's life became a raging river. The crude reality was that he had to face the consequences of his action. He summoned enough courage to talk to his wife, but then decided it would be better to have his mother speak to Darah first. Like a coward on his way to a battlefield, he walked upstairs and found his wife standing in front of an open closet; there was a suitcase packed with shoes and clothes.

Without any form of introduction and a surprising calm, she said, "I overheard your conversation with Hagathe."

Even though Darah spoke in a soft voice, her words echoed like thunder in a field. "What did you say?" he asked, refusing to believe his ears.

She repeated the terrifying revelation before losing her composure and slapping his face, not once but twice, and then again, while sobbing and calling him a sang sale, an undignified lowlife.

Brahami later drove to his parents' home to finish his mea culpa and to find allies. Once he arrived, his body dropped into a chair like that of a tired old man. Resting his elbows on the table, he held his head and watched his parents eat their breakfast of hot banana cereal.

"You look exhausted," his mother said with a worried look. "Didn't you sleep last night? Is something wrong? Would you like some breakfast?"

"Easy, Maud. How many questions are you going to throw at him at once?"

"I don't want anything to eat," Brahami answered a bit too curtly. "But coffee will do me good," he added in a softer tone, removing his elbows from the table. He lit a cigarette and abruptly broke the silence. "Hagathe's baby is mine." He then threw his head back to blow out smoke but mostly to avoid looking at his parents.

His father raised his eyebrows. "How could you have done that?"

"Kyrie eleison!" his mother exclaimed, peering upward to address heaven. She reached for the rosary beads in the pocket of her skirt.

"Maud, the Lord's mercy has nothing to do here," Brahami's father said in an even tone, although he was upset thinking his genealogical tree was about to be tainted with crude peasant blood. "Don't you have any respect for the name you carry?"

Monsieur Bonsang came from a pedigreed mulatto family. His father often bragged about his ancestor, a mulatto slave owner whose patriarch was a Frenchman from Normandy, who had come to Saint-Domingue as

Napoleon's envoy after the 1791 slave revolt and had fallen in love with a free black woman of the affranchi class, who bore him two sons and a daughter. Thus began his family lineage.

"Sometimes you do something, even though you know you shouldn't. I mean—"

"My son," his father interrupted, "you should know better than to have sex with every woman who excites you. Being responsible and mature means exercising self-control. Does Darah know?"

"Yes."

"How is she taking it?" his mother asked.

"She's devastated. I thought we might raise the child as ours. But I didn't have a chance to tell her that."

"Wait for her to regain her calm before suggesting it. If she doesn't agree, your father and I will raise the child. What do you think, dear?"

"I have no objections," Brahami's father reluctantly told his wife.

The week that followed Hagathe's departure from the house, Madame Bonsang noticed that the maid had left her belongings behind. She asked her husband to drive her to Monn Nèg. Brahami gave them money for Hagathe and requested that they keep it a secret from his wife. He left the room but returned moments later to say he thought he should accompany them. Brahami's father expressed his approval.

"I think you're making the right decision. Hagathe is, after all, carrying your child."

Brahami drove at a moderate speed, absorbed in thoughts of how he would feel seeing Hagathe again.

"Monn Nèg shouldn't be far from here," his father said. "Slow down."

Brahami stopped in front of a booth next to a house off the road. On a small blackboard, a sign read, Borlette. First prize 100 gourdes. Second prize 50 gourdes. Third prize 25 gourdes. He stepped out of the car and walked toward a man who recorded names and numbers in a notebook.

"Bonjour. Could you please tell me how to get to Monn Nèg?"

"Wi, mesye," the man answered. "You just turn left when you

reach the second crossroad. Who are you looking for?" There was suspicion in his voice.

"We're looking for a woman named Hagathe who used to live in the city."

"Which Hagathe is that?" asked a woman, taking a five-gourde bill out of her bra.

"I don't know her last name." Brahami turned to his parents, who looked at each other, shaking their heads. He was amazed that they only knew the servant by her first name, even though she and her mother had worked in their home for decades.

"Who's her mother?" asked an older man.

"Her mother's name was Acéfie. She died a few years ago," Brahami responded.

"Acéfie was Lamercie's daughter," the older man told the others. "Ti Jean, take them over there."

The sound of the approaching jeep aroused curiosity. It had been quite some time since a vehicle had ventured off the main road. Children ran around grinning and waving. Women left their cooking. Men in the fields leaned on their hoes to watch. A man in cutoff faded jeans nearly fell from a coconut tree.

Lamercie, Hagathe's grandmother, saw the approaching vehicle, moved the pipe away from her mouth, and walked toward the visitors. Madame Bonsang wiped the sweat on her forehead with a white embroidered handkerchief.

"We've brought Hagathe's belongings," she said.

"Mèsi anpil." Lamercie thanked her and invited them to sit under the mango tree, where a mild breeze would keep them cool. "Hagathe is washing clothes in the river. I'll send someone to get her."

Half an hour later, the young boy returned and said he had looked for Auntie Hagathe but could not find her. Brahami suspected Hagathe did not want to see her former employers. How is it possible not to find someone who is washing clothes by the river? The Bonsangs entrusted the money and Hagathe's belongings to Lamercie, who gave them plantains and coconuts to take back to the city.

* * *

Time passed. No one ever mentioned Hagathe and her baby again. But eventually a letter from Latham changed everything. Brahami had often wondered about Hagathe and whether she had given birth to a boy or a girl. At some point, he had even considered going to Monn Nèg, but decided that creating a tie with the former maid and her child would further complicate his life. Visiting Monn Nèg with the Winstons and Latham gave him a legitimate excuse to see his child.

CHAPTER 9

'Tis virtue, and not birth, that makes us noble:
Great actions speak great minds, and such should govern.
—John Fletcher

B rahami dabbed a handkerchief across his forehead with an unsteady hand. As I watched, I was surprised that his growing discomfort provoked a cynical joy in me. "Is it a Haitian custom for the powerful lord to take advantage of the weak servant?" I asked, unable to contain the knot in my chest.

Perspiration pearled on his forehead again. "Let's go for a walk," he said.

As we strolled along the quiet street, he put his arm around my shoulder. Though the gesture seemed natural, it was untimely. I couldn't control the anger and resentment that suddenly flared, and I shrugged his arm away.

"I may have good intentions," he said, "but I always take the easy route. What happened between your mother and me is a perfect example. I went along with Darah's decision not to have you in my life because it was easier."

Glancing at his profile, I noticed his obstinate chin looked aristocratic, although the way he had abandoned me was less than noble. "What do you mean?"

I wasn't sure if he heard me, and at that same moment a barking black dog ran out of a gate. Brahami bent down as if to pick up a stone that wasn't there. The dog changed direction and ran back to the housekeeper, who closed the gate behind them.

I managed a faint smile. "It's interesting how you chased that dog away."

"That was *kaponaj*."

"What's that?"

"*Kaponaj* is, oh, I guess you can say, intimidation," he explained. "To survive in Haiti, you have to know how to intimidate before someone else gets the upper hand."

"A brilliant concept!"

"Your mother could have used *kaponaj* on me, you know."

"Why didn't she then?"

"She was too naïve."

"Meaning?"

"She could have threatened to make a scandal, for example, to get something out of me, like money to raise you."

My anger was on the rise again. "Why did you think it was all right to touch her?" I blurted.

"I would have stopped, if she had asked me to . . ." He spoke in a courteous voice, coated with irony.

"When I asked you about my mother earlier, you became uncomfortable and I had an urge to add to your discomfort. Would that have been *kaponaj*?" I asked, this time in a more neutral voice.

"I guess."

At six o'clock in the morning, colorful tap-tap buses, lopsided from the weight of mercantile goods, chickens, and goats, drove servants to other people's homes and laborers to factories and construction sites. Women traveled on foot or on a donkey's back from one town to another to sell food staples and secondhand clothing. Those with strong and erect backs carried large baskets of fruits and vegetables on their heads, swinging their arms like soldiers on their way to battle. The more fortunate women sat on donkeys loaded with merchandise on either side, beating the animals' flanks to move them along. One woman who clutched the end of a tether in her hand stood with her legs astride. Her other hand held her dress up and away from the beer-colored liquid that poured from her upper thighs, that foamed and disappeared into the earth. The donkey nodded, looking as tired as an old slave. A few feet away, another woman squatted to relieve herself as well.

As the car crossed the rusty metal bridge that separated the capital from the northern rural areas, I saw a small girl who reminded me of the time I'd rode in a jeep with John and Margaret away from Monn Nèg. Water had rushed in the river, making gentle whooshing sounds. The burning summer heat, at that time, had filled me with happiness and fear.

Looking down again from this same bridge during the trip back to Monn Nèg, the scene was desolate. The dried-up river exposed its rocks to the sun. Women bent over puddles of muddy water to bathe their naked babies. Brown hills stood bare against the horizon, void of their green cover and precious topsoil. What had happened over the years?

When Brahami announced we were approaching our destination, my heart skipped and jumped in anticipation. Monn Nèg seemed vaguely familiar. More houses had been built on land that used to be vacant. There were fewer trees and I was surprised to see cars on the unpaved streets. The compound was packed with people dressed in mourning colors. Some sat on wooden chairs or straw mats. When the two jeeps pulled up, the men removed their straw hats.

A woman rushed toward us, unable to hold back her tears. "I am Marie Ange, your godmother," she said, grasping me in a warm embrace. "Come, you must see your great-grandmother at once," she went on in a rudimentary French with a singsong lilt. She smiled and held me at arm's length. When she finally let go, she led me to the matriarch, a thin, toothless, elderly woman in an immaculate white dress that had been through many washes. A white scarf covered her bristly gray hair. She strained to peer at me as she leaned her stooped figure on a cane.

"*Pitit mwen*, my child," she said in a stirring voice. She took my hands into hers and heaved a wounded sigh. Her hands were rough, but her eyes shone with kindness and wisdom. She hugged me and kissed my cheeks with wet lips, before disappearing behind a closed door.

I sat on a low bench next to Marie Ange, who washed cups and saucers in a plastic basin. "Your mother bought these sixteen years ago after the Bonsangs first came here," she said, "just in case they showed up at our door again." She rubbed a handful of soapy straw on a saucer. "But they haven't been used since you left with the Winstons."

Jésula, Marie Ange's mother, interrupted and could not have picked a worse time to talk about money. "Do you know Hagathe didn't pay me for the merchandise I picked up for her last week?" she said.

"*Ou finn deraye*, you've lost it. *Manman*, with all due respect, I don't think you should be thinking about money right now. People are right to say your head isn't straight because of all the spirits dancing in it," Marie Ange snapped, placing the cup she had washed in a wicker basket to dry.

Jésula burst into a wail. "I need to find some money to pay for a Mass for Hagathe's soul to rest in peace." She sobbed and took a handkerchief from her dress pocket to blow her nose. "My poor niece, you have to forgive me if I hurt your feelings." She looked at the sky with great expectation. "Your body isn't even in the ground and I'm talking about money you owe me. I'm sorry. You have to give me a number to play so I can have enough money to pay for a Mass so your soul can rest in peace."

The other women laughed, but Marie Ange shook her head in disapproval.

* * *

"I'd like to view the body," I said, having savored the last drop of the black, overly sweetened coffee that Marie Ange served.

"I'm coming with you," Mom said, and led me by the hand the way she used to when I was a young girl.

Hagathe lay under a white sheet on a table in the middle of the room. As I contemplated the lifeless body, I fell into deep meditation recalling the day she told me to go with the Winstons. "How would you like to go to New York with Mesye and Madan Winton?" she had asked.

"Do they live in a pretty house with beautiful things like in the book you gave me?"

She nodded yes.

"Are you coming too?"

"*Mwen pa kabap*, I can't," she said. "They're going to take care of you while I'm sick." She took a deep breath. "You will go to a nice school." Streams of tears rolled down her cheeks. The morning sun, streaming through the window across from the bed, brought life to her saddened face.

"*Manman*, what's wrong?"

"Go play," she ordered, and turned her head away from me.

I stood in respectful silence until I heard Marie Ange say that they were ready to wash the body. Mom then led me to a corner of the room. Lamercie, who had worked as an undertaker and a midwife, was no longer strong enough to perform those rigorous jobs. Marie Ange later told me that she could only do those tasks for family members. At the head and feet of the body my great-grandmother lit candles; she then washed the body with fresh leaves soaked in water and changed the cotton balls that sealed the body's openings. Because my mother's mouth had remained open when she died, her lower jaw had to be tied shut. "The corpse could release a poisonous odor that would endanger lives," Marie Ange explained.

When I left the room, a man in a black polyester suit, whose high cheekbones reminded me of Jésula, approached me. He introduced himself as Uncle Dieudonné; and as he hugged me awkwardly, I could smell alcohol on his breath. Before I could speak to him, Marie Ange said that they were ready to head to the church. As he walked away, another episode from my awkward past came to mind.

That day, dressed in a pastel blue dress with a white collar and white sandals purchased in a fancy boutique, I no longer looked like a child from Monn Nèg.

"What's your name?" Dieudonné had asked.

"Iris," I answered, showing a gap where two front teeth used to be.

"Do you want to go with those people?"

"Yes. We're going to New York."

"Everyone dreams of going to New York. You're lucky."

The fragmented recollection of isolated moments like this troubled me. Images flashed before my eyes without my being able to thread them together, to see a total picture.

The professional mourners' wails resounded like confused dialogues, and sent eerie chills down my spine. When the wailing subsided, two men placed the pinewood coffin on top of small cushions on their heads that were made by tying a rag into a circular shape.

Lamercie stayed at home. It was considered bad luck for the elderly to attend funerals. I walked between Mom and Dad. Jésula, Marie Ange, Magda, and her children followed. Pépé, Cynthia, Brahami, his parents, and Madame Dufour rode in the jeeps. The vehicles drove along the wide road. The procession took a shortcut, winding through roads so narrow that we, at times, had to form a single file. When we walked into town, people who watched made the sign of the cross.

Inside the church, I inhaled the scent of burning candles and frankincense. People whispered and pointed at me. Father Leblanc droned on and on about eternal life. He then read a verse from the Bible: "*For God so loved the world, that He gave His one and only Son, that whoever believes in him shall not perish but have eternal life.*" My mind drifted. A desire to remember more about my life with Hagathe haunted me. Caught in a nightmarish world of forgetfulness, I stared at a mahogany statue of the Virgin Mary holding Baby Jesus.

Father Leblanc's voice again echoed in my ears and I tried to focus on his words. "Because God made us in His own image, man is a spiritual being. That is why we need to have an intimate, personal relationship with Him. Eternal life means loving God, and loving God shows itself in love for people." Thoughts about Hagathe returned to my mind, and I no longer listened.

Finally we reached the cemetery. People shrieked and wept. Marie Ange fainted. Thunder pealed, but the rain never came. Mother Nature's *kaponaj*.

The villagers and townsfolk surveyed the soft drinks, bread, tea, coffee, cassava, rum, and sardines next to bags of rice, beans, and ground corn laid out for them. Men played cards and dominoes, while drinking white rum spiced with cinnamon sticks straight from the bottle. The women drank tea or coffee and sat on low chairs or on mats spread over the dirt floor. Some sat with no cushion at all, their cotton skirts or dresses tucked between their legs; feet on the ground, knees side by side. Children played tic-tac-toe, moving pebbles from the holes they dug in the ground. Those who had walked a distance recovered from fatigue and hunger and slept under shelters made of fresh palms. Tin lamps with rough wicks lit the yard.

"Did Hagathe have a good send-off?" Lamercie asked.

"People whispered a lot during the church service," Jésula told her mother. "I guess they were trying to figure out who the white people were. I tell you, the last time people were so excited in church was years ago, when the first person from town who had gone to live in New York came home."

"What happened?" I asked.

Jésula laughed at the memory. "I guess that woman wanted to show us country folks how they dress in the place where she came from. She showed up in church for the celebration of St. Christopher's Day dressed in clothes that didn't seem like cloth and made her look like a big white cat with a black face. She had on shoes that came up to below her knees. The poor woman fainted in the middle of the packed church. I guess her body couldn't take the heat."

Lamercie joined us in laughter. "I remember that day," she said.

Marie Ange called me inside the bedroom, where Hagathe's body had been displayed. She handed me a red cotton undershirt that she took out of a brown paper bag. "*Tan pri*," she begged. "Wear this to bed every night for the next two months," she whispered. The seriousness of her voice alarmed me. "Your mother never got over being separated from you."

"What's this supposed to do?"

"It will keep her away from coming to get you when you're asleep at night."

"How is she going to come for me if she's dead?"

Marie Ange shrugged. "I guess you don't know about these things."

I put the undershirt in my bag and cannot remember what I did with it. I do know that I never did wear it and that Hagathe never did come for me—that is, until much later.

"Tomorrow," Marie Ange went on, "I have to go back to the cemetery to put an eyeless needle and a spool of thread on her grave."

I cast a questioning look at her.

"It will take her mind away from wanting to come get

you," she said. "She'll be too busy trying to thread a needle she can't thread."

Early the next morning, after everyone else had left, I sat on Madame Dufour's front porch with Pépé. A local bus drove by, raising a cloud of dust. Curious passersby stared at us and whispered to one another. "They're the beautiful people of the city," a boy about fourteen years old told his two friends.

"*Sak pase?* What's up?" Pépé asked, as she slapped her right shoulder, killing a tropical marsh mosquito.

The three boys grinned. "I told you they speak Creole," one of them said.

"Where are you from?" asked another.

At that moment, Madame Dufour came out. "*Allez, foutre!*" she yelled, chasing the boys away.

"They weren't bothering us," I said.

"You don't know these people. You give them this," Madame Dufour measured her hand, "they'll take that," she showed the length of her fleshy arm. "These people don't know their place."

I didn't think the boys had done or said anything offensive. Somehow, I knew better and left the matter alone. On an impulse, I announced, "We're going for a walk."

"You should visit my brother-in-law's mills to see how we make sugar and rum. I'll ask the priest if his driver can take you."

"Why did Madame Dufour treat those boys that way?" I asked Pépé when we were alone. "They didn't do anything wrong."

"She probably thought they were being fresh."

At the mill, workers clad in rags carried sugarcane stalks from the field to a large basin. Bulls plodded around the basin in a circle, grinding the juice from the cane. The workers brewed and simmered the liquid until it was the consistency of molasses. Women in tattered clothes gathered under a tent to cook cornmeal and red beans over wood fires.

Madame Joseph sat under an almond tree, fanning herself. A young girl massaged her legs. As we approached she exclaimed, "I must have a sixth sense!" Dismissing the girl, she slipped her feet into plastic slippers and stood up to meet us. "I was just thinking about the beautiful people in the city, and *voilà*! You must be my daughter's friends."

"Actually, we're not. We're staying at Madame Dufour's in town and she suggested we stop by the mill," said Pépé.

The workers gawked. Even the bulls had stopped to stare. "Haven't you seen people before? You're so uncouth," Madame Joseph, Madame Dufour's sister, snarled. "When are you going to learn to mind your own business?" With their heads down, the men went back to work.

She led us to a veranda, and just beyond I gazed at a tree trunk with bare stunted branches and at the barren mountains on the horizon.

"The landscape used to be green," said Monsieur Joseph, who had joined us. "It was a jungle when I was a young man." He waved his hand and remarked, "Look at it now."

"You must meet our daughter Chantal. You're the kind of people she should know," Madame Joseph stated emphatically.

Chantal wore fashionable red shorts, a white T-shirt, and gold hoop earrings. Her fingernails and toes were painted red. Pink sponge rollers covered her head. She suggested that we move to the living room where four mahogany armchairs formed a circle around a coffee table on which cheap porcelain figurines were arranged. A framed black-and-white photograph of a worn-out Papa Doc with his arm around Baby Doc's shoulders decorated a wall. Next to it was a picture of Monsieur and Madame Joseph on their wedding day.

"This is why I am always telling you the living room must be dusted first thing in the morning. I never know when someone will show up." Madame Joseph surveyed the room and focused her annoyed eyes on the barefooted *restavèk*, who was no more than twelve years old. "What an embarrassment you are. Get out of my sight!" she ordered. She then turned a smiling face to Pépé and me. "How long are you staying at my sister's?"

"I'm leaving tomorrow morning," Pépé told her. "But my sister is staying a little longer."

Madame Joseph's face lit up. "Then you can invite my daughter to a New Year's Eve party." She smiled broadly, turning hopeful eyes on her daughter. "Chantoutou, these girls can introduce you to decent people in Port-au-Prince."

The daughter returned a smile, then asked what we were going to wear to the party.

"We haven't given it a thought," Pépé answered.

"Don't worry, Chantoutou, we'll give you money for a new dress," Madame Joseph said, smiling at her daughter.

As I can recall, the idea of going to a party was never discussed. I only remember Pépé mentioning that she and her family usually spent New Year's Eve with her Auntie Suzanne and her family.

The *restavèk* entered the room with a tray of five glasses of lemonade, which was way too sweet for my taste. Chantal suddenly announced, "That boy down the road sent me a love letter."

Madame Joseph kissed her teeth, barely making an audible sound. "He thinks he's your equal, just because he goes to school in Port-au-Prince." She turned to Pépé and me again. "You will introduce my daughter to some decent people, right?"

Pépé smiled without committing herself. I said nothing.

As the driver pulled out of the yard, I thought about the social dynamics in Haiti and the unusual circumstances of my birth. The barrier between Hagathe and Brahami was bigger than the chain of mountains on the island. I began to have some understanding of the distress Brahami must have felt when he learned of Hagathe's pregnancy.

"Are you going to call her?" I asked Pépé, leaning back in my seat.

"Who?"

"Chantal."

"Are you kidding?"

"Why do you think she brought up that boy?"

"To feel important."

"I can't believe how the mother talked to the young girl!"

Pépé shrugged. "People here are like that."

I could not help but think about my mother's life as a domestic servant and wondered if the Bonsangs treated her with the same arrogance and scorn, stripping her of her dignity.

"In all the years I've been driving Father Leblanc to that woman's house, she has never, not even once, offered me a glass of water," commented the driver, a middle-aged, dark-skinned man with salt-and-pepper hair.

"How long have you been working for Father Leblanc?" I asked.

"Over twenty years. I've been around since the beginning of their relationship."

"Whose relationship?"

"It's almost official now. Madame Joseph and Father Leblanc have been lovers for a long time. People say it started with her opening her heart to share her disappointments in love. The more she confessed to him, the more his excitement for her grew. He would invite her to share a meal or an afternoon snack. As time went on, they shared more." The driver smiled, showing his tobacco-stained teeth. "When it became clear to her that he would never leave the priesthood, she married Monsieur Joseph. Father Leblanc celebrated the wedding. But that didn't put a stop to their relationship. Everyone, except her husband, notices the daughter's resemblance to Father Leblanc. The priest has lunch with them twice a month, and she visits him whenever she can. Only God knows what happens behind closed doors!"

The driver parked the car off the road, next to a woman crouching in front of a tray of mint candy and cigarettes set on a wooden bench. He asked for a loose cigarette and searched his pockets for coins that weren't there. When I offered to buy him a pack, he gladly accepted. A few feet away, a woman in a torn dress sat under a rubber tree, rocking a naked toddler with ashen skin, a huge belly, and reddish hair. The child was sobbing and inhaling his mucus.

"Is the baby sick?" I asked the mother.

"She's hungry."

My heart tightened. I reached into the pocket of my jeans and handed five gourdes to the woman, who thanked me with a litany of prayers.

"How long has Father Leblanc been in this parish?" I asked the driver, watching him light a cigarette and inhale deeply.

"Father Leblanc came here from France during President Lescot's antisuperstition campaign," he said. "Even now, he whips parishioners who practice *vaudou*. That's why people are discreet when it comes to those things."

That evening when we reached Lamercie's home, people were already gathered in the yard. Those who lived far away had spent the night. Some of the women prepared and served food, while others helped to set up an altar for the first day of prayers in one of the two rooms.

The luminous hues from an oil lamp revealed a bouquet of wild flowers and a wooden cross that had been placed on a table covered with a white cloth. Candles on both sides of the table brightened the room. Underneath the table a woman placed an enamel plate of boiled plantains, yams, and dried codfish, along with a glass of water and a cup of black coffee. The *pè savann*, the bush priest who conducted Catholic prayers, shouted, "Be quiet!" to the people outside and berated them if they did not participate in a prayer or a song. When it was over the people called out, "Amen!"

The next morning, Marie Ange took me inside the room where the prayer had been held the night before. She handed me an aluminum box that contained a stack of gourdes, my mother's elementary school certificate, all of the Christmas cards and pictures she had received from the Winstons and me, and the deed to the land Acéfie had purchased before she died. There was also a picture of Brahami standing in front of the Louvre in Paris that later I would tear into pieces.

"Is there anything here you want to keep?"

Marie Ange smiled and said she would like the Christmas cards and the pictures.

"You should also keep the money and the deed."

"B-but they're yours," she protested.

"I don't need them."

"*Mèsi.* The deed to the land will be here should you ever return to build something. This is home, *ou konprann?*"

"Yes, I understand."

"I have something else for you." She lifted the mattress and took out a book from a brown paper bag; it was faded by time and humidity. "Do you remember this?"

She handed me the first book I'd ever owned. As I turned the pages, the sight of a ballerina leaping across a stage reminded me of the day that I braved the hurricane. As I recall, my Haitian family and I were inside the house where we rarely spent time, except to sleep or when there was a hurricane. I sat on a bundle of soiled clothes wrapped in a sheet that the grown-ups would wash in the river when the sun returned. Suspended in the air, the ballerina's legs stretched into a horizontal line. I later peered out of a hole in the door and listened to the blasting wind, as forceful as a rushing train. Leaves whirled wildly as the wind scattered them away. Like them, I wanted to float in the air. That afternoon, giving in to a sudden impulse, I opened the old wooden door to face the wind. Oblivious to its fury, I spread my arms under the torrential rain. But instead of flying up in the air, like the leaves and the dancer in the short fluffy skirt, I was blown into a pool of mud. My mother ran to me, and struggled to get us back inside. As soon as Marie Ange closed the door, Hagathe lost her composure and pulled me onto her knees. Her arm, stronger than I ever imagined, went up and down. Her palm landed forcefully on my behind. Her anger matched the wind's fury.

CHAPTER 10

Life, you know, is rather like opening a tin of sardines.
We are all of us looking for the key.
—Alan Bennett

Staring at the barren mountains that stood naked and hurt, with no place to hide from the merciless sun, I tried to recall more details of my life with Hagathe. Her features appeared but were suddenly swallowed by a cloud of smoke from Lamercie's pipe. My memories grew hollow and more distant.

Lamercie sat on a straw mat, pulling smoke from her pipe. "Get out of here!" she yelled, waving a hand in the air.

"Why can't I sit with you?" I asked, shocked that she would chase me away.

"I was talking to those evil spirits walking around in broad daylight."

I thought she was losing her mind, but said nothing.

Wearing a blank expression on her face, she told me, "You can't see them. Three little men went by walking on their hands. They were no more than twelve inches tall."

I had heard from Marie Ange that Lamercie had come back from death and that she was exceptional because the caul over her head at birth allowed her to see supernatural beings. Mean spirits couldn't hurt her, and she could communicate with good ones. "Marie Ange told me that you died and came back to life," I said, thinking it was the right time to bring up the topic.

"I came back to life because my time had not come."

She peered into the distance, hands cupped around her clay pipe. "The night I was supposed to die, my mother dreamed of a black man dressed in flaming red pants and shirt, holding a machete high above his head. Ogoun Badagris, the spirit of fire, talked to her all the way from Guinen. He told her Koksanbèk, the toothless sorcerer, was about to make a zombie of me and that Gran Bwa, the spirit of medicinal herbs, could bring me back to life." She paused, puffed contentedly on her pipe, taking her time.

"When the sun woke up early the next morning," she continued, "my mother went inside the peristyle and came back with the spirit of Gran Bwa dancing in her head. The spirit went to the mountains and returned with leaves that he used to fix me a drink and a bath." Lamercie took her time again, puffing and blowing smoke. And I waited. Above her head floated a halo of wisdom that inspired awe. "Minutes later, I sat up and rubbed my eyes."

"How did your mother know your time hadn't come?" I asked.

"She couldn't know for sure," Lamercie explained. "She just took a chance. But if God, our Granmèt, wanted to take me from this life, it would have happened anyway."

Once again, I doubted her sanity. "Could it be that you were just in a coma?"

"Call it whatever you want," she snapped. "But I'll tell you what happened. I saw my soul leave my body and then I came to a wooden door and knocked. A voice told me I had to go back because my job here was not done yet. Soon after that, my mother entered the room where I was sleeping."

"Do you think Hagathe could come back?" I asked in a hopeful but only half-serious voice.

"I gave her a dose of poison to make sure she really died."

"Why would you poison her?"

"Vilanus's family is still going around saying he died because of Hagathe. I was afraid they would turn her into a zombie to take revenge."

"How would they do that?"

"The night of the funeral, they could take her body from the coffin and revive her with herbal medicine. I poisoned her to make sure that wouldn't happen. Being a zombie is worse than being a slave. At least a slave can hope for freedom." Lamercie removed her red scarf from around her waist and tied it around her head.

"I was planning to visit my mother this summer," I told her.

"Learn to recognize her messages." She threw her hand in the air, this time to chase a mosquito. "Your mother's spirit is right here. She's listening to our conversation." Lamercie flashed a toothless grin that lit up her face. "If you want," she said, "we can call her in a *govi* so you can talk to her."

"That won't be necessary," I said, not wanting to venture that far into Lamercie's mystical world. But I did ask her to tell me more about Hagathe's complicated life.

CHAPTER 11

*True kindness presupposes the faculty of imagining
as one's own the suffering and joys of others.*
—André Gide

When Lamercie saw Hagathe from a distance, she removed the pipe from her mouth and spat on the dirt floor. Only an hour ago, she had told neighbors her granddaughter would be coming home because the night before she appeared in her dream, asking her to make room for her to sleep.

"You must be hungry," she said, as soon as the younger woman settled.
Hagathe held her waist, stretched her lower back. "I'm just tired."
Lamercie examined her discreetly but kept her suspicions to herself. "Sit down and have some ginger tea," she said.

Days later, after a breakfast of cassava pancakes and avocado, Lamercie told Hagathe she must greet the spirits. That afternoon, Lamercie and the other women carried rum, water, and candles to pay their respects. The older woman knocked three times before opening the door. Once inside, she lit candles, poured water and rum libations.

They all sang and clapped until the spirit of Papa Ogoun, the Yoruba god of fire, inhabited Jésula's body. The fierce spirit of war and thunder let out mixed cries of joy and anger through Jésula's lips.

Marie Ange brought forth a red scarf that Lamercie tied around Papa Ogoun's head. She tied another around the waist, a third one around the right arm. She then passed a machete and a bottle of rum to the spirit, who shook hands with everyone. Staring at Hagathe long and hard, he shook one hand then the other before spinning her around three times.

"Manzè Hagathe. It's about time you fulfilled your duty," the spirit said in his powerful voice.

"Papa Ogoun, you must excuse her, she's innocent, wi," Lamercie pleaded. "She came home tired. That's why she didn't come to the peristyle sooner."

The explanation seemed to appease Papa Ogoun. "Manzè Hagathe," he said, "the father of your baby will have another child, who will put an end to the hatred in his wife's heart." The spirit who inhabited Jésula's body brandished his machete and speared it into the dirt floor. Next he poured rum into an enamel washbasin and struck a match that he dropped into the liquid, igniting flames that danced furiously around the rim; red and gold entwined and twisted in a celebration of life.

Papa Ogoun ordered Hagathe to remove her clothes except her underwear. In his powerful voice he sang as he rubbed flames on Hagathe's stomach, arms, legs, and back to bring vigor into her body and give her strength for upcoming struggles.

With excitement in her voice, Lamercie said, "Wi, Papa Ogoun, make her strong enough to fight like a warrior and ward off bad luck!"

As Jésula's body fell to the floor she slowly regained control of herself. Papa Ogoun had left the world of mortals.

Lamercie watched the older children dive off a rock, and listened to their laughter. A woman balancing a bucket of water on her head approached. Behind her, a young boy followed.

"Bonjou, man Cicie," the woman said, addressing Lamercie in the way that the villagers did, out of respect for her age and wisdom.

"Bonjou, fammi," answered Lamercie, who referred to most of the people of Monn Nèg as family since they were usually related through marriage or one ancestor or another.

"What are you doing here?"

"I'm waiting for someone with strong legs to bring Hagathe to me. I can't go down these steep paths like I used to."

The woman asked the boy to hurry, knowing it had to be important for Lamercie to come to the river herself. And she was right.

Late that afternoon Brahami had arrived at Lamercie's with Latham and the Winstons. Because the old woman feared Hagathe might find an excuse not to come, as she had done years ago, she decided to look for her granddaughter herself.

When Lamercie found Hagathe, she whispered, "Mesye Bonsang is here with two white people and a foreign black." As they walked back to the house, Hagathe remained absorbed in her own thoughts. Lamercie held her hand and respected her silence.

"Bonjou-mesye-dam," Hagathe greeted everyone as they entered the yard.

Brahami shook her hand but avoided looking at her. "What's your name?" he asked, picking up his daughter on an impulse.

"Iris."

He wiped perspiration from his forehead and turned to Lamercie. "My two friends are from the United States," he said, pointing to the Winstons. "They have come to Monn Nèg to study Haitian culture. Since I don't know anyone else in the countryside, I thought of bringing them to your home. I hope it won't be too much of an inconvenience for them to spend time with you and your family."

"I'm honored," Lamercie said, intertwining her fingers as if in prayer. "We don't have much, but we share whatever the Good God gives us. The only problem is, I have no place for them to sleep." She tightened the red scarf over her braided gray hair. "Our home is small. Hagathe will talk to Madan Dufour, who lives alone in a big house in town, but you should leave now, before it gets dark."

As Lamercie watched them climb into the jeep, she whispered to her daughter Jésula, "Iris is the spitting image of that man."

"Uh-huh. She's just a few shades darker than him and her hair is coarser."

CHAPTER 12

*Memory is deceptive because
it is colored by today's events.*
—Albert Einstein

nnumerable memories remained lost in the flow of time, swept away to an inaccessible place beyond consciousness. My eyes wandered toward a blossoming mango tree. Its green leaves moved to the rhythm of a soft breeze. Despite the light of day, everything seemed strangely blurred. The longing for the sight of Hagathe, her voice, her touch, the aroma of her bosom, continued to haunt me. My soul descended deeper into an abyss of unsolved mysteries.

The afternoon sun filtered through tree branches. I was lying on Lamercie's mat of plantain twigs when a flashback sprang up as quickly as a flame from a struck match. Another fractured episode of the past flitted without being conjured, providing a faint glimpse of a scene, as images and words found their way out of my subconsciousness. The memory of the first time I saw John, Margaret, Latham, and Brahami suddenly came to mind.

Hagathe, Marie Ange, Magda and her children, and I strolled down the hill toward the river. The two women stopped to talk with people they met on the way, while we scampered around them. As usual, I was the object of attention because of my cinnamon complexion and thick, dark-brown hair. To counter the effects of the evil eye, Lamercie had provided me with protection in the form of special baths and colorful beads that I wore around my waist and underneath the dresses Hagathe made for me on her Singer sewing machine. We walked in a single file and stopped a few times to clear the slippery dirt road for the women and young girls who carried buckets and calabashes on their heads. There was no running water in the houses, but it was the rainy season and the river had overflowed with plenty of water to spare.

As I enjoyed the pleasure of being in the cool water and playing games that my older cousins had taught me, a boy raced down the hill calling out, "Manzè Hagathe, Manzè Hagathe!" The urgency in his voice echoed above the river's constant symphony.

The boy whispered something in Hagathe's ear.

"Grann Lamercie is up the hill waiting for me and Iris," Hagathe told the other women, as she tied a bow at the waist of my dress with unsteady hands. She then told me, in a near whisper, that she wished she had brought better clothes for us to wear and a comb to fix my wild hair. She did the best she could, using her fingers and her hands, to transform my hair into two braids.

My thoughts began to spin like a wheel. Beads of sweat dripped from my brow as I tried to untangle the thread of memories, unable to recall what happened next.

Brahami's driver brought Pépé back to Monn Nèg. As she left the jeep she announced that she had something to tell me. Making herself comfortable next to me on Lamercie's mat, she said, "You remember the man who came to talk to you the day of the funeral?"

"Yes," I nodded.

"He's a ruthless Tonton Macoute in Port-au-Prince. Papa recognized him."

"The only way for most Haitian men to find a better life is to become a Tonton Macoute," I said. "Papa Doc gives them no other choice."

A line of tension appeared across Pépé's forehead. "People aren't allowed to criticize *him*," she whispered, as if afraid to even say his name. "We could be accused of being *kamoken* and sent to jail."

"What's a *kamoken*?" I asked, trying to put thoughts of being locked up in a dung-plastered prison out of my mind.

"Anyone who is an enemy of Duvalier."

"Let's ask Marie Ange."

She was peeling plantains under a breadfruit tree. When she noticed us, she asked "*Sak pase?*"

"Not much," I said. "I just wanted to ask if it's true your brother is a Tonton Macoute."

"That's what I hear," she admitted. "People in Monn Nèg and in town are still talking about how he got rid of Vilanus, the country Tonton Macoute who made life miserable for us here."

"So he's a legend."

Marie Ange straightened her back. "I guess you could say that."

"What happened?"

She took a deep breath and set aside the calabash bowl where freshly peeled plantains floated in water.

CHAPTER 13

The fascination of shooting as a sport depends
almost wholly on whether you are at the right
or wrong end of the gun.
—P.G. Wodehouse

Dieudonné had not been back to Monn Nèg since the day that the shrewd country doctor, who rose to the national palace, proclaimed himself president-for-life. All over the country, his followers herded peasants into trucks and dropped them off near the national palace in Port-au-Prince, ordering them to shout, "Long live Papa Doc!" After the celebration, some chose to stay. Others, like Dieudonné, had no choice because after the trucks left, they could not pay their way back home.

Months later, Dieudonné heard that Doc was recruiting new members for his militia. He joined a group of recruits and repeated the pledge, "I believe in Papa Doc, the almighty father, creator of the nation, who can protect us. I swear to kill without hesitation, even if it is my father or my mother who brought me into this world, to safeguard the power of Papa Doc, the only one able to lead the country."

His zeal and determination caught the attention of Manman Lalo, the fearless leader of the Defenders of National Security. Dieudonné came to her in a room furnished only with a wooden table and two wooden chairs.

"Did you understand the words you just pledged?" Manman Lalo asked, while signaling for Dieudonné to sit in the chair across from her.

He crossed his right leg over the other. "I meant every single word I said. Only Papa Doc can make me somebody."

She examined his faded clothes and noticed the hole that freed his big toe in his right shoe. "We're going to take care of you," she said. "If you return to me within three weeks, with the names of seven kamo-kens, I will take you to Papa Doc. He will give you more than enough money for a beautiful home. He is very generous, you know. You will have everything you want, even the women of your choice."

Dieudonné grinned. "The names may be hard to find. I only have a few friends here. But I will do my best, wi."

"It's good that you have some friends." Manman Lalo smiled. "They can lead you to enemies of our regime." She took a stack of new gourde bills out of her denim shirt pocket. "Here's money to get yourself some decent clothes. Go to bars, dance halls, and restaurants. Get invited to people's homes."

Dieudonné smiled at the sight of money and, true to his word, three weeks later, he handed her a list of not seven, but seventeen names scribbled in childlike handwriting. He had outdone himself.

"I knew we could count on you," Manman Lalo said. "I'll find out when Papa Doc can see his new Defender of National Security."

Days later, riding in a chauffeur-driven Ford with Manman Lalo, Dieudonné was on his way to the National Palace to meet the man who decided when the rain should fall and when the sun should shine in Haiti. During the ride, he thought about his life in Monn Nèg and how he was about to become an important man, one who would have money to buy expensive liquor and afford a light-skinned woman. He was definitely ready to reap the benefits of his loyalty to Papa Doc.

Years later, when Dieudonné realized that the young girl who the Winstons wanted to adopt was his cousin's daughter, he immediately approved the papers that normally could take up to three to four years. Thoughts of his family in Monn Nèg clouded his mind. He poured himself half a glass of Rémy Martin and gulped it down to erase the memory, but blurry visions of his mother and his grandmother continued to haunt him. He tightened his jaw, and reconsidered his decision to never return to Monn Nèg. This time, he took a longer gulp from the bottle and wiped his mouth with the back of his hand. It was time to show his family how successful he had become.

* * *

Lamercie shielded her eyes from the sun with one hand, and then squinted and peered as the sound of an engine brought the others to see the well-dressed man in the car.

"Rete!" Marie Ange cried out. "It's Dieudonné, wi."

Lamercie lowered the pipe from her mouth. "Gras lamisèricod! Lord have mercy!" she exclaimed.

Dieudonné jumped from the vehicle and handed out plastic cars and dolls to his young relatives. The children, thrilled to have their first store-bought toys ever, ran off to play.

Lamercie could not hide her suspicion. "Pitit mwen," she said. "We're happy to see your affairs are good, but I hope you are not doing anything dishonest."

Relieved that he had left his gun in the glove compartment, he told his grandmother not to worry.

"What brought you here after so many years?" his mother asked.

"I've been thinking about all of you. But I wanted to have a job before coming home."

"What kind of job could a black man with no education get that would pay so well that in just four years you can buy a car and good clothes?" Lamercie squinted as she spoke.

"I'm not doing anything wrong."

After a moment of uncomfortable silence, Dieudonné thought he should leave. "I was just passing through," he announced. "Now, I must return to the city for important business. I promise to come back soon."

Next he visited an old friend whom he thought would be more impressed with his success. Dieudonné parked the jeep under a tree and removed his gun from the glove compartment, making sure it was visible to Barilus, who sat under a tent made of dried coconut leaves.

"I can't believe it. Look at you. You're even carrying a gun! Hats off!" Barilus handed his friend the bottle of cheap liquor that he had been drinking.

Dieudonné grimaced at the burning sensation as it went down his throat. "It's been awhile since I've had clairin," he said, trying to suppress a hiccup.

"You don't look like a man for clairin anymore. You probably drink

Barbancourt rum or whiskey from the white men's country," said Barilus, as his wife emerged from the shack wearing a dress with a hole on the side that freed a breast; a five-month-old baby rested on her hip. She kept a respectful distance, grinning and staring at the local man who had made it big in the city.

Barilus rubbed his stomach. "I've been dying for some eggplant sauce with salt pork and crabs over white rice. But we can't afford it."

Calling to Barilus's wife, while opening his wallet, Dieudonné ordered, "Go to the market and cook us a meal."

"Have you seen your family yet?"

"Right before coming here."

"Did they tell you about the problem they had?"

"I wasn't there for long."

Barilus told his friend about Vilanus and Hagathe. At that moment, Dieudonné understood the urgency of the white people's request to adopt Iris. Suddenly he announced that he would avenge his cousin Hagathe's honor.

"If you teach him a lesson, he'll never look at another woman. Never!" Barilus emphasized, encouraging his friend to take action.

Dieudonné was convinced that this was an opportunity for him to show the people of Monn Nèg that now he was a powerful man. In the process he might even earn his family's approval. With Barilus at his side, he set out to find Vilanus.

Dieudonné stopped the car a few yards from Vilanus's house. "Go tell that bastard someone from Port-au-Prince is here to see him. Tell him to come at once!"

Barilus found Vilanus dozing on a chair propped up against an avocado tree. His latest woman, a willing conquest, scratched his thinning hair with a comb. The handsome rooster he had been pampering for next Sunday's cockfight pecked at grains of corn nearby.

Vilanus followed Barilus, pleased to know someone from Port-au-Prince was looking for him. As they walked to Dieudonné's jeep, he told Barilus he was going to make Hagathe beg for forgiveness. He rambled on about how he would make her suffer before accepting her apology.

Hagathe would even ask him if that daughter of hers could live with them, which he thought was good because in a couple of years she would be ripe enough to take her mother's place in his bed.

The sight of Dieudonné behind the wheel came as a shock. "My friend, I'm happy to see you again," Vilanus lied, extending a hand that Dieudonné ignored.

"You never cared that much about me," Dieudonné sneered.

"You're wrong about that," Vilanus disagreed. "I always knew that you would become somebody."

Dieudonné held up a hand. "Just tell me what happened between you and Hagathe."

"You know how women are," Vilanus offered, staring at the gun Dieudonné carried on his hip. "Sometimes you've got to let women know who wears the pants. Perhaps you can help me knock some sense into your cousin."

"Do you know who you're talking to?"

"You may someday need a country Tonton Macoute to take care of some problem here," Vilanus replied. "All I'm saying is that you can count on me, wi." He scratched his head. "Look, you and I, we understand each other. We can't let a woman—"

A sharp slap across the face caused Vilanus to lose his balance "Get in the car!" Dieudonné barked at Barilus. "I need more clairin."

While Barilus went to buy the liquor, Vilanus pleaded, "Look, Dieudonné, let's forget the whole thing. If you want, I'll apologize to your cousin, and we can spend the rest of the day drinking like good friends, sa ou di? What do you say?"

"If you know what's good for you, you'll keep quiet," Dieudonné warned, then pondered what he was actually going to do.

As he resumed drinking at Barilus's house, he ordered the country Tonton Macoute to sit in a corner. A half an hour later, the man tried to escape.

"Come back here!" Dieudonné shouted as Vilanus ran toward the nearby sugarcane field. He reached for his gun, aimed, and fired. Vilanus kept running until a bullet tore into his flesh.

Dieudonné continued drinking. Late that evening, he dumped the body at the police station and reported to the officer in charge that he and Vilanus had been drinking together when Vilanus insulted Papa Doc. He had wanted to arrest him, but Vilanus had tried to run away. That was when he had been forced to shoot him.

CHAPTER 14

What is water,
that pours silver,
and can hold the sky?
—Hilda Conkling

On our way to the outdoor market Marie Ange, Pépe, and I walked past the police station where Dieudonné had dropped Vilanus's body. A growing hostility toward the dead man set in. I quickened my steps to dilute my anger, as I thought about the pain that the Tonton Macoute had inflicted upon my mother.

The market was teeming with people. Vendors with large hats sheltering their heads from the harsh sun yelled, "*Men mwen wi pratik*, here I am, customers!" Marie Ange waved and stood in front of the people from whom she wanted to buy things. Women sat on low chairs or squatted in front of fresh spices, onions, fruits, and vegetables arranged in piles on mats. Some had a pyramid of rice, ground corn, or a variety of beans. Under tents others sold cut-up pieces of beef, pork, and goat.

There were women selling freshly caught and dried salted fish. Except for a few small crabs, there were no shellfish in sight. Marie Ange said they were usually sent to the city for the wealthy, or sold at the beach to people in fancy bathing suits, who either had them cooked straight from the sea or took them home. The fish vendors were louder than the other market women and were more likely to pick a fight. They argued while gesticulating or standing with their hands on their hips, bragging about the freshness of their fish.

People pushed their way around the marketplace. "*Bèt, bèt, bèt!*" announced that their mules or donkeys were coming through. Marie Ange, who balanced a straw bag on her head, warned us to move quickly when a mule almost knocked us to the ground. Leaving the most crowded area of the market, we passed vendors who sold secondhand clothes, donations from charity organizations in the United States. A few feet away, men and women who sold live chickens, pigs, and goats bargained with customers.

After an hour of watching Marie Ange haggle with vendors under the hot sun, we made our way back to Lamercie's, leaving behind the smells of animal, vegetable, and human essences. That afternoon Pépé returned home with the driver.

Feeling the effect of the suffocating hot air, I thought it a great idea when Marie Ange, Magda, and the children invited me to the river to bathe. As soon as we reached the river the children jumped in. Two of them pounded the water with their fists, making sounds like talking drums. A few adults stood waist deep, while others floated on their backs, enjoying the cool water on a hot, sunny afternoon. A woman who sat on a rock holding a tub between her leg stroked a denim shirt one hand over the other. Slightly hunched, her breasts swayed with her vigorous movements.

Under the still, cloudless sky, the refreshing water pushed its way over my shoulders and chest, past my hips and legs, washing away my worries. From an early-childhood memory, stories suddenly emerged of people living in a world below the river. I shivered and climbed out of the river, trying to imagine a life underwater. I sat on a rock and recalled a story Lamercie—or Jésula, I'm not sure who—used to tell about a girl who was in love with a fish that she met by the riverbank every day at dawn. The fish eventually took her to his underwater kingdom, though I forgot the rest of the story.

When I left Monn Nèg at the age of five, I left behind everything and everyone I had known. Now, the questions about my former life followed me like an invisible shadow. People, places, and experiences emerged from darkness to become a life beyond conscious memory. The river that knew the mysteries of my ancestors had caused my mind to wander in its flow. The river remembered the paths it traveled but couldn't return to them, just like I couldn't return to my past.

Although I took pleasure in bathing in the river, eating local food, and being reacquainted with Haitian life, I felt more like a tourist who willingly blended into a new culture, knowing the experience was only temporary. Sooner or later, my life would resume its course away from the pastoral setting. It would have been different if I had never left. But now, another culture and another life had laid claim to me.

Marie Ange came out of the river and sat down beside me. "What's the matter?" she asked.

"Nothing. I'm trying to tan a little."

"Why?"

I shrugged and listened to the trickling of the river. The washerwoman was spreading white clothes on rocks so the warmth of the sun would dry them and make them whiter. "I was thinking about stories I must have heard as a child about people who lived underwater."

"You know, Mesye Charles, the rich merchant in town, people say he spent seven years under this river and came back with mystical knowledge and wealth."

"What should I call you?" I asked my godmother, breaking the silence that suddenly fell between us.

She smiled broadly, looked away as if to better remember. "You used to call me Ninninn."

"Ninninn, did my mother talk about me?"

The question brought a wave of sadness over Marie Ange's face. "After you left, she practically stopped talking, unless it was to tell us about something you did or said, or to wonder what you were doing at that very moment. On every birthday you've had, since the day you left, she would buy special treats for the spirits of Guinen so they would protect you." Marie Ange went back to the river to splash her face with water from her cupped hands, washing away her tears. She returned to sit next to me on the rock.

Though I realized I was upsetting her, I wanted to know more about the mother I hardly knew. "How did she die?"

"Hagathe was never the same after the rape."

The word "rape" stirred unrelenting horror, brought chills to my body. "Did she ever talk about it?"

"People don't talk about those things."

"Why not?"

She ignored the question and went on saying, "She had headaches that wouldn't go away. One day, she stayed in bed and the headaches came with a fever. I made cow-foot soup to bring strength to her body." Marie Ange closed her eyes, took a deep breath, and sighed. "When I came in the room she was soaking wet. She ate the soup and told me she didn't think she would live much longer. She asked me to go to town to telephone Mesye Brahami and tell him you were with his white friends and that she wanted to see you. With a shaking hand she wrote down his telephone number. Then she dropped her head on the pillow and took her last breath. Just like that." Marie Ange shook her head as though she still could not believe it had happened.

"She should not have sent me away," I said, then realized my tone was more accusatory than intended.

The words had an explosive effect on Marie Ange, whose nostrils flared.

"Oh, no! Your mother wanted the best for you. There are people in this country who send their children to a faraway town or city just to make sure they have something to eat and can go to school. That doesn't mean they have no heart." Tears flowed down her cheeks as she spoke, and her voice became increasingly intense.

"How did my mother feel about my father?" I asked, remembering she kept a picture of him.

The sun had dried her tears, and Marie Ange gazed at me for what seemed a very long time. "The women in our family haven't been lucky when it comes to love. I'm going to ask Ezili Fréda to make your luck better than ours." She then peered at me with a faint strangeness. "She's the goddess of love, you know. I want her to make you seductive and irresistible for the man you will fall in love with." A quick smile brightened her face. "I don't want you to suffer like the rest of us."

Silence fell over us. I listened to the uninterrupted sounds of the flowing river and the children's laughter. So many questions continued to flow through my mind, producing a bewildering flood of incoherent images. My curiosity to know more about my mother's life grew even more urgent, and I knew my godmother could help me. Although reluctant at first, she agreed to tell me everything she knew about her cousin, who was more like a sister.

CHAPTER 15

The stone that is rolling can gather no moss;
For master and servant oft changing is loss.
—Thomas Tusser

Hagathe had been busy shopping and preparing an elaborate menu for Brahami's welcome home party. The regal dinner was a gastronomic feast, with a table laden with stewed conch, chicken in Creole sauce, red beans and rice, djon djon rice with jumbo shrimp and crabs, homemade guava ice cream, and sweet potato cake for dessert. When Hagathe first glimpsed Brahami that day, she thought he looked like one of the fancy white men she had seen on the screen when movies were shown in the town's square. This was before she moved to the capital with her mother.

One night while his wife was in France, Brahami came to the kitchen after dinner and looked at her in a way that made her feel something she'd never felt before. He told her that the conch was the best she had ever cooked. Flattered by the compliment, Hagathe smiled. Without her usual reserve, she stood, though felt nailed to the spot. A veil of embarrassment covered her. Even though she was uncomfortable, she waited for him to say or do something; and when he touched her, he provoked an unfamiliar rush through her body. She stuttered and pleaded in her confusion, feeling a persistent desire to welcome him between her thighs.

Pressed against the kitchen's mosaic floor, she inhaled the scent of his citrus cologne. Staring at the ceiling, she imagined Darah's face looking scornfully at her. She closed her eyes to keep the mistress of the house away and to bask in the glory of having Brahami on top of her. But even with her eyes closed, she could see Darah's face; and for a short, glorious moment she became Darah and welcomed the delightful pain with an urgency that made her breathe heavily and her heartbeat quicken.

After Brahami left the next morning, Hagathe cleaned the bedroom. She examined Darah's clothes and shoes, and wondered how she would look in such fine attire. She imagined herself being served by a maid, speaking beautiful French, and entertaining high society. The door, slammed by a breeze, brought Hagathe back from her fantasy. After her moment of daydreaming, she examined her sad image in a full-length mirror and continued her work.

The more Brahami avoided her, the more she felt drawn to him. Even though she realized he lacked interest in her, the flame of her silenced passion peaked. She longed for the feelings she had experienced that night in the kitchen and became more withdrawn than usual, except for occasional sighs that were like groans from her inner soul, providing the kind of relief one experienced after coming up for air from a long-held breath underwater.

One morning, as she was tidying the family room, Hagathe looked inside a photo album and saw a picture of Brahami. Without thinking she slipped it into her skirt pocket. Darah appeared soon after she had returned the album to the shelf.

"Are you all right, Hagathe?" Her voice was filled with concern.

"I'm fine, wi, Madan Bonsang."

Darah gazed at the maid. "You look tired. You should go home next month to rest for a few days. You haven't had a vacation in years."

Hagathe was touched by Darah's kindness. It would be easier for her to bear her sorrow if Darah were unkind to her. "Should I get the coffee ready for you, Madan Bonsang?" she asked.

"Please."

That afternoon when Hagathe brought in the mail, she expected the couple to be in their room, where they napped after lunch. But Brahami was reading the newspaper, his head resting on his wife's lap. Darah held a magazine in one hand; the other caressed her husband. Suddenly she dropped the magazine and unbuttoned his shirt.

Hagathe crept out. She was accustomed to keeping a low profile even when yearning to be noticed. In her room in the servant's quarters, she *took the stolen photo out of her pocket and brought it to her lips. It was a reminder of the life and the man she could never have. Yet she imagined the smile on Brahami's face in the picture was meant for her, and the risk she took by stealing it made her think of the seriousness of the situation if Darah were to find out her husband had been with her. She remembered the pride on her mistress's face when she overheard a conversation one day between the lady of the house and her best friend, Suzanne, as she served them coffee. "He only has eyes for me," Darah had said, her voice breathing confidence. "I'm sure he'll never betray me."*

Hagathe swallowed the bitterness in her throat and found a place for the picture in the square tin box where she kept her elementary school certificate, the deed to the land her grandmother had purchased, and the book from which she had learned to read and write. It was the only book she ever owned.

Hagathe saw Brahami in a different light that morning when he asked her if the child she was carrying was his. The question filled her with bitterness and, for the first time ever, she held his stare. What she saw was treachery and cowardice. Moments later, when she heard Darah scream, she sensed that there was trouble in the Bonsangs' home. When Brahami's mother came over later that morning, and she heard Darah scream again, she was convinced that the household's peace had been shattered. Suspecting the disturbance was about her, Hagathe quietly went upstairs. Though it was not her habit to eavesdrop, she felt compelled to know what was going on. Her ears perked up when she heard the older Madame Bonsang speak.

"Ma chérie, blessings often come in a disguise. Hagathe's child could be the child you've always wanted. You and Brahami could raise it as your own."

"I could never love a maid's child as my own. In fact, I don't ever want to see her again," Darah huffed.

"If that's the way you feel, I will raise the child myself."

"I will never speak to you again if you do that."

"How can you talk to me like that, ma fille?"

In a softer voice Darah said, "I want a child of my own."

Hagathe's heart chilled; her body trembled with rage. She was hurt that the Bonsang ladies were deciding her baby's fate without consulting her, the mother who, to them, was just a pitit soyèt, from illiterate stock.

Because she wanted the best for her baby, she would have allowed them to raise her child, but not if it caused turmoil in their family. She wiped her tears, took a deep breath, and left the house. After walking a mile and not knowing where else to go, she realized that Monn Nèg was her only option. She did not know how she would get there. She had no money. She felt hopeless but knew that even if it took days she would get to her village.

As she walked under the pitiless sun, Hagathe thought about her life. When she was ten, Monsieur and Madame Bonsang had allowed her mother, Acéfie, to bring her daughter to live in their home, expecting that she would help with small tasks around the house. Since her all-too-brief childhood, Hagathe had worked from daybreak until past nightfall, resting only after serving supper and retiring to her room. When she was sixteen, her mother grew ill. Hagathe's duties increased, and although her intention had been to continue to high school, she never made it. Torn between her desires to be educated and her duty to help her mother, Hagathe decided to settle for sewing lessons twice a week, while she continued to perform most of Acéfie's chores.

Her mother's stomach pains became unbearable. Instead of going to the doctor Madame Bonsang had recommended, Acéfie went to a doktè fèy. The bush doctor gave her medicinal herbs that were supposed to chase away the dead spirit that inhabited her stomach. For a while, the teas she brewed made her feel better, but the pains came back sharper than before. In the end, Acéfie returned to Monn Nèg to die. Hagathe inherited her mother's job, and her limited education brought no greater reward than her mother's meager pay.

Hagathe realized how lonely her life had been after her mother had passed away. She recalled the evenings that they spent together after supper had been served and the dishes were put away. Most of all, she remembered the stories her mother had told her about her life in the Dominican Republic and about her father's death on October 16, 1937, when the drunken President Trujillo ordered Dominicans to kill Haitians and cut them into pieces. According to Hagathe's mother, that was

Trujillo's way to avenge two decades of Haitian occupation and to chase away the shadow of his own Haitian ancestry.

As she continued her journey, the sun's rays beat down on her head. Tears drenched her face. Her vision blurred. Her knees weakened and she crumpled to the ground.

People rushed from their houses and gathered around her. An elderly woman knelt beside her and lifted the pregnant maid with her left arm. With her right hand, she slapped Hagathe's face to revive her. "Get some water," she said to a woman, who ran to a house across the street. The old woman poured the water on Hagathe's face. When Hagathe began to move she asked, "What's your name?"

"Hagathe, wi," she said in a feeble voice, staring at the mole that looked like a black bean on the old woman's forehead.

"Where do you live?" the old woman asked, while giving Hagathe water to drink.

"I'm on my way to Monn Nèg," Hagathe uttered and sipped the water.

"Monn Nèg! Oh oh! She'll never make it on foot," the woman who had brought the water said. "She's pregnant, wi."

Grann, as everyone called the old woman, suggested they contribute money to pay for her transportation to Monn Nèg. She took Hagathe to her home to wait for the next tap-tap bus. After waiting for nearly three hours, she fed Hagathe dried codfish, ground corn, red bean soup, and mashed eggplant. Hagathe, who had not eaten since the night before, chewed absentmindedly under the watchful eyes of Grann, who was a mambo. A desire to help prompted the vaudou priestess to share with Hagathe a message a spirit had communicated to her.

"Remember what I'm going to tell you," she said, and paused. "You're going to have a girl. What a future she has ahead of her! Some people from a faraway place will ask to raise your child. I know it is hard for a mother to give up her child, but you should think of her future and let her go."

Hagathe nodded, though she did not understand what the old woman meant. Grann handed her a mixture of white, pink, and red powders sealed in a fresh leaf and sewed in red cloth. Hagathe then noticed the woman was missing the pinky finger on her left hand.

"Always carry this on your body until your child is born. Your family back home will take care of the rest. I see they know and serve the spirits of Guinen, wi. Now, it's time to go on the road. But before you go, I have something else to give you." She disappeared inside the house and returned with a loaf of bread and an avocado.

As Hagathe boarded the tap-tap, the old woman held her hand tightly and said softly, "Take care of your child."

When Hagathe stepped off the bus and looked around the familiar sugarcane field, she breathed in the intoxicating fragrance of ripe mangoes. Walking at a slow pace, she heard the unmuffled laughter of gossiping women. The piercing cries of children playing mingled with angry sounds of men screaming at each other while playing dominoes.

"Rete!" Marie Ange let out a wondrous cry when she noticed her cousin from a distance. "It's Hagathe, wi, oh, oh!"

Marie Ange ran to meet her cousin. "We thought we'd never see you again," she said. "The last time you came home was before Hurricane Hazel." She hugged Hagathe and rubbed her swollen stomach. "There's a little one there, wi," she whispered in her cousin's ear, then led her toward the other women. It was unusual that Hagathe should arrive empty-handed, so they knew something was amiss. But no one uttered a word. They were just happy to have her home.

"Where's cousin Dieudonné?" asked Hagathe.

Marie Ange sucked her teeth noisily and rolled her eyes. "Probably out somewhere drinking like a good-for-nothing."

She proposed that Hagathe wash up and offered her a loose dress to wear. Where thatches of palm formed a washroom, Hagathe poured water from a calabash into a basin. After cleaning up and changing her clothes, she sat next to Lamercie under a mango tree.

"How was your trip?" Lamercie asked, taking her pipe from the pocket of her faded denim dress.

"It was good. Thanks to God, our Granmèt." Hagathe watched Lamercie pick up a piece of burning charcoal with her fingers and was reminded that her grandmother was a kanzo. The hot charcoals could make a pot on top of them brew, but the piece did not burn Lamercie's *fingers.* "*Adye! On my way home after walking in the hot sun for such a long time, I fainted. A woman called Grann helped me.*"

"Everyone *called her Grann?*" Lamercie asked. "*She has a missing finger and a mole on her forehead?*"

Hagathe nodded.

"*How do you know?*"

"*I know the woman you met. My grandmother initiated her. Grann always had powers,* wi." *Lamercie shook her head.* "*A spirit of Guinen claimed her when she was twelve. When she turned twenty, the spirit visited her in a dream to give her an ultimatum: either she served the spirits of Guinen, or she would lose a finger. So Grann became a Protestant, thinking the spirits can't hurt Protestants.*" *Lamercie smiled knowingly.* "*She lost a finger just the same! When the spirit threatened to take another one, she quickly accepted.*"

As the night approached, Hagathe pondered Grann's story until sleep seeped through her weary mind. The next day, she woke up two hours later than everyone else, except Dieudonné, who had come in long after the others had gone to sleep. Marie Ange brought her cousin a breakfast of cassava and black coffee.

When Dieudonné woke up it was close to noon. He was still drunk from the night before. "Cousine mwen," he greeted Hagathe with a kiss on a cheek. "What did you bring me from the city?" As usual, he spoke at the top of his lungs, making one believe the friendliest conversation was a quarrel.

"You shameless parasite," his mother Jésula butted in. "All you do is take, take, take. Oh, pitit!"

Dieudonné sucked his teeth and walked away. Two hours later he returned and waited for his mother to prepare for him a plate of cornmeal and a slice of avocado.

That afternoon Hagathe and Marie Ange walked past sugarcane fields. They sat by a stream, where they watched cows graze in a nearby field and slipped off their sandals and dipped their feet in the sparkling rivulet.

"If you want to talk I'm here for you," Marie Ange said in a soothing voice, while peeling a mango with her fingers.

"You're the only friend I've ever had."

Marie Ange watched tears well in her cousin's eyes. "It must be hard living with those rich people," she said. "They're so different."

"They don't think we have feelings."

As Hagathe began to tell Marie Ange about Brahami and that night in the kitchen, the deep bellowing sound of a cow rose from the field.

"I'll do whatever I can to help you and your baby," Marie Ange promised her cousin.

Weeks later, when the young boy told Hagathe her former employers wanted to see her, her first reaction was to gather the clothes that were drying by the riverbank and head home. But just as immediately, she recalled what Grann had said to her. Some people from a faraway place will ask to raise your child. The words echoed in her mind and she opted not to see the Bonsangs, certain that they wanted her baby. She recalled hearing them discuss that possibility. Having spent most of her life doing what the Bonsangs demanded of her, she now enjoyed the freedom of not seeing them if she did not want to.

When she returned from the river Lamercie explained, "They just wanted to give their regards and leave you these things. You should use the money to start a business."

Hagathe folded the clothes she had washed and placed them in a wicker basket to be ironed. Later she headed to the spring to be alone with her thoughts. She listened to the murmur of the water flow over the rocks while recalling how Brahami's arms felt caressing her, holding her close. Though it was hard for her to recall exactly how it felt when he was inside her, she did remember whimpering, putting her clothes on, and washing away the blood that was still fresh on the floor, then going to her room and curling up on her iron bed and pulling the sheet over her head.

The following week Hagathe bought a Singer sewing machine and still had enough money left to build a small shop made of woven twigs plastered with mud, and topped with a thatch roof. It was a place where she sewed and sold peanut and coconut candy and food staples. She was at her sewing machine one afternoon when water poured from between her legs, like bubbles from a bottle of champagne. The liquid seeped into the dirt ground, leaving a large design behind. Her joy became fear when she felt fierce cramps in her lower back and below her belly button.

"Oh! Jesus-Marie-Joseph. Manman Acéfie, pray for me!" Hagathe cried out.

Marie Ange, who was in the shop with her, gasped and panicked, wishing their grandmother would come home. Lamercie was a midwife who the people of Monn Nèg often called upon to deliver their babies, but now she was gathering fruits and vegetables in the fields to sell at the market on the following day.

"Adye! Hagathe kase dlo. Ro-ro-ro-roye!" Marie Ange announced when Hagathe's water broke. "Somebody please go get Grann Lamercie!" She led Hagathe to the bedroom, and between contractions Marie Ange uttered the prayers that she had learned in catechism.

Hagathe felt sharp, quick pains that she tried to suppress by biting the pillow and rocking her body from side to side. She groaned and wailed as the pain became more intense. Marie Ange held her cousin's hand, wiped sweat from her forehead, and urged her in a calm voice to push, push, push.

Between sharp breaths Hagathe pushed as hard as she could. She heaved and pushed again. The pains subsided for moments that she found too brief; and they started again, each time sharper, tearing her insides more and more. She pushed and pushed and pushed. Nothing happened. She summoned determination and doubled her efforts until a little head covered with blood and mucous appeared. The shoulders followed and then the rest of the body. Hagathe let out a cry of deliverance from the brutal pain, then heard a piercing sound that was a salute to the world.

"The baby is here, wi!" Marie Ange shrieked as she ran toward Lamercie, who had just arrived. Hagathe was holding the baby against her chest when her grandmother entered the room. The umbilical cord still connected, the afternoon heat enveloped her as her sweat mixed with blood. Lamercie cut the cord and wrapped it in a white cloth. She then set out to bury it under the mango tree. When she returned, she announced, "She's going to be a lucky one."

* * *

Hagathe never stopped longing for Brahami, though she would not see him again until years later when he brought the Winstons to Monn Nèg. When that moment Hagathe had prayed for finally came, she was apprehensive. What could Brahami possibly want from a poor woman like herself, ignorant of worldly matters? How could she have thought he could feel anything for her other than lust or the curiosity to find out if women like her were different in their lovemaking?

As she accompanied the Winstons to Madame Dufour's, Hagathe sat in the backseat of Brahami's jeep, between John and Margaret. Seated on her lap, her daughter shielded her nervousness.

"How old is Iris?" Latham asked, as Brahami drove them back to Lamercie's.

"Five," Hagathe replied as she kept her eyes focused on her shoes, which were too tight on her feet.

"How is she doing in school?" asked Latham.

"She will start next year."

"The child has no future here," Lamercie said, as the women shared a supper of corn porridge and discussed the Winstons' desire to take Iris to the United States. "Children need to be educated nowadays. How can we poor folks of Monn Nèg help her? If you want your child's fate to be different from yours, let her go." She puffed on her pipe, watching the smoke rise. "We must consult the spirits," she decided.

"Oh! Oh!" Jésula cried out. "You're going to call the spirits and I'll be the one paying the consequences. I'm going to become a Protestant. That way, they'll have to find another horse to mount."

Lamercie offered water and rum libations, and lit candles to implore the spirits to come. Marie Ange's body suddenly jerked then fell to the floor. Papa Ogoun had taken over her words and actions.

"Aïbobo!" Lamercie greeted the warrior spirit who had come to guide them. With Jésula's help, she tied red scarves around his head, arms, and hips.

"Papa Ogoun, it's about time you found another horse," Jésula joked. The spirit rolled his eyes. "It's not up to you to decide who my horse should be," he said, and began to sing in a powerful voice that was so unlike Marie Ange's.

Ogoun's children don't bother a soul
They've declared war on them
Ogoun must fight, fight, fight.

The spirit gulped rum from the bottle and resumed singing:

Ogoun, man of war
drinks, drinks, drinks
but never gets drunk.

"I dare say you've got a problem. A big one." He paused and set his eyes on Hagathe. "Mother, tighten your belly. The moment has come to decide what's good for your child, to give up the joy of motherhood as a sacrifice. Do you know about Solomon's judgment?"

No one answered.

"Damnit! I'm talking to you!" the voice roared. "Do you know the story of Solomon's judgment?"

"Wi, Papa Ogoun," the women answered in chorus.

Papa Ogoun nodded, took another gulp from the bottle, and offered to share his rum. Everyone declined. "Manzè Hagathe, I'm here to tell you your child will be miserable if she stays here. Aïbobo! I must leave now. Another spirit has a message to communicate to you, wi."

Papa Ogoun shook everyone's hands vigorously, first the right, then the left. He sat on a chair, covered his head with a red scarf, and returned to his Yoruba village in West Africa. The spirit gone, Marie Ange sat down, looking drained.

Papa Guede then took over Jésula's body, a favorite steed. He moved his hips energetically and suggestively. "How the fuck is everybody today? I know all you women are happy to see me 'cause no man fucks better than Papa Guede," the spirit said, making the women laugh.

"Papa Guede, when are you going to stop using foul language?" Lamercie asked. She then lit a cheap cigar for the spirit.

"Woman," Papa Guede replied, staring at Hagathe, "you're going to be attacked. When that happens you'll know your daughter must go."

"What else can I do?" a hopeless Hagathe wanted to know.

"You can always take another job in the city, working for some rich family."

"Papa Guede, that's something I swear I'll never do again."

"Very well, then. Send her to white man's country. That's all I have to say."

The next morning, Hagathe was on her way to town to buy merchandise for her shop. As she walked through the sugarcane field, she reflected on her conversation with Margaret, finding it hard to believe she had confided in a stranger. But Margaret's kindness and the fact that she treated her like an equal, in spite of the obvious differences in their lives, made her open up. The sincerity in her eyes, which reminded Hagathe of the sea, Mèt Agwe's kingdom, reflected warmth and understanding in a motherly way that was so much like Aïda Wedo's energy. She decided she would ask her grandmother to tell Margaret about the spirits of Guinen. Hagathe wondered what Margaret meant when she used words such as "environ" and "erudite" that sounded like important words she wished she understood. While she tried to make sense of Papa Guede's message, she saw a shadow appear in the sugarcane field and prayed for her safety as she hurried along.

Despite what the spirits and Lamercie had told Hagathe, it was what happened next that made her realize she had to let her daughter go. Vilanus, the Tonton Macoute, who had been less than subtle about wanting her favors, emerged from the field and stood before her. He was wearing the Tonton Macoute uniform of blue denim shirt and pants, a red scarf around his neck, and dark sunglasses. His narrow, reddish eyes accentuated his evil nature and made him look like a wild beast.

"Beautiful woman, why are you trembling? Are you that happy to see me?" he slurred as his body swayed from side to side.

"I don't want to have anything to do with you," she said.

"You don't think I'm good enough for you, uh?" He moved closer, bringing his face inches away from hers. "You must really think you're hot shit going around with white people!" The smell of cheap liquor on his breath repulsed Hagathe. She tried to walk away, but he seized her arm. "I'm going to show you how much better we dark-skinned men are. When I'm through with you, you'll never want one of those pale men inside you again."

She took a deep breath, shook loose from his grip, and moved again to walk past Vilanus, who grabbed her by the arm again, knocking her to the ground. She tried to bring her knee to his groin but missed. She bit his neck. He howled in pain and hit her head against a stone. He lifted her dress, and pulled down her panties. "I'm going to fuck you real good. You and your light-skinned daughter ain't better than the rest of us," he said, penetrating forcefully, with vengeance.

CHAPTER 16

The lion had need of the mouse.
Angels their failings, mortals have their praise.
—Edward Young

Y ou need to spend time with your father," Lamercie
had said, picking up her pipe. She struck a match
and looked away from me, indicating that she was
through talking.

The truth was, it was only out of decency that I had told
her and Marie Ange that I didn't want to go when Brahami
sent his driver to pick me up to spend New Year's with him
and his family.

The Christmas tree in Brahami's living room reminded
me of the phone call that led to my sudden return to Haiti,
yet I looked forward to taking a shower without having to
squat in front of a bucket, using a cup to pour water over
my body; not to mention the luxury of using an indoor toilet
instead of a latrine.

While waiting in the living room for the dinner guest to
arrive, I picked up an album with black-and-white pictures
of Brahami and his friends in Paris. Both he and Latham had
an eccentric appearance that I still saw in Latham, who almost always wore a French beret, either for style or to hide
his thinning hair. As for Brahami, he was now a prosperous gentleman who wore pure linen suits. Quickly turning
the pages, I came across a photograph of his welcome-home
party in which Darah was wearing a beautiful white dress
and a flower in her hair. In another photograph, a woman in

a black dress and a white apron stood behind a table covered with a white lace tablecloth, laden with food.

"Who is this?" I asked, suspecting who it might be.

Darah leaned closer to me on the sofa. "That's your mother," she said, but avoided looking directly at me.

The casualness of her tone did not match the feelings inside me that the picture evoked. Aware of the place my mother occupied in that class-conscious society, I thought about the life that would have been mine had I not left. I had a clearer view of Hagathe's aspirations and the life she lived within the cloister of Haiti's social limitations, and that freed me of any doubts I might have had about the decision that she'd made to let me go to America with the Winstons.

Brahami turned to Darah. "Have you seen the picture I took in front of the Louvre? I want to give it to Iris." He then turned to me. "Latham took it one afternoon after we had spent hours studying Delacroix's paintings for an assignment."

"It must be in one of the three albums," Darah answered dismissively. Then almost immediately she announced that the guest had arrived.

I closed the album, hoping that no one would mention the missing picture that only days ago I had torn to pieces.

"Doctor Georges Buisson," Brahami greeted his friend.

Later that evening, we sat on the veranda after dinner and the maid asked if we preferred coffee or tea. I asked Pépé to tell her I would like lemongrass tea.

"How is it that one knows more Creole than the other?" Georges asked after the maid left.

Brahami lowered his eyelids. "One grew up in Haiti and the other didn't."

The sudden pain in his eyes aroused sympathy on my part, and I wanted to come to his rescue. "When was the last time you two saw each other?" I asked, changing the subject.

The lines on Brahami's face softened. He shared with me

how Georges fell out of grace with Papa Doc, sought asylum at the American Embassy, and left Haiti in 1961. "This is his first trip back."

"Baby Doc has given amnesty to political exiles. I guess the boy is smart enough to realize foreign currency will help the country's economy," Georges explained.

"Georges used to be Papa Doc's adviser," Brahami added.

At that moment, Darah excused herself and so did Pépé, who said she had calls to make. As I took the lemongrass tea that the maid handed to me, I pictured my mother doing her job. "So you knew Papa Doc well. What was he like?" I asked in order to divert the thought.

"At first he was a doctor with modest tastes," Georges said, reaching for the sugar bowl. "A lot of us thought he would continue the social ideology we fought for in 1946. But he turned out to be a ruthless dictator."

"Papa Doc knew he was going to be a puppet to the army," Brahami said. "So he created a militia to counterbalance their power."

Georges took a sip from his cup. "That was a wise political move."

"An act of *kaponaj*," I said. Brahami smiled at the private joke between us.

Georges soon wished us a goodnight, leaving me alone with Brahami.

"His great-grandfather, his grandfather, and his father were prosperous planters from Jérémie," Brahami began. "But he didn't continue that tradition. He became interested in science at an early age. While pursuing our studies at Saint-Louis de Gonzague, his knowledge of Haitian rural life and his analytical skills impressed me. Unfortunately, I'm not as committed as he is to the destiny of Haiti. I guess I don't have what it takes."

I inhaled the scent of flowers in the clean air. "Like what?"

"Passion."

"How come he didn't even know I existed if you are good friends?"

"He left Haiti several months before you did."

That didn't answer my question. But I gathered no one outside of Brahami's immediate family knew about me.

When I went downstairs the next morning, Brahami had already gone to his office and Darah was in the living room listening to Charles Aznavour lament an Italian mother's death on a radio program that featured French music. She lowered the volume and told the maid to bring my breakfast.

"I've been waiting for a chance to talk to you," she said, leading me to the dining room.

I was under the impression that she did not care much for me and I had avoided her. I also knew, from what Marie Ange had told me, that years ago she was the reason her pregnant servant had run away. I kept my head down and buttered a slice of bread. Darah turned off the radio and sat down across from me.

"You must be upset with me for what happened to you and your mother. I have been thinking that if I talked to you, you would understand what happened and perhaps you would not judge me too harshly. Pépé is close to you, and I don't want a cloud hanging over your relationship with her."

I took a bite from the buttered toast and listened.

CHAPTER 17

But for the multitude whose hope is selfish worldly happiness,
Such fare not better singly, than those who missed it doubly.
—Martin Farquar Tupper

While Brahami was abroad for his studies, Darah had wondered if he would return from Paris changed. His smile revealed the same charming dimples. As soon as they were alone with an after-dinner sherry Brahami told her, "Your letters made me happy. I'm sorry I didn't answer the last two. I was busy with my thesis and preparing to come home."

"I thought some French girl took all your time."

"No one could keep me away from you."

In his letters to Darah, Brahami usually wrote about his studies, his travels outside of Paris, and the cultural events he attended. Those letters stirred in her a desire to travel to France, the land of her ancestors, as she often claimed. She, in turn, usually wrote that she yearned to see him again and that she would wait for him, even if it took an eternity.

In the days that followed his return, Darah helped Brahami get reacquainted with the city and its surroundings. Pleased to be with one of Haiti's most adored beauties, Brahami and Darah often went on picnics in the cool mountains of Kenscoff. On Sunday afternoons he visited her at home. Their parents watched them discreetly and hopefully.

One such Sunday, Darah's friend Suzanne and her husband of two years went with them to the Rex Theatre to see Rio Grande. After the show, they went to Bicentennial Square, which President Estimé had built in downtown Port-au-Prince to beautify and modernize the city. Lumane Casimir's melodious voice blasted from loudspeakers and water gushed from fountains. American tourists disembarked from a cruise liner to purchase mahogany souvenirs and colorful paintings from street merchants. Suzanne and Gérard sat on a bench facing the bay, while Brahami and Darah strolled along the promenade, enjoying the salty air.

Brahami led Darah to a secluded area where they sat on a bench near a bush of wild red roses. "I'd like your permission to ask your parents for your hand," he said.

One evening after they were married, Brahami was surprised to find a bottle of wine at the dinner table. That treat was usually reserved for special occasions. "Are we celebrating something?"

Darah filled a glass for each of them, lifted hers to eye level.

"To our love."

After a dinner of grilled fish, baked sweet potato, and a tomato salad, the couple sat on the veranda, taking in the evening breeze.

"Something is bothering you. What's wrong?" he asked.

"I'm okay."

"Tell me what's on your mind."

"I saw my gynecologist yesterday. I might not be able to conceive if I don't get the fibroid removed."

"I'm sure you'll be fine," he said and took her hand into his.

After the fibroid had been removed, Darah was still unable to conceive. Her doctor recommended a specialist in Paris. Since Brahami's architectural firm was thriving, he could not take time off to accompany her. Instead, her mother and mother-in-law traveled with her to Europe. There, the doctor could not find anything medically wrong with her reproductive system. After numerous tests he concluded it was anxiety that had impeded conception.

Months after her return from Paris, Darah still had not conceived. She shared her despair with her closest friend, who advised her to get a card reading. "I told you the woman who read my cards helped me when I didn't know where I stood with my husband," said Suzanne.

"I don't think Brahami would approve."

"He doesn't have to know."

"I can't bring her to my house."

"We will go to her. How about tomorrow evening?"

The streets of Bel Air were noisy even after dark. Darah watched, as Suzanne drove through the raucous neighborhood. People who could not afford electricity gathered around lampposts to play cards or dominoes. Students formed study groups at other lampposts, hopeful that education would help them escape a life of deprivation. Others stood around women who sold fried foods, plantains, sweet potatoes, fish, and pork. Lovers strolled, looking for secluded places to share a moment of intimacy. A breeze roused putrid odors of garbage.

When Suzanne pushed open the wooden gate of an alley, Darah could not hide her contempt for the surroundings as she stepped into a muddy puddle that the torrential rain had left behind the night before.

A boy greeted them. "You want to see Man Clara?" he asked.

They answered yes and followed him past wooden houses with sheet steel roofs.

Clara welcomed Suzanne with a broad smile. "It has been a long time since I've seen you. Come in." Dressed in a white cotton dress and a white scarf covering her hair, she called one of the young girls playing osselet, a game in which the knee bones from goats are spread on the floor and the player throws one at a time up in the air. The object of the game is to catch as many bones as possible before the one tossed comes back down. "Ti fi, go get me some matches," Man Clara called to one of the girls.

"This is a good friend of mine," Suzanne said, placing her hand on Darah's arm.

The mambo took the book of matches from the young girl and lit a candle while Darah observed, with great curiosity, a table covered with bottles of hot peppers steeped in white rum, dark Barbancourt rum, red Manischewitz wine, cheap perfume, syrup, and other articles that were unfamiliar to her. The walls were covered with pictures of Catholic saints, some of which she could not identify.

Clara took a white enamel cup of water from the table, poured three drops on the floor, and invited the women to sit at a table on the other side of the room. As Clara shuffled a deck of cards, she told Darah to relax. "If you're here, it's because you want the truth, and I'm going

to tell you just that. Cut the cards in three piles with your right hand."
Clara spread the cards and slipped into deep concentration. "You just
came back from a trip. Oh, oh-o-o! You went to white man's country.
You were not alone, non. Two older women were with you. You saw
doctor there. But you not sick."

Darah cast a questioning look at Suzanne.

"I see you're married. Your husband is worried lately, right?" Darah nodded, and Clara went on, "It has to do with another woman. But
don't worry. He loves you and will do whatever you say." Another pause.
"You want a child, wi." Darah nodded again. "You will have one, but
not right now." The mambo put the cards in a pile and spread them out
again. "Your husband will have a child with another woman before you
have yours. Madame, I know it will be hard, but try to be kind to that
other woman and her baby."

"Never!" she uttered between her teeth. Even though she doubted
the possibility of another woman in her husband's life, Darah was still
resentful.

The mambo shrugged. "Ask yourself a question." She spread the
cards, examined them. "I already said you will have a child. But not
right now."

"Can you give her some medicine to help her conceive?"

"But I already said she'll have a child, wi." Clara sounded annoyed.

The consultation was over, and the mambo walked the two women
outside and bade them good night. "What do you think of the reading?"
Suzanne asked her friend when they were back in the black Chevrolet.

"I wonder who the other woman is."

"You should have asked her."

"Can we go back?"

Suzanne drove away from the stench of garbage. "It's probably better not to know," she asserted.

The thought of a rival whirled in Darah's mind so much so that she
began to go through her husband's pockets and other personal belongings, without ever finding a clue to confirm if there was another woman.
She even began to go with him on his evenings out with Georges, and
concluded Man Clara didn't know what she was talking about.

It promptly came to light one morning when Darah didn't find her husband in the room when she woke up. She figured he was in his study and went downstairs to make sure Hagathe had his breakfast ready. As she approached the kitchen, she overheard the conversation between her husband and the maid. Her chest suddenly heaved and, as if Erzulie Dantô had taken control of her mind, she could only think of how to avenge her pride.

Two hours later, when Darah became aware of her mother-in-law's presence, her sobs became violent once again. The older Madame Bonsang suggested they pray to restore peace in the home and in their hearts. She opened the Bible Darah kept by her bedside table, read to her daughter-in-law in a clear voice: "And it came to pass that when the sun went down, and it was dark, behold a smoking furnace, and a burning lamp that passed between those pieces."

Later that day, Darah turned down her mother-in-law's invitation to come home with her. After a meal and a nap at her parents' home, she went to visit Suzanne. "So, this is what Clara was talking about. It makes sense now. Just wait, you'll have your child," Suzanne promised.

In the days that ensued, she vacillated between feeling cheated and humiliated. But with time, she was able to forgive Brahami, who became even more attentive toward her. "Nothing like that will ever happen again. I've learned my lesson," he told her one evening.

Darah became more and more absorbed in her tragedy. She struggled with desperation and hope; an obsessive longing for motherhood haunted her. Fearing her barrenness was a punishment from God, she lit candles in as many churches as she could find and distributed coins to the numerous beggars that paved the churches' entrances to calm any possible wrath. During that time, she had a recurring dream in which she saw herself swimming in a pool of still, dark water.

Her mother suggested a trip to Lourdes to ask St. Bernadette and the Immaculate Conception to intercede on her behalf. Along with people who suffer from incurable diseases and physical handicaps, she bathed in the miraculous water of the grotto to change her intrinsic fate. During a candlelight procession one evening, she vowed to only wear white and blue until she was rewarded with the desired child. Seven months after she returned from her trip, she dreamed she was in a river of crystal-clear water, and soon after that her doctor announced she was six weeks pregnant. From that moment on, she contemplated her naked body every day. The fuller it looked, the happier she felt.

The sun was shining at its strongest one afternoon when a brief rainfall moistened the dusty ground and a fresh earthy smell lingered. Darah was resting next to Brahami after lunch when the moment she awaited finally came. Not even the pains could overshadow the happiness she anticipated when she gave birth to their daughter with little difficulty, assisted by Haiti's best obstetrician.

Espéranza Bonsang's birth also brought happiness to her father. He went to the only florist in the capital, ordered a basket of each variety of flower. Never had the nurses and doctors of the hospital seen so many flowers in a patient's room. While Darah was still in the hospital, Brahami told her to think about a date for their daughter's baptism. Suzanne would be the godmother. Brahami's first cousin, with whom he had shared an apartment in France, would travel from Paris to be the godfather.

Months later, the same mulatto elite that had attended Darah and Brahami's wedding gathered for the lavish ceremony. They brought with them luxurious gifts to honor the baby who, by virtue of her birth, seemed destined for a good life.

CHAPTER 18

There are two things for which animals are to be envied:
they know nothing of future evils, or of what people say about them.
—Voltaire

D arah poured hot, steaming coffee for her daughter, who had joined us at the dining table. "Flora and Pierre called you back this morning. They want to meet you and Iris at L'Auberge de Grand-Mère."

"They are my two oldest friends," Pépé said, turning to me.

I watched her take small, quiet sips; and I realized, at that moment, that she was almost flawless and that her good nature was probably the result of having lived a life free of adversities. The straight line of her life was definitely the opposite of the intricate spiral that described mine. It also occurred to me that Pépé never had to struggle to transcend the troubling feeling of not belonging; the inescapable feeling of being abandoned; the haunted desire to retrace a past to find the assurance of kinship and acceptance.

"You are so lucky to have the Winstons in your life. They're good people," Darah said out of nowhere, leaning back on her seat as if expecting to hear some kind of confidence from me.

I would have agreed with her, without any hesitation. But she could not have picked a worse moment to remind me that my family wasn't my family.

"I am," I said. My throat suddenly felt dry. I considered the inability to introduce my parents without having dubious eyes set on me, trying to decipher the circumstances of my birth. Then I considered what the alternatives might have been. "I really am," I added in a more cheerful voice, dismissing the shadowy feelings that had entered my heart.

We met Pierre and his sister that evening at L'Auberge de Grand-Mère, a reddish gingerbread house with off-white windows, nestled in the hills of Pétionville. They were both students at the University of Puerto Rico and were home for the holidays.

"How do you like Haiti?" Pierre asked, keeping his dark, emerald-colored eyes set on me.

"This country seems to be divided into two groups that share the same geography but not much more," I replied, unfolding a napkin.

"*Bueno*," he said, touching the image of Che Guevara on the red T-shirt he wore. "That is precisely why we have to consider another system. We need to end class struggles."

Flora, his sister, shrugged and rolled her eyes. "Come on, Pierre," she protested. "I'm tired of hearing that nonsense. I keep telling you Haiti was like this before we were born and will stay like this after we're gone."

Pierre filled a glass with ice water. "You could be more sympathetic."

Despite the physical resemblance between the two siblings, they apparently held very different views on life. "*Qué va!* Sympathy won't change anything," said Flora.

A waitress came to the table and left with our order.

"The way I see it," I said, "one group is meant to serve and the other to be served."

Pierre leaned his elongated torso forward, close enough for me to sniff his lavender cologne. "That man over there hasn't stopped staring at us. I think we should drop this conversation."

I turned around, but the man had his back to me. I only saw the young woman across from him, who was clad in a red satin dress and bedecked in jewelry. After a second look, I realized she was none other than Chantoutou from the Joseph sugarcane mill, and I wondered if Pépé saw her.

Flora curled her upper lip. "Doesn't she look fit for Mardi Gras? They are the nouveau riche that immigration and macoutism have produced."

Pierre shook his head to signal that the conversation should stop.

Flora, however, went on saying, "Nowadays, if you look around our institutions, the people in charge have names like Barilus, Célius, or even Alcius Charmant."

The three of them laughed, though I didn't understand the joke. "Alcius Charmant is how Haitians call the sounds of excitement people make during lovemaking," Pépé explained. "Names with those endings usually mean a person is rooted in Haitian peasantry."

"It's what we call *mounn monn*," Flora said.

Pierre leaned across the table again. "Flora, please! You need to cut it out!"

The man in the polyester suit started to lead Chantoutou out of the restaurant. As they got closer, I realized it was Dieudonné, my uncle, the Tonton Macoute. It seemed odd that he did not approach me, like he had the day of Hagathe's funeral. Could it be that he did not recognize me? How about Chantoutou, who was so eager to spend time with Pépé and me—why didn't she stop by to say hello?

On New Year's Eve, a popular song blared through the yard, which was decorated with red and green balloons and other Christmas decorations. A singer, who satirized Haitian society through his music, sang that women have to become mistresses to keep their jobs. While Pierre and Flora entertained inside, their parents sat outside with a circle of friends. The guests were mostly mixed-race kin of generations who enjoyed Baby Doc's political era, having recovered the power they had lost during Papa Doc's reign; they seemed proud of their mulatto identity.

Pierre kissed my cheek. The soft hair from his beard tickled my face. "*Hola, guapa!* Good to see you again," he said.

Couples held each other in an embrace or danced inches away from one another. Knees slightly bent, they swayed their hips and glided their feet on the mosaic floor. Pierre's eyes darted around the room. Holding himself with quiet dignity and his head slightly bowed, he asked me to dance.

He led me outside for fresh air when the music stopped, still holding my hand. His sister wore a look of disapproval on her face, as did his mother. But Pierre did not seem to notice, or maybe he just didn't care.

"Iris is a marvelous dancer," Pierre said to Brahami, walking by the circle the older generation had formed outside.

"I hope you'll give me a chance to dance with her," Brahami teased.

"Whenever you like."

"How about now?" Brahami said, already on his feet.

I followed him to the dance floor.

"I'm sorry I've been an absent father to you," he said, holding me at the waist. Even though he spoke softly, the words resounded loudly in my ears. I stole a glance at the man whose genes I carried, thinking he had never been the provider, the responsible, dependable, problem-solving presence John Winston was for me.

"I'm sorry too, Brahami."

"Why do you call me by my first name? You should call me Papa."

I wanted to tell him our relationship was too accidental for me to be able to do that. But all I managed to say was that I needed to get used to the idea.

The smile on his face disappeared and his hands grew cold. He looked at me with sad eyes. "*Eh oui*, the past is like spilled water," he said. "There is nothing I can do except admit I was wrong."

It was five minutes before midnight, and the younger and older generations came together for a toast. Tonton Macoutes in nearby villas as well as in the more crowded areas downtown shot bullets in the air to celebrate, in boisterous revelry, another year of power.

Pierre and I sat by the pool. A bright moon and a blanket of stars hovered above us. He crossed his lean legs and asked if I had made a New Year's resolution.

"No," I told him.

"You have to make one."

"All right. I will not hold grudges and will be more tolerant of other people's flaws and weaknesses."

Music and laughter came from the house. "Life would be much more pleasant if we could all do that," Pierre said, and then let out a sigh.

"What is your resolution?"

"I'm going to be more involved in my country's destiny."

He placed his empty champagne flute on the ground next to his chair, stretched out his legs, and rested his head on the back of the chair. "How about a quick run to our beach house tomorrow?"

It was a little past two o'clock in the afternoon when Pierre picked me up in his father's Isuzu jeep. As we headed south, beyond Champs de Mars, children from working-class neighborhoods strolled in brand-new clothes and shoes. Colorful bows that looked like butterflies decorated the young girls' pressed hair. Pierre slowed down to allow them to cross a street that had no traffic light and no stop sign. As he stepped on the gas again, a woman carrying a large basket of fruit on her head walked in front of the car. Pierre yielded and blew the horn.

Soft sunrays floated above us. Waves grew high and spilled foam over the warm sand, leaving blades of kelp and seashells ashore. The sea then pulled them back, like a protective mother who refused to let go of a rebellious child. A blanket of crystal drops covered my brown skin when I emerged from the water.

"You look like a *sirène*," Pierre said, smiling flirtatiously.

I shook salty water out of my wild hair. "A what?"

"A Haitian mermaid."

"Why?"

"Because you are mesmerizing."

The sun glistened on the waves. A flock of seagulls flew east, toward the Dominican Republic. A fisherman in a canoe cast a net into the sea.

"Even the fish have deserted Haiti," Pierre said softly, gazing silently at the fisherman. "I'd like to take you to La Citadelle."

I stopped playing in the sand to look at him. "Where would you like to take me?"

"To La Citadelle. Henri Christophe built the fortress to protect Haiti from foreign invasion," he explained, staring at the barren mountains on the horizon.

"I have to go back to Monn Nèg tomorrow."

"We could leave at dawn and come back at night."

I buried a big toe in the sand that was warm on the surface but cool an inch below. "I wish I could."

"Too bad. La Citadelle is the Haitian version of the Great Wall of China," Pierre said in a passionate voice. He broke into an enigmatic smile, rested flirtatious eyes on me again. "I like you, Iris." The dim glow of sunset covered us. He pushed my matted hair away from my face, brought his oval suntanned face close to me, and his lips met mine.

I thought about the looks on his mother's and his sister's faces when they saw us holding hands at the party. I also thought about Darah's nervousness and the anxiety in

Brahami's eyes when Pierre picked me up hours ago, and I wondered what they would do if they knew what had just happened.

The sun suddenly disappeared behind tall mountains, and I was basking in the warmth of my first kiss.

CHAPTER 19

As the smell of the sea cleaves to the sea-plant for long years,
so the love of the dead clings to the living.
—Thomas Toke Lynch

H*onè*," greeted a woman who had come to see my godmother.

Marie Ange removed a stone from the red beans that she was washing. "*Respè*," she said, looking up from the bowl.

The woman pulled up a chair to join us under the mango tree. "Are you coming to the *kandianwon* tonight?" she asked Marie Ange. "The one at Mambo Lolotte's."

"I forgot it was tonight. I'll come get you, but I have to take this girl to town first," Marie Ange replied.

"Where are you going?" I asked.

"Nowhere," Marie Ange said, and winked at her friend.

"You just said you were going somewhere," I insisted.

"This child is so curious." Marie Ange studied me briefly. "I don't think you'll be interested. We're going to a *vaudou* ceremony."

Mom's lecture at Yale University immediately came to mind, and the flame of my curiosity grew. "I'm going with you."

Mambo Lolotte was a huge, moon-faced, light-skinned woman. She sat in a rocking chair while a young woman brushed her long, thick, soft hair. A man who had come from the outskirts of Fort-de-France to celebrate a spiritual union with Erzulie Fréda, the mulatto spirit of love, seduction, and vanity, was sitting next to her. He was to marry Erzulie Dantô, a fierce spirit who would kill to protect her children.

Several initiates who were present changed into white dresses, their heads tied in white scarves. Along with them, two men were dressed in white: white short-sleeved shirts, tight white pants, and white scarves tied tightly around the waist. Mambo Lolotte and her sister-in-law, also a priestess, dipped fingers into a white enamel bowl. They skillfully drew ritual diagrams on the ground, inviting spirits to appear. Wildflowers, drinks, cakes, and fruits lay on a table, next to the center pole. On the right, an icon of Mater Dolorosa represented Erzulie Fréda, whose face conveyed pain and ecstasy. She held a bleeding heart and tears fell from her eyes. On the left, with two parallel cuts on one cheek, was the black virgin representing Erzulie Dantô.

Pictures of Papa Doc, Baby Doc, and his glamorous wife decorated the peristyle's dried-palm roof. Together, they represented the trinity of modern Haitian politics. I studied Baby Doc's boyish face, his wife's scornful stare, and the patriarch's cunning eyes. I asked why their pictures hung inside the peristyle, but no one was able to tell me.

The ceremony finally began. Mambo Lolotte recited one Our Father and one Hail Mary. The initiates sang songs that created a world of mysticism and took control over their lives as they communicated with invisible spirits. Their guttural voices greeted the spirit of Damballah Wedo, and they proclaimed their loyalty to him.

Bonswa Damballah Wedo
kouman nou ye
O Dan nou mache ak nou de

One of the initiates dropped to the floor, hissed, and

slithered on the ground. *"Kee-kee-kee-kee-kee."* The Daho-mean snake god had come.

"Papa Damballah! What an honor to have you here!" Mambo Lolotte exclaimed as she offered the spirit a white saucer on which there was a raw egg smothered in flour. She then covered the spirit's head with a white scarf.

"Kee-kee-kee-kee-kee."

Mambo Lolotte removed the scarf. The egg's shell, bro-ken into pieces, lay in the saucer. The yolk was gone.

"Kee-kee-kee-kee-kee." Pleased with the offering, the spirit returned to his world of mystical knowledge. The woman whose body he had inhabited shook the dust off her dress.

Other *hounsis* sang and danced to the next god in the pantheon, holding up the sides of their wide skirts, show-ing lacy petticoats.

Some additional spirits came but did not produce the same energy as Papa Ogoun, who had now inhabited Mambo Lolotte. "Hey! hey! hey! hey!" The warrior spirit bounced inside her large body as she moved with surprising agility.

The *hounsis* hurried to remove the white scarf on the horse's head and replaced it with a red one. One of them handed the spirit a bottle of rum and a lit cigar.

"Hey! hey! hey! hey!" the spirit cried, then blew smoke in the air. The rhythm of the drums thundered. Papa Ogoun walked to the horse's sister-in-law, vigorously shook her hands, and knocked his head against hers.

"Hey! hey! hey! hey!" The sister-in-law now jumped, beating on her chest. She, too, had incarnated the spirit of Papa Ogoun.

In the stillness of the night the voices grew louder. The clapping accelerated when other *hounsis* also became the spir-it of Papa Ogoun. The energy subsided only when the spirit left them. Mambo Lolotte dropped her 250-pound heft on her custom-made rocking chair. Other horses fanned themselves with red scarves and wiped sweat away from their faces.

To cool themselves they drank soft drinks and beer. Minutes later Mambo Lolotte resumed the ceremony. Shaking a beaded rattle, she closed her eyes and sang to Erzulie Fréda. Suddenly the spirit of feminine beauty inhabited her fleshy body. Gazing around the room, she pulled back the corners of her lips, flared her nostrils, and raised her eyebrows. "Oh! oh! oh!" she said in a singsong voice.

Led by a senior *hounsi* who carried a flag, the effeminate pair escorted her to a room, dancing to the rhythm of the drums. They emerged from the room with a perfumed and coquettish Mambo Lolotte wearing a pink satin dress. With her pink perfumed handkerchief, the spirit wiped the face of her husband-to-be. She then came to me and stared intently as though she wanted to uncover my most intimate thoughts.

"Stand up," she ordered without the slightest trace of a smile. She asked me to close my eyes and sprayed cheap perfume on me. "You will find true love, but never forget a rose comes with thorns." Even though the words didn't completely make sense to me, they made me feel hopeful and uncomfortable all at once. As I was about to take my seat again, my eyes met Marie Ange's.

The adepts sang "Veni Creator," turning to Catholic rites. The man from Martinique and the spirit uttered, "I do," and Erzulie Fréda proudly placed a ring on his finger. The bush priest read the legal act of marriage and the couple's mutual obligations. While the Martinican man agreed not to engage in any sexual acts on Fridays, the spirit, in turn, promised to protect him.

"We forgot to bring a flashlight," Marie Ange suddenly realized. "How are we going to find our way home?"

"You will have to sit here until the sun comes up, *wi*," Marie Ange's friend joked, but then became serious. "I'll guide you home, if you like. We must leave now. I have to get home to my children."

As we began to find our way in the darkness among the roaming spirits, we left behind a people engaged in the tenuous solace of magic and beliefs.

Unable to get back to Madame Dufour's at such a late hour, I slept at Lamercie's. Lying in the darkness, I tossed and turned, haunted by a vivid yet hazy memory of Hagathe and the memory of being cuddled in her arms. I was a little girl again, touching her face as she rocked me to sleep. Before long, I fell asleep and dreamed of a woman standing on water. Though it was a vivid and brightly colored dream, I could not remember the words she spoke. It was the barking of Lamercie's bony dog that penetrated the walls of the shabby room and woke me up at dawn.

I found Marie Ange in the yard, sweeping the dirt floor. "Good morning," I said. "How are you?"

"Not bad, thank you," she replied. "How was your night?"

"There was a black butterfly hanging above my head when I woke up. It flew away as soon as I sat up."

"That was probably your mother paying you a visit," Marie Ange explained. "She probably came to give you her blessing. You need to visit her grave before you leave tomorrow."

The pinkish hue of the early morning served as a background for the chirping of birds. Careful not to disturb the stillness of nature, I took off my sandals and sank my feet into the uncut grass, still wet with dew. I breathed the smell of moist earth that reminded me of my childhood. The image of a carefree barefooted young girl running flashed before my eyes. Then I heard Hagathe's protective voice telling her to be careful. I realized then that my soul drew energy from the blood in my veins, like the roots of trees draw water from the soil. As I inhaled the earthy fragrance in the air, visions of Hagathe's casket being covered with dirt came to me. *Ashes to Ashes, dust to dust.* Despite the distinct experiences that separated us, my mother and I had formed an entity, connected by silent and invisible ancestral blood. My roots were deep and I could draw inner strength and spiritual nourishment from them. That realization became the source of a promise to myself to always remain deeply rooted as I continued my quest to reach for the sky.

Peddlers walked down a hill with baskets on their heads on their way to the market. Thoughts of my mother continued to occupy my mind, and I remembered throwing away her picture to avoid being reminded of a life I was eager to forget. Overwhelmed with sudden anxiety, I looked across the landscape hoping to uncover the deepest secrets of the earth and to find communion between the spiritual and the material. The fragrance of the grass and the beauty of the trees softened my heart. Tears that had eluded me for so long rushed to my eyes, emerging from the depth of hidden feelings, liberating me of the anger, sadness, and fear Hagathe's untimely death had provoked in me. Peering out to the hillside, I examined the earth that had succumbed to erosion. The best of Haitian Mother Earth had been washed to the sea. She stood naked, barren, watching her fruitlessness become a source of hunger and unrest.

The sun was partly visible behind the mountains when Marie Ange and I left for the cemetery. I followed her quick steps until we reached bright-blue, hot-pink, and lime-green gravestones whose architecture resembled the houses that people lived in.

"This is food and drinks for Baron Samedi, the lord of the cemetery," Marie Ange explained, pointing at a four-foot wooden cross where people had left cups of black coffee and cassava pancakes.

A few feet away from Hagathe's grave, a woman in a white dress poured a coffee libation. I kneeled down on a step, believing Hagathe's strength had rested in her ability to endure pain. The tears that once flowed from her eyes nourished my soul. The memory of her telling me to go with the Winstons returned and brought forth a river of silent tears that drenched my face. I had finally found the strength I needed to continue my journey despite bewildering images of the past.

About two hours later, the sun reached the mountaintop. The heat rose and the air turned humid. As I readied to say goodbye to Lamercie, she stretched out her slender arms and led me inside. She sat on her bed and examined me in solemn silence, then motioned for me to sit next to her. Her eyes were wet, but no tears fell. "We have been transplanted to this land, but we're Africans," she said. "My grandmother, who was one of the last slaves from an island not far from here, used to tell me that when I was a young woman with fresh breasts coming out of my chest."

"Which island?"

"I don't know," she snapped. "She never told me. I don't think she knew either." Lamercie stared in the distance, as if to better remember. "Coming from a noble family of warriors, she hated the work she had to do in the fields."

"How did she get to Haiti?"

"Let me finish the story," she said, sounding annoyed that I had cut her off. "She met a man on the plantation who spoke Kikongo, the African language she knew. That was my grandfather. He had heard about another island where blacks were free. He was a smart man; used to be his king's adviser. He stole a boat and they got away one night. They made it to the shores of Haiti and settled in Monn Nèg. We've been here ever since. She used to speak to me in her language. Now, I don't remember much. My grandmother raised me because my mother died from a fever soon after I learned to walk. At night, she would tell me stories about her family in Africa. She also told me not to forget that I am

African and that she hoped that her children would return to Africa someday. My grandmother's face appeared to me on the ground when I was about to dig a hole to bury your umbilical chord, and a song she had taught me long ago that I thought I'd forgotten came back to me. That's how I know her spirit is connected to yours. The song went like this:

Mama aaaa
Mu nkoku ibuidi
Simbi
Umbabakidi
Mama aaaa

"I saw her in my dream last night. She told me that you have an African water spirit dancing in your head and that Africa is where your soul belongs. That's the message she gave me."

"Grann Lamercie, what does the song mean?"

"I knew you were going to ask," she said, and took a deep breath. "If I remember correctly, the song is about a girl telling her mother that she fell in the water and the evil Simbi spirit has kept her prisoner."

"What was your grandmother's name?"

"Nlunda a Kinkulu. But everyone here called her Lunda. She told me most names in Africa have a meaning. Hers means keeper of traditions."

PART TWO

CHAPTER 1

Exile is terrible to those who have, as it were, a circumscribed
habitation; but not to those who look upon the
whole globe but as one city.
—Cicero

How is it going?" Latham asked when I answered the phone.

"Not so well."

"What happened?"

I stepped over my dance bag and sat on the bed. "I'm frustrated with the finale."

"Why is that?"

"It's choppy and long."

"You have a week to pull it off," Latham reminded me. "I'm bringing a special guest. So make it good."

"Yes sir," I replied in a military voice, saluting like a soldier, forgetting he could not see me. "Who's coming with you?"

"It's a surprise."

"Somebody I know?"

"You don't know him, but he wants to meet you."

I hung up the phone, rushed to the dance studio to be alone with my art. Then something that had happened earlier that day came to mind, forcing me to reflect. I was packing the books I had accumulated over the years when I found a letter from Brahami. The words he wrote were meant to erase any trace of bitterness in my heart, but I prefer to believe he was only trying to make peace with himself. Afraid of being abandoned again, I doubted the sincerity of his words, knowing the sex with Hagathe was obviously a mistake he regretted. The fact that his blood flowed in my veins never made a difference until I accidently showed up in his life two decades later. Yet, I knew I was being unreasonable and wanted to forgive him. I also knew it was unrealistic for me to assume that he should have gone against the norms of society and keep Hagathe and me in his life. The thought of making peace with him lingered in my mind and made me think of going to Haiti again. Perhaps we could take walks together like we did the day I met him. Perhaps he could tell me things about Haitian culture, like *kaponaj*. Perhaps he could teach me to love and trust him the way I loved and trusted John Winston. Perhaps.

I peered at the audience from backstage, spotted Latham in the second row, next to a brown-skinned man in a shirt-collar jacket and a burgundy scarf with triangular beige designs, tied into a V-shape around his neck.

The production portrayed the historical and cultural journey of an African-American slave. The first act captured the middle passage; the second was about the life of slaves on a Caribbean island; and the third was set on a Southern plantation in the United States. The movements represented a cultural symbiosis that blended classical and ethnic movements. My idea was to utilize a variety of dance forms and techniques, marked by history and geography. The only drawback was that I had to use white dancers because of the small number of black students on our campus.

The head of the dance department, who had once argued against ethnic dance forms under the pretense that they were too spontaneous and did not require specific training, ran backstage when the performance ended. "A plus! Bravo! Bravo!" she exclaimed, hugging me.

I hurried off to find Latham, who introduced me to Ngwendu, the director of the National Arts Institute of

Zaire. "There are good techniques and sensibilities in your work," he said in one breath. "You have talent."

"The ambassador to the Zaire mission told me about Ngwendu coming here with a troupe. He's trying to recruit a dance instructor for the Zaire Arts Institute," Latham explained. "So I brought him here to see your performance."

"You should come to our performance at Carnegie Hall next week," the director suggested. "I would like some feedback from you."

Driven by the beat of drums amid a décor of huts and trees that replicated life in an African village, dancers in grass skirts and colorful beads at the waist, neck, and ankles enticed the audience with rhythmic movements of the hips. In a choreography that depicted a royal wedding, they twisted their bodies into provocative forms. The sound of the drums called to me, reached the pulse of my soul, and revealed memories of a distant life.

When the magical moment ended and the lights brightened the theater, still under the spell of the performance I said to Latham, "I am so glad that I came."

After leaving the white-and-gold interior of Carnegie Hall, we were on our way in a taxi to a reception at the Zaire mission.

"Iris made some interesting comments about the performance," said Latham to the director, who had joined us for the ride.

"I'd love to hear them."

I smiled and hesitated while thinking, so Latham took it upon himself to speak on my behalf. "Iris thinks rigorous training in modern and classical techniques would give the dancers more stage presence and would bring more depth to their movements."

I was afraid the director would find my comments insulting, but he nodded in agreement and encouraged me to elaborate. "The movements should be more uniform," I said. "There are too many individual variations."

He looked at me intently, then smiled. "You are right. We need to develop our technique. I have visited a couple of dance schools here, looking for an instructor. But after seeing your work, I have decided that you should be the one to train our dancers." He paused and smiled again. "Send me your curriculum vitae and two recommendation letters. I'm going to highly recommend you to our *commissaire d'état*." He then nodded, as if to approve his own idea.

His words took me off guard. "I—I don't know," I managed to say. "I was thinking about going to Haiti for a year."

"To do what?"

"Maybe teach English, I'm not sure."

"You are a great choreographer! You cannot give up your art. Take my card," he said. "Africa needs her long-lost children."

I had considered a career in dance, but Mom and Dad were strongly opposed to the idea. They said I needed to keep other options open. So I majored in both dance and anthropology, to compromise.

"What if you get hurt?" Mom had said.

Dad, on the other hand, had reminded me of the competition in the field. "You cannot rely on talent alone. So much has to do with luck. Besides, you may later decide that all of the sacrifices that you must make aren't worth it."

Caught in my never-ending process of indecision, I called home as soon as I turned in my last paper before graduation and finally gathered enough courage to talk to Mom and Dad about my plans. A week earlier, I had told them that I was going to start applying for jobs; but I changed my mind after one visit to the placement office. The only possibilities were entry-level positions with insurance companies, banks, and department stores. None of which appealed to me. And now, I was torn between going to Haiti to be with Brahami, and the possibility of traveling to Zaire.

"How are you?" Mom said immediately upon hearing my voice.

"I'm fine."

"How was the dance performance?"

"I loved the dancers' enthusiasm. So much energy!"

She abruptly changed the subject. "How's the job search coming?"

"I can't imagine taking a nine-to-five job."

"What do you plan to do then? Have you thought of graduate school?"

"I'm thinking about going to Haiti for a year. Maybe I can get a job teaching English." I was sure the long pause on the other end meant she didn't approve and that she needed to weigh her words before speaking.

"What's the matter?" I asked.

"Haiti isn't a good idea," she said, and asked me to hold on a second.

As I waited for her to come back to the phone, I looked out of my window and watched students who were playing Frisbee. They didn't seem so worried about their future.

"Your dad wants to speak to you," Mom said, coming back on the line.

"Your mom just told me about your new plan."

"There was an article in the *New York Times* recently," Mom added from the other line. "A Peace Corps volunteer was arrested and beaten because the government didn't approve of what he was teaching,"

I listened to Mom's rhythmic breathing and heard Dad cough. "Excuse me," he said. "You grew up in a country and a home that encourage freedom of speech. You know that you can get in trouble for doing that over there."

"Haiti is my country as much as it is theirs. They can't stop me from going there."

"But they could make you wish you hadn't." The seriousness in Dad's voice made me shiver.

"Think about it," urged Mom.

"I'll be sure not to make any political statements in public," I said, hoping to convince them it was safe for me to go.

"But your words could be misinterpreted," Dad clarified.

The possibility of being locked up was suddenly enough to make me reconsider.

I went through piles of papers, looking for Ngwendu's card. As I read the information on it, I felt Lamercie's bony hands around my shoulders and remembered the story she had told me about Nlunda a Kinkulu, the keeper of traditions. Taking it as a clue, I sat at my desk to compose a letter to the director. While trying to find the appropriate words, I contemplated a fusion of the grace of classical movements with the fiery sensuality of African dance and remembered a proverb I had heard in Monn Nèg: *When you can't get the mother to breastfeed you, find the grandmother.*

Soon after, I moved with Cynthia into the one-bedroom apartment that Mom and Dad kept on the Upper West Side. Cynthia hosted a dinner party. She was about to begin her residency in tropical medicine at Johns Hopkins University. That evening I met Paul, a Wall Street broker who had the body of a professional athlete; his hair was the color of dried straw; his eyes, which he kept on me from the moment he walked into the apartment, were as blue and warm as the Caribbean Sea.

"How come you and Cynthia are sisters?" he asked, taking a seat next to me on the sofa.

"Because we are."

Leaning closer to me, he smiled and said, "You two must be twins because she gave me the same answer."

"Why did you ask?"

"I'm sure I'm not the only one to wonder about that. How about a movie tomorrow afternoon, or should I ask big sister first?"

"She will probably tell you that it's up to me."

After we had been dating for about three months, Paul and I were walking back to my apartment after a matinee performance of Carlos Saura's *Carmen* at Lincoln Center. I reveled in how the director had cleverly used an Italian art form to express a cultural reality that had originated in southern Spain. "Wouldn't it be great to tell an African story with modern dance techniques?" I said, thinking about the work that I would be doing in Zaire.

Paul stopped, forcing me to do the same. "Why this fascination with Africa?"

"It's my heritage," I said, looking into his bluish eyes.

"What's that supposed to prove?" he snorted.

I looked away, watching a flock of migratory birds fly away from Central Park in search of a warmer place.

"My ancestors were Polish, but you don't see me trying to dance the polka," he blurted.

We continued our walk to my apartment and I wondered how to explain to Paul the potency of African heritage in my veins and what he would think if I were to tell him that I saw Lamercie on the sofa in my living room in my dream last night. She was smoking her pipe and telling me Nlunda a Kinkulu was happy that I was going to the land of our ancestors.

A week later, a yellow cab sped north on Sixth Avenue, taking us home from a dinner party at one of Paul's colleague's homes. "What's the matter?" he asked. "You looked bored all evening."

I held on to the black strap above the window, watching

the city lights. "I got tired of all of the talk about money and power," I answered. But the truth, in fact, was that I was preoccupied with thoughts of the letter I had received from Ngwendu that afternoon, informing me that the *commissaire d'état* of culture and education welcomed my idea of integrating modern and classical techniques into the institute's program.

Paul rolled down the window to let in the cool autumn air. My mind, at that moment, traveled back to the fight in the school cafeteria years before. *Go back to Africa!* the girl had said.

Once in the apartment, I filled the kettle with water, sat across from Paul while he drummed his fingers on the dining table. The kettle's whistle summoned me back to the kitchen.

"I got the job at the National Arts Institute of Zaire," I said, returning to my seat at the table.

"I'm thrilled," he said with tight lips.

I poured steaming hot water into a ceramic mug. "Aren't you happy for me?"

"Roving Iris," he said and sighed. "I'd love to plant you in my garden." He left the apartment without even looking at me.

I threw the comforter back and reached for the alarm clock on the night table. I had stayed in bed much longer than I intended. I fantasized about the work that I would do in Zaire as I envisioned women in grass skirts executing steps from the nation's rich folkloric repertoire, combined with the controlled technique of Martha Graham.

I left the apartment without drinking the four glasses of water and eating the grapefruit that I usually had for breakfast and responded to the wind's crisp kiss with good humor. Autumn rays sneaked through clouds, providing adequate warmth. I quickened my steps toward the subway.

Two construction workers stood on a corner, eating a quick breakfast of buttered rolls and coffee. One of them looked me up and down and said, "Ooh, mama. You look so-o-o-o good! Take me wit ya!"

The other one laughed. "Uh, uh, uh!" he said, shaking his head. "Baby's got back!"

The train emerged from the dark tunnel with people packed like cookies in a box. Some forced their way out of the two sliding doors, but twice as many rushed to get inside. An ageless woman wearing a white scarf paced the platform. "Why you do dis to Haitians? What we Haitians do to you? We boat people but we good people!" Some commuters watched with faces void of expression. Others dozed or flipped newspaper pages. The Haitian woman continued her plea for justice, walking up and down the crowded platform.

Another train roared through the tunnel, then came to a stop. I entered a packed car with the help of people pushing from behind. Four stops later, I made my way out of the crowd, hurried to the fifth floor of a walk-up building, two streets away from the dance studio where the Haitian instructor had taught. After graduation when I returned to the city, I had stopped by to see him but he was no longer teaching there. No one seemed to know where he was.

In the locker room, I kicked off the boots that I wore over my black tights, and took my ballet slippers out of my bag. While I was pulling my large beige sweater over my head, the clear energetic voice of the dance instructor reminded me that I was late for class.

After class, I called to tell Mom and Dad about my decision to accept the job offer in Zaire. Mom was at the university, but Dad told me it was a good idea and that he was sure Mom would also think so. "It's not often a recent college graduate finds an interesting job like this," he said.

That night, I dreamed of walking a long rocky road. The

more I walked, the farther the end of the road seemed. My arms stretched out to the sides and I fell on a tree. I woke up suddenly and tried in vain to give meaning to the dream. Finally, I fell asleep again.

When I called Paul the next morning, his secretary told me that he was home nursing a cold. I bought chicken noodle soup from around the corner to take to him. During the bus ride downtown I experienced a sense of guilt about my imminent departure but managed, somehow, to convince myself that I probably dated him because I was bored, or perhaps it was because he reminded me of the boy I had a crush on in high school. Then again, it could simply be that I needed someone to be with in a city where one could feel lonely among a multitude of people. Another possibility could just be that I was ready to discover my sexuality, having been one of the few of my generation to remain a virgin throughout college.

"I'm leaving for Africa next week," I said, setting the soup and a spoon on a tray.

"Where are you going?" he asked, as if he didn't remember our last conversation.

"I'm going to visit Felicia, my friend from Wayberry College, before heading to Kinshasa. She's working in Dakar right now."

Paul raised his eyebrows. "Are you sure you know what you're doing?"

"My mind is made up."

He studied me briefly and in a disdainful voice said that he couldn't believe I was giving up life in New York City for Africa. "What makes you think you'll find an El Dorado in that wild place?"

I ignored the question.

He picked up the *Wall Street Journal* on the coffee table and started reading.

"I guess I'll be leaving now."

"Lots of luck to you," he said, without seeing me to the door.

The January cold energized me as I walked among people rushing to buses and subway stations that would take them away from Midtown Manhattan at the end of their workday.

It was no easy task preparing to travel for an indefinite period. Mom, Cynthia, and Pépé had different ideas on what I should take. I spent days deliberating because each suggestion confused me more. As I was going through my belongings, I came across the book I'd had when I was a child and that Hagathe had kept for me. I opened it to the page where the ballerina leaps across a stage and I smiled at the thought that dance turned out to be so important to my life, after all.

When the doorbell rang, I was surprised to find Mom and Dad standing there. I had turned down their invitation to dinner because I still had too much to do and they had agreed that the next day we could have a late lunch on our way to the airport.

"We're not staying," Dad said, handing me a box carefully wrapped in bright blue paper and a red ribbon. "We wanted to give you this before tomorrow."

My heart raced as I untied the ribbon with shaking hands, thinking it was odd that they would make a special trip to the city just to give me a present. The sight of Hagathe's picture in its original frame stirred a twinge of regret and guilt and reminded me of all the times I had wanted to recover the picture that connected me to my essence. I stared at Hagathe's face with a feeling of wholeness, as if I had found a part of myself.

It was snowing outside. Big round flakes. Watching through the living room window, I wondered when I would see snow again. I had visions of New England winter wonderlands when a robe of the purest white covered the ground to form a perfect bliss. But snow in Manhattan was not very appealing. In just a few hours, it would become a dirty grayish slush.

As I moved around, making sure I had packed all that I could possibly take with me, the silence in the apartment made me sad. I turned on the television and listened to a talk show about Reaganomics. People were arguing about that a lot in those days. Some called it "voodoo economics." I don't know why. The controversial economic policy advocated activities to boost tax revenues, meaning tax cuts for the rich and job loss for unskilled workers. I had heard enough. I turned off the set, watched snowflakes from the living room window, and finally dozed off on the couch.

CHAPTER 2

I am a part of all that I have met;
Yet all experience is an arch wherethrough
Gleams that untravelled world, whose margin fades
For ever and for ever when I move.
—Alfred, Lord Tennyson

Darkness had cast shadows everywhere when the plane landed in Senegal. Eager to embrace my new journey, I welcomed the hot air and rolled up my sleeves, forgetting about the snow and the cold weather I had left behind. Felicia kissed me three times on my cheeks. "That's the way they do it here," she said. I followed her out of Yoff Airport, past men and women dressed in bright traditional outfits. Their hands gesticulated to make their point as they talked. The men's guttural voices contrasted greatly with the women's high-pitched speech.

As the car traveled along the shore toward Dakar, I rolled down the window to listen to the waves crashing against rocks. The lamenting sounds of the sea boiled over, reminding me of the suffering voices of Ibo, Nago, Congo, Mandinga, Wolof, and Yoruba souls that never reached American shores and whose bones carpeted the bottom of the water kingdom. The ocean that betrayed thousands of men, women, and children roared menacingly like a wild beast about to attack a prey. I breathed the salty air, stared into darkness, and thought of Nlunda a Kinkulu, the keeper of traditions, the runaway slave who found freedom on the shores of Haiti and who probably had listened to this same ocean from an overcrowded slave ship on her way to the New World.

"Welcome to the land of *teranga*," Felicia said, opening the door to her apartment.

"*Teranga?*"

"That's like Southern hospitality."

We sat in the living room drinking mint tea, talking about our days at Wayberry College, and listening to Sarah Vaughan, the sassy divine one. *Nice work if you can get it*, she sang in her melodious voice.

I took off my shoes, wiggled my toes. "Here I am in the motherland!"

"I've been thinking about this motherland stuff . . ." Felicia said, shaking her head.

"And?"

"I should let you get to know Africa before we talk about it. I don't want to influence you in any way." She got up to play the other side of the cassette, leaving me wondering how she felt about being in Africa.

"I wonder if Jamal ever made it to this continent. He said he wanted to come here after graduation."

"No idea," Felicia answered. "But I did hear that he and Wanda had plans to get married. And let me tell you something, Wanda is one sister who couldn't make it in Africa. She's too intolerant."

"*Allahu, Akbar!*" a deep male voice chanted from a nearby tower.

"That's the *muezzin* calling people to the first of the five prayers of the day," Felicia informed me, and pushed the stop button on the boom box.

The *muezzin* announced a new day filled with hopes and promises and invited the rising sun to come forth. Windows and doors opened as Dakar slowly woke up. My eyes, though, were still heavy with sleep.

* * *

After I slept for a few hours, Felicia's boyfriend, who was way over six feet tall with dark, smooth skin the color of grapes, came to take us to lunch. The strong smell of spiced incense filled the air. Proud men dressed in heavily starched and embroidered robes circulated amidst the bustling crowd. Their elegance contrasted sharply with the weary beggars who crowded the sidewalks. The men made their way to the mosque to worship and praise the prophet Allah for his wisdom and guidance. From the sidewalk, I could see them seated reverently on their mats, facing east and rolling beads with faithful fingers.

Ousmane took a few coins from his pocket to give to a leper whose left hand had been eaten away by disease. He also gave to a woman who sat nearby, the mother of triplets.

Walking past Independence Square, we headed east to an open-air restaurant overlooking the harbor that served French-influenced Senegalese cuisine under a thatched roof. I ordered *thiof*, a local fish stuffed with fresh parsley and other spices.

"What are your plans for tomorrow?" Felicia asked Ousmane, sipping white wine and leaning back in her chair.

"I must go to my village," he answered.

Felicia leaned forward. "How long are you staying?"

"Just a few hours."

"You should take Iris with you," she suggested. "I have to work tomorrow. There's a consultant coming from Washington."

"How far is your village?" I asked Ousmane.

"Two hours north of Dakar."

Hours later, Ousmane parked his car in front of the home of Jean-Luc and Marguerite, both French expatriate doctors. A few inches taller than her husband, Marguerite was a talkative brunette who chain-smoked as she spoke about her parents' farm in Normandy. When the maid, who had brought us a cold ginger drink, was out of sight, Marguerite told us that she recently fired one of her servants, a boy, because she saw him plant something in the yard. "I'm sure it's *maraboutage*. I know about African magic," she asserted.

"These things don't work," Ousmane said.

"I know what I'm talking about," Marguerite insisted, rolling her eyes. "It's probably still there 'cause I didn't want to touch it."

"Let's see what it is."

Ousmane went into the garden with Marguerite to dig up the soil at the spot but found nothing. After he tried a few more places, they gave up their search and rejoined Jean-Luc and me. No longer concerned with African magic, Marguerite asked Ousmane when his brother would be returning from France. "With so many students returning home with advanced degrees from Europe and North America, Africa doesn't need technical assistance from foreigners anymore," she said, reaching for her cigarettes on the coffee table. "They're ready to develop their own land." She took a cigarette out of the pack and shrugged. "So they say."

Her comment made me think about my contract with the government of Zaire, though I saw no reason to be concerned. After all, I was one of Africa's children returning home.

While Ousmane and Jean-Luc discussed their mask exporting business, Marguerite watched the smoke from her cigarette rise and disappear. "I used to think Africa was a haven for foreigners. You'll see." Her words sounded like a warning against some unseen danger. The thought made me as uncomfortable as I had been when Felicia alluded to her disillusionment with Africa.

"What don't you like about Africa?"

"I came here after the country's independence some twenty years ago, when there was a surge of cultural energy on the rise. But now I'm afraid politics is destroying this

"Spirits can communicate with her, even without the cowry shells."

The kettle boiled on the hot plate. The smell of fresh mint lingered in the room. Ousmane took one of the glasses from the tray, poured the liquid into it. His right hand held a kettle that he slowly lifted above his head. The tea foamed as it filled the glass.

"You should think about what she told you," Ousmane urged, pouring the tea from the glass back into the kettle. He repeated the process a few times before serving the *ataya*. The first round was bitter, the second sweet, and the third sweeter.

"The cowry never lies," Ousmane told me on our way back to the main road. "The prophet was hiding from his enemies in the desert, and a cowry player told them where he was. That's why he banned the practice." He paused. "It's too bad you will be gone. I'm having a ceremony next month for a female spirit who is fond of me." He pulled a handkerchief from his back pocket and wiped the sweat from his forehead and neck. "I have to do it so she doesn't interfere with my intimate life with women," he added in a conspiratorial voice. "I am having some problems with Felicia."

"How can you have a personal relationship with a spirit?" I asked, then suddenly recalled the ceremony at Mambo Lolotte's in Haiti.

"Africa existed before Islam came," he said and shrugged.

"Why do you think she gave me this concoction?"

"For protection."

It sounded more like paranoia to me. But I didn't tell him that. Instead, I asked him why he had told Marguerite that African magic didn't work.

"White people have no business knowing about these things."

"What do you think *really* happened?"

great country. The bureaucracy is becoming too much of a maze. Greed is everywhere."

I wanted to hear more, but Ousmane said that it was time to pick up Felicia, who had gone to her office after lunch.

The following morning, Ousmane picked me up. Driving at a moderate speed on a dirt road, we passed cloistered brown huts where women with small children strapped to their backs pounded wooden mortars. Their upper bodies leaned forward then back in a continuous movement. As the car sped along on a deserted road, a young barefooted boy about ten years old, dressed in beige and brown balloon pants and a sleeveless top, chased a flock of sheep away from a peanut field.

The blue sky merged with the ocean on the horizon. "My village isn't very far," Ousmane said. "The car is going to attract too much attention," he added, and parked it off the main road. "Everyone expects me to solve their problems."

A young man about seventeen years old jumped off a minibus before it came to a full stop. Three men sat on the roof on top of bags of rice; two sheep kept them company.

"*Asalam waaleykum,*" Ousmane greeted the people as we stepped inside the vehicle.

"*Waaleykum i salam,*" everyone answered in chorus.

There were seven people in each of the four rows that were meant to seat five. The woman on my right sat at the edge of the seat, a sleeping baby tied to her back. A toddler, about two or three years old, stood between her legs as she engaged in a conversation with a woman next to her.

"*Fi bakne,*" Ousmane soon told the driver, who came to a full stop.

He pushed a wicker gate that opened onto mud huts in a yard. A couple of children and two sheep ran around playfully. A full-bodied woman sat on a mat inside one of the huts, looking like a baobab tree in the middle of an open field. She smiled broadly when Ousmane's face appeared through the green and yellow tie-dyed curtain that partially covered the wooden door. He kept his hand in hers throughout the lengthy salutation. A brief conversation followed in Wolof before Ousmane turned to me. "She wanted to know who you are. I told her you're a friend from America."

Koumba, the big buxom woman, looked at my cutoff jeans and burst into laughter, showing teeth stained with tea and kola nuts. She spoke again in Wolof, clapping her hands. Ousmane then told me she was happy to have an American in her home. "*Astou!*" she called out after she was done inspecting me.

A girl entered the hut and listened to Koumba's instructions before leaving again. She came back minutes later with a wooden bowl that contained three different kinds of leaves and a cup of water that she placed on the floor. She then squatted in a corner.

Koumba had thick, wooly hair that she wore in loose braids. Each ear bore a row of colorful hoop earrings. A dark design covered her lower lip down to her chin; the same black ink darkened the soles of her feet and intricate orange designs decorated the palms of her hands. She removed a bag of cowry shells from her chest, tossed them on the mat where she sat, and patiently studied their positions. Ousmane nodded, smiled, or frowned as she spoke.

"She's good," he said after they repeated the process. "You want a reading too?"

"Why not?" I said on an impulse.

Koumba laughed when Ousmane told her what I wanted to know. She signaled for me to come closer, then tossed the cowry shells.

"You're going on another journey. Things will work out if you honor your spirits. But you should be patient. *Legi,*

now, you should remember the sun always com[ ] rain." Ousmane translated. He listened to Kou[ ] then said, "She sees you in a triangle, but thing[ ] out. You need to prepare a meal of ground whea[ ] to feed as many poor children as possible."

Koumba spoke once more. "She wants to [ ] those *toubabs* around you are."

"I don't know what a *toubab* is."

"White people."

"Tell her I know a lot of white people."

"She said she doesn't want to read for you an[ ] cause you're not cooperating."

"I didn't mean to be disrespectful."

Puzzled by what Koumba had told me, I wor[ ] this type of reading was an art or a science. I still dor[ ]

She put her shells away, mixed fresh leaves in a[ ] bowl. Then she pulled a basket containing bottles o[ ] and oils from under a wooden bed. She added some[ ] to the bowl, filled up two bottles, and handed one [ ] mane and one to me.

"We have to rub our bodies with this before g[ ] sleep at night," Ousmane explained.

The young girl returned with a plastic tub of wa[ ] which two halves of a lemon floated. She took the [ ] away after we washed our hands then brought in a[ ] of *ceeb-u-jen*, the national dish of rice, fish, and veget[ ] and a spoon for me. Ousmane and Koumba skillfully [ ] handfuls of rice into balls with their right hands, an[ ] them in their mouths.

After the meal, the young girl brought in a hot [ ] a kettle of water, fresh mint leaves, sugar, and a tray [ ] four glasses, each about three inches tall. The woman [ ] something to Ousmane, who then turned to me. "She [ ] you're not going to do what she asked."

"How does she know that?"

"Maybe the boy did plant some charm to keep his job but removed it after Marguerite saw him."

Back in Felicia's apartment, I poured the liquid Koumba had given me in the toilet bowl. I didn't like its strong smell and didn't want it on my body. Besides, I didn't see how it could actually make a difference in my life.

Felicia was in the kitchen, washing lettuce. I stood at the doorstep, watching. "You still haven't told me what you think of Africa," I said.

She turned to face me. "I love it here. I've embraced the culture as my own." She turned her head away from me and sliced a fleshy tomato. "But sometimes I think people here aren't so accepting."

I shifted my weight. "Be more specific."

"Hand me that cucumber, will you?" She uncovered the fish the maid had prepared earlier and turned on the stove.

"What's bothering you?" I insisted, studying her reaction.

"Ousmane and I are in love. The problem is his family. They think it would be better for him to marry the girl they choose for him," she said, peeling a cucumber. "Sometimes I think he needs to stand up to them, although I understand the strength of family ties here."

"Have you met them?"

"I've been to their home a few times. They're very warm and kind."

"Just like Ousmane."

Felicia mixed oil, vinegar, mustard, salt, and pepper to make a salad dressing. As she shook the jar, I felt her anger rise. "They're hung up on blood ties and think blacks from the Americas are sons and daughters of slaves."

"They obviously don't know their history," I said, sharing her anger. "You should tell them Toussaint Louverture was the grandson of an Arada king."

We carried the fish and salad to the table and took our

seats. "Isn't it a shame that I thought I was coming to the land of the ancestors and get slapped with this?" As she poured the dressing over the salad, she continued softly, "Of course we're not going to generalize, but it does say something about what some Africans think of us."

"When they get to know you better they will change their minds."

"Why are you staying only one week?" she asked, switching the conversation topic. "That's not enough time."

"I have a job waiting for me, remember?"

"I've been thinking," Felicia said as she lifted a piece of fish from her plate.

I watched her as she ate. "What have you been thinking?"

"Are you sure you want to go to Zaire? There is a famous dance school in Dakar. Maybe you should try to get a job there. I hear Zaire is a tough place."

"It can't be that bad if it produced a great man like Patrice Lumumba."

"Look at what they did to him."

Felicia and I boarded the ferry to Gorée Island, along with tourists who, like me, were trying to piece together fragments of a dark passage. Thick with foam, the turbulent sea changed from indigo blue to dark green. I wished that I could penetrate its mysteries. Homes with red-tile roofs that sheltered European traders stood in the distance. Children ran and played in the streets where, centuries ago, captives had been assembled and branded, chained and shackled, before sailing to a life of slavery in the Americas. Women in colorful clothing sold man-made artifacts. With the ruins of the past in the background, fishermen repaired boats and nets.

"This was once a lavish mansion where wealthy traders lived comfortably in the sun-filled rooms upstairs overlooking the sea. The dark cells served as a warehouse for captives," said the curator of the Slave House, with a thoughtful look on his face. He then turned to one of the small cells. "Here sat about thirty men with only a cloth around their waists."

I shook my head in disbelief. "Where did they sleep?"

"Right there, sitting down." He then pointed to a small space under the stairs. "This is where they locked up the rebellious ones who would be left behind. Traders didn't want rebels because they were bad merchandise, a risk to the business." He walked over to a rectangular opening into a dark hallway that led to the sea. "That's the Door of No Return."

I imagined Nlunda a Kinkulu sharing the fate of thousands of others, and I wondered what her thoughts were when she embarked on that long journey to the unknown. As we left the island, soft moonlight reflected on the sea whose dark waters hid the ambitions and secrets of slave traders. Suffering moans of captive spirits who never lived to leave the island echoed in the wind. Koumba Castel, the defeated old spirit that protected Gorée, wandered in the sandy streets.

CHAPTER 3

The ships are lying in the bay,
The gulls are swinging round their spars;
My soul as eagerly as they
Desires the margin of the stars.
—Zoë Akins

When the plane reached Lomé, a slender woman boarded and sat next to me. She fell asleep almost immediately. About an hour later, as we were about to land in Douala, she woke up and looked at me for the first time. Navy-blue pumps matched the cloth wrapped around her waist, making her look even more elegant in her traditional attire.

"Where are you going?" she asked.

"Kinshasa."

"So am I. My name is Citoyenne Nbutongi. Call me Marie Madeleine."

"Iris Odys. Pleased to meet you. Is Citoyenne your first name?" I asked, even though I knew the French word meant *citizen* in English.

The question brought a smile to her face. "The titles *mister*, *miss*, and *missus* are for foreigners. Zairians are either *citoyen* or *citoyenne*," she explained. "We also must use our African names. But I like the name Marie Madeleine." She studied me briefly and asked where I was from.

"The United States," I said, wondering why she would introduce herself as Citoyenne Nbutongi if the word *citoyenne* means *madame* or *mademoiselle*.

The stewardess served drinks then rolled the cart away. "I wanted to be a stewardess," Marie Madeleine said, looking pensive.

"Why did you change your mind?"

"I didn't have the connection to make it happen." She rested thoughtful eyes on me then asked if this was my first trip to Kinshasa.

I told her yes and she continued to examine me. A few seconds later, she said, "Then you must work for your embassy or an American company, because you don't look like a missionary."

"I will be working for the National Arts Institute. What do you do?"

"I am a businesswoman." She took a sip from her glass.

"What kind of business?"

"I am a *mbana mbana*."

"Meaning?"

"I buy and sell whatever I can get my hands on. This is a business trip for me. Prices are good in Lomé. So I go there to buy merchandise." She finished her drink. "That's what most of the women on the plane do."

Glancing around the plane I noticed that, indeed, most of the travelers were women. As the stewardess walked down the aisle collecting empty cups, Marie Madeleine watched her.

"What is it like in the United States?" she asked.

"Compared to what?"

"I don't know. Everyone dreams of going there. I've heard people can make a fortune just like that." She snapped her fingers. "Everyone there is rich, right?"

"It's not like that," I stated.

"You must invite me there. I am a hard-working woman. I could become a millionaire in no time."

"*Ladies and gentlemen, in approximately ten minutes we will land in Kinshasa's N'djili Airport...*" the rehearsed voice of the stewardess reverberated throughout the plane.

"Someone's picking you up?" Marie Madeleine asked, looking into a pocket-size mirror, powdering her face.

"I guess the director. I sent him a telegram."

"A telegram! Do you know if he got it?"

"I hope so."

"Stay with me until you see him," she urged. "Things can get nasty at this airport."

When the plane finally landed in Kinshasa, the women became restless. Men in military uniforms, rusty rifles in hands, pulled them to the side. A woman who had wrapped cloth on her back, pretending she was carrying an infant, raised a defiant hand to attack the soldier who tried to take her cloth away. Two women held her back. The soldiers continued pulling women aside, trying to seize their merchandise. One of them looked me up and down before taking away my carry-on luggage. He said something in Lingala, the widely spoken Bantu language in the city of nearly seven million people. Marie Madeleine told me he said the bag looked heavy so it probably weighed more than the five-pound limit. He wanted me to pay a tax.

"This makes no sense," I said.

Marie Madeleine whispered, "I'll handle this."

Again, the man spoke to me in Lingala.

"Excuse me," Marie Madeleine replied in French, taking quick steps, while pointing a finger at the soldier. "My sister isn't going anywhere without me. She doesn't deal with people like you. She grew up with civilized people." She then turned to me. "Come along, my dear."

A man in a green uniform led us inside a room and slammed the door behind him. He dropped my bag onto the floor, sat behind a desk, and took out a piece of paper that he handed to Marie Madeleine; she ignored it. "I do not deal with people like you. Get your superior on the phone and tell him Colonel Bangawa's wife would like to speak to him. If it is trouble you want, I'll give you trouble."

The man put the paper down, scratched his head. "*Citoyenne*, pardon, eh. I don't want any trouble," he said in hesitant French.

"I didn't think so," Marie Madeleine replied, and signaled for me to follow her as she picked up my bag on her way out.

Ngwendu was not at the airport, so we took the first taxi in sight. As I closed the back door of the brown Peugeot, I let out a huge sigh of relief. Marie Madeleine pushed down the lock and asked me to do the same on my side.

"Papa, *démarrez!*" She told the taxi driver to pull out.

"So your husband is a colonel?" I asked when the taxi turned onto the main road.

"I don't have a husband," she said and laughed.

Night had spread its black shawl over Kinshasa and its outskirts. Palm trees rose like El Greco's elongated figures, hovering above, like spirits in the shadowy night.

At the Intercontinental Hotel on Avenue Batelela I was given a room that faced the pool on one side and overlooked Brazzaville, Kinshasa's twin city, on the other. After a long shower I slipped between the ironed sheets and fell asleep wondering what had happened to Ngwendu.

Two days later, Marie Madeleine picked me up in a taxi to take me to her home for lunch. The vibrancy of the crowded *cité* reached me as soon as the car turned onto Kasa-Vubu Avenue toward the Matongue district, where most of Kinshasa's inhabitants lived. Unlike the people of Senegal, who were predominantly Wolofs, usually with a deep chocolate complexion and a tall lean frame, the people of Zaire were of varied shades, height, and shapes. Through the taxi's open window, I could hear loud conversations and electrifying music. On potholed streets, the car bounced to the rhythm.

When Marie Madeleine opened her gate, a multitude of children came running to greet her. Even though it was Saturday, they wore their Sunday best. Two of the children were hers; the others were her younger brothers and sisters. She led me to her living room furnished with four chairs and a coffee table with a vase of plastic flowers on it.

A woman in her late forties sat erectly on one of the four chairs. When she saw me standing behind her daughter, she rose to shake my hand. "So this is l'Américaine," she said, showing yellowish teeth. "My daughter is lucky to have an American friend." She continued to study me with a strange gleam in her eyes.

Marie Madeleine turned to the children, who sat on a long bench. "Go get Huguette," she told them.

Immediately, I saw the resemblance between the two women. "My younger sister Huguette is studying law at the university." Pride shone in Marie Madeleine's eyes.

Huguette wiped her hands on the wrapper tied around her waist and accepted the hand I offered. "Please excuse me," she said, "I must go. I don't want to burn the food."

The children stared at me and snickered as Marie Madeleine ordered them out of the living room and announced that she was going next door to buy us drinks.

She left me with her mother who, only seconds later, leaned forward and lowered her voice in confidentiality. "Can people really find money in the streets where you come from?" The intensity in her eyes made me uncomfortable.

"There are poor people living in the United States too."

She cast an incredulous look at me and remained silent until Marie Madeleine came back with beer and soft drinks for the children. On the other side of the living room Huguette set the dining table for her sister and me. She and her mother ate outside with the children. I was hungry and helped myself to the mashed plantain topped with a spicy meat sauce and cassava leaves.

As she cleared the table Huguette asked, "Did you enjoy the food?"

"The beef was so tasty."

"That was monkey meat."

"Oh!"

Marie Madeleine pushed the coffee table away and turned up the music. "This is Zaiko Langa Langa." She started to dance, moving her forearms up and down. Her mother and sister soon joined in. The children followed. They suddenly turned to me. "*Bina! Bina! Bina!*" they cried, clapping their hands.

"They want you to dance," Marie Madeleine explained.

I joined in without inhibition. Even Marie Madeleine's mother, whom I initially thought of as sullen and stiff, loosened up.

A few days later, Marie Madeleine called me from the hotel lobby and invited me to come downstairs and have a drink with her and her friend.

As their eyes roamed the room, both women maintained fixed but friendly smiles. They wore much too much makeup.

"You should come with us to Un-Deux-Trois," Marie Madeleine said as her eyes continued to survey the bar.

"What's that?"

"It's the place where Franco, our famous musician, and his band perform. Every Friday is ladies' night."

Moments later, the two exchanged words in Lingala then asked to be excused. "We'll be right back," Marie Madeleine said as she walked away, adjusting the wrapper with precise movements around her hips.

An Asian man in a dark Maoist suit stared at me intently, forcing me to look away. Very shortly, a waiter came to me and said, "That Chinese man wants to know what you're drinking."

In a curt voice, I responded, "Tell him nothing."

Looking around the hotel bar, I suddenly realized that I was the only woman there. The Asian man walked up to my table and in heavily accented French asked if he could sit down.

"Excuse me?" I said in English, hoping to discourage him.

"You American?" he continued in English, as he sat down on a chair across from me. "I lonely Chinese man looking for company." He broke into a smile that was more like a grimace, revealing brownish teeth.

"I don't want company."

As he stood up, his smile disappeared. It was then that I noticed he was only about four feet tall.

When she finally returned to the table, Marie Madeleine asked, "What are you thinking about?"

"I talked with the director yesterday. He said he wasn't at the airport because he had not received my telegram."

"You've been here a week, and he's only returning your call now?" There was suspicion in her voice.

"He said he was visiting his family in Kikwit," I told her. "He asked me why you didn't take me to a more modest hotel."

Marie Madeleine ordered another round of beer, then lit another cigarette. "What's going to happen now?"

"I'm waiting to sign the contract."

"Kinshasa is a nasty bitch. People here only get a good job when they have influential family members. You're not even from here." She blew out smoke. "I bet you don't have a contract because the men in the offices are waiting for you to become so desperate you'll do anything for a job."

I held up a hand.

"You think I'm kidding, but that's how it works here."

"I don't think you're kidding."

"I guess it's not the same for you. You're an educated foreigner with American dollars." She puffed on her cigarette. "Anyway, I don't understand why you left a country like the United States to come to a place where life has nothing to offer but misery, especially for women!"

The waiter brought the beer Marie Madeleine ordered. "The Asian man said to put it on his tab."

Marie Madeleine turned her head, smiled, and winked at the Chinese man. She then poured the chilled beer into tall glasses. "Some women must swallow their pride to get or keep a job. Do you think going to Lomé to buy merchandise is enough for me to support myself, my two children, and my younger brothers and sisters?" She flicked ashes from her cigarette. "Where do you think Ana is right now?"

"I don't know."

"Working."

"Working?"

"Yes, working!"

It took a second or two, but I finally understood what she meant. "I hope you girls use condoms."

"Come to think of it," she said abruptly, "you probably shouldn't hang around me. The big shots in town know who I am. You don't want them to think they can buy you the way they buy me."

"Come on!"

It was now her turn to hold up a hand. "I know what I'm talking about." She paused for a moment and said, "I'm leaving for Lomé again in two days. I'll be gone a week or two. When you leave this hotel, give your address to Huguette. And by the way, you can tell the director I chose this hotel because it is where foreign people with foreign currencies come. Unless I can prove to the desk clerk that I know somebody staying here, he would want a cut from the money that I make on my back." Suddenly she stood. "Take care of yourself," she said, and kissed my cheeks before walking over to the Chinese man's table. I couldn't hear what she said to him but saw that she sat down. I wondered if I would ever see her again.

The shadow of the night swiftly settled. In its embrace, I fell into the deep sleep of a disillusioned soul.

CHAPTER 4

The nuts from a palm tree don't fall
without dragging a few leaves with it.
—Congolese proverb

The man who carried my suitcases to the room bowed his head slightly and extended his right hand to receive the generous tip I gave him, flashing a smile that uncovered his teeth filed into sharp triangular shapes.

"*Mèsi mingi.*"

"*Elokoté*, you're welcome," I said, happy to use the Lingala expression I had learned at Marie Madeleine's home.

I looked around my room in Paix Retrouvée. The guest house that Ngwendu recommended had belonged to a Belgian family before the country's independence and had since been transformed into a commercial lodging. The simple furnishings in the room consisted of a wooden table and chair, two twin-size beds, and a nightstand between them. There were no dressers or closets, nor carpets covering the cement floor. I left my two suitcases on one of the beds then opened a door to a small bathroom with chipped-paint walls.

That night I tossed and turned and finally dozed off until thunder woke me. When the wind's violent howls turned into whispers, I got out of bed. As my feet landed in a puddle of water that had leaked in through cracks in the window, I let out a cry of disgust and returned to bed, gazing at the ceiling that so desperately needed to be painted.

A sudden desire to call home emerged as I realized that Mom and Dad were probably worried by now because I hadn't contacted them since I left Dakar. The manager told me that I should go to the post office in order to place the call. I filled out the mandatory form and waited to be connected. I finally dozed off in the unbearable heat of the poorly ventilated room. A guard tapped me on my shoulder and told me the office was closing for lunch and that I could return in a few hours, and I did. When I questioned the clerk, to whom I had given the form, he told me that he still couldn't get the call through. I waited there until closing time.

At the guest house, I ran into the manager. "How's your family?" he asked.

"The clerk kept telling me he couldn't get through," I answered in a voice filled with exasperation.

"I suppose you didn't give him a *matabiche*."

"I don't know what you mean."

He touched his chin. "It's a tip people expect before they do you a favor."

"But he's not doing me a favor. It's his job to make the connection, isn't it?"

"If you really want to speak with your family, give him ten zaires with the completed form, and you'll see."

I returned to the post office the next morning, filled with renewed optimism. The clerk smiled at the sight of the bill, and I was connected to New York in less than five minutes. As I listened to the phone ring, it occurred to me that it was only four o'clock in the morning in New York. I had thought it best to call when they still had sleep in their eyes; that way they wouldn't ask too many questions. By the second ring I was tempted to hang up, nervous about what I would say. But I was glad I didn't because hearing their voices brought me more joy than I expected.

"Latham was planning on calling the Zaire mission tomorrow to trace your whereabouts. We were worried," Dad said.

"Are you making interesting friends?" asked Mom after a few minutes of catching up.

"Oh yes, some very interesting ones," I said, thinking about Marie Madeleine and her family.

"How about the job?" Dad wanted to know.

"I haven't started yet. I'm doing some cultural immersion first." It was getting harder for me to mask the truth, so I became eager to get off the phone. I told them I only had a few seconds left, promised to call again, and hung up in a hurry.

My soul was wrapped in darkness when I woke up in the middle of the night. I sat on the porch, staring at the leaves shimmering on the trees in the front yard. The whisper of a cool breeze, flirting with the leaves, broke the stillness of dawn. I felt Lamercie's presence next to me and wished I could communicate with Nlunda a Kinkulu's spirit, the way she could. My restless soul suddenly woke from despair and echoes of ancestral drums vibrated in my mind as a river of determination flowed in my veins.

The silhouette of a woman elegantly dressed in the traditional wrapper approached. Her cautious steps were like those of an adolescent coming home after curfew. As she got closer, she smiled and said, "You're the woman from America, right?" But before I could answer she went on, "The manager told me about you this morning. My room is next to yours." She paused and yawned. "Sorry, I'm beat. I had to work double shifts because my colleague couldn't make it to work." She held her back, then stretched her upper body. "I'd love to talk with you more. Can you have breakfast with me at La Voix du Zaire? That's where I work."

"Sure."

"I have to get some sleep," she said, pushing the door open. "*Lobi*, eh."

"Yes, see you tomorrow."

The taxi drove us through a street that was more like a mud

river that the early-morning rain had left behind. As the car turned on Kasa-Vubu Avenue, echoes of OK Jazz and Tabu Ley blasted. La Voix du Zaire, with its twenty floors, starkly contrasted with shacks in the surrounding shantytown.

"That's an impressive building," I said to Amba, stepping out of the taxi.

"It's not occupied to its fullest capacity."

"Why is that?"

"We don't have enough technicians to operate the sophisticated machines. A total waste."

While waiting for our order in the employees' cafeteria, Amba examined her face in a compact mirror. "How did you land in Kinshasa?" she asked. "People don't come here to visit. I mean, it's hardly a vacation place. Foreigners are usually here to work."

"I did come to work but it's turning out to be some kind of vacation."

"What happened?"

"The director of the Arts Institute invited me to start a dance program," I said. "But my contract hasn't come through."

"That's Zaire for you."

"I'm thinking about packing my bags."

"To go back home?"

Even though I missed the security of home, going back would be conceding defeat. "No, I'd try to get a job in Dakar."

Amba waved to a couple that walked by. "My father sent me to Liège where I went to school and lived with missionaries," she said. "I could never make it to class because I was always tired from cooking, cleaning, washing, and ironing for them. So I ran away. Life was even more difficult for me, until I met some people who helped me get on my feet." She sipped coffee and continued, "Being here is not that much better either. Life is so rough; people blame it on independence and wish colonization would come back. If this is independence, who needs it?" She broke into cynical laughter. "Have you tried finding out why the *commissaire d'état* hasn't done anything? Your dossier is complete, right?"

"Uh-huh."

"That's strange. I know the Arts Institute needs a dance program and they don't have any other job applicants."

"How do you know this?"

"I get around."

"Every time I try to get the *commissaire d'état* on the phone, his secretary tells me he's not there or he's in a meeting."

"I think I'm beginning to understand." Amba leaned forward. "I'll ask the general for the number to his direct line."

"I don't know how to thank you."

"*Mbote,*" she greeted me hours later when I opened the door to let her in. "I have the number for you. Throw on some clothes, and let's go for some beer and food."

The restaurant was another private home transformed into a business that catered to middle-class professionals. Their menu featured local food like *fufu, chikwangue, saka saka, soso, makemba,* and *loso.*

"Lotodo, *pili pili,*" Amba called to the young girl who waited on us, asking for hot pepper sauce. As soon as the waitress was out of sight, she looked around the room. "There's a lot of controversy around the *commissaire d'état,* Citoyen Bolingo. People wonder if *authenticity* means the same to him as it does to the *maréchal,*" she said in a lowered voice.

The young girl brought the *pili pili* to the table and left.

"Citoyen Bolingo is a very powerful man. Even the *maréchal* respects him." She unfolded the banana leaf to uncover the *chikwangue.*

I listened to her without interest, too busy thinking about what I was going to say to the *commissaire d'état* when I called him the next morning.

"The general contacted him," said Amba, "and just as I thought, his secretary hadn't told him about your phone calls."

"Why would she do that?"

"She's a bitch!" she smirked.

"Come on."

"Citoyen Bolingo told the general he'd heard about you from the UN ambassador and thought you were still in Senegal."

"He never got my dossier?"

"His secretary obviously made sure of that. There's a rumor that she's madly in love with him and thinks every woman is a potential threat."

"I still don't understand why she would do that."

"The woman is obsessed."

He picked up the phone on the second ring. "Citoyen Bolingo speaking."

"This is Iris Odys. I'm sorry to bother you. I got your number from—"

"Ah! Mademoiselle Odys," he interrupted. "I should be the one to apologize to you. I'm sure you have a poor impression of our Zaire."

"Not really," I said, to be polite.

"I'll personally make sure your paperwork is taken care of."

"Thank you."

"Don't mention it. Let me know if there's anything else I can do."

A day later, I received an invitation from the *commissaire d'état* to come to the director's office to sign my contract. As an expatriate, I was entitled to a furnished villa, a standing guard, a servant, and a car. Immediately after signing the contract, I moved out of my desolate room to a three-bedroom villa with two bathrooms, a large living-dining room, a veranda, and a backyard. Amba helped me buy plants, paint-ings, malachite and ivory sculptures. African fabric pillows and upholstery completed the décor. My photograph of Hagathe once again found its place on my night table.

CHAPTER 5

Love walks backward with her mantle on her shoulders
and covereth a multitude of sins.
—Rev. J.M. Gibbon

I had been teaching at the National Arts Institute for a month when I first saw him. Right leg resting on the bar, my arms went up and down and to the side. "*Plié*, two, three, four. Up, two, three, four. *Relevé*, two, three, four. What's going on?" I asked the students, who seemed distracted. I followed their gaze toward the entrance and there stood Ngwendu along with a distinguished-looking man of dark chocolate complexion.

"*Plié*, two, three, four. Continue without me," I said, walking toward the visitors.

"Mademoiselle Odys," the director said, "please excuse the interruption. Our *commissaire d'état*, Citoyen Bolingo, wanted to meet you."

Probably in his late thirties, his brown, raw-silk tailored suit with the Maoist-style collar accentuated his shoulders. A discreet smell of aftershave lingered in the air around him. His slightly bowed legs added to his manliness.

"I've heard a lot about you," he said.

"Nothing bad, I hope."

"On the contrary." He let go of my hand and his lips parted into a smile, showing gleaming white teeth. "In fact, the director is one of the many people who raved about your talents. I just wanted to extend my apologies for the mix-up with your contract. Can you stop by my office tomorrow around four?"

"Sure," I said, already charmed by his baritone voice.

"Are you in trouble?" one of the students asked when I returned to them.

"I don't think so," I said but thought that maybe I was. I continued with the class though my mind was focused on the *commissaire d'état*'s smile and the sound of his voice.

Having stayed in the shower too long, I hastily chose a peach suit, appropriate for a business meeting. I examined myself in the mirror and smiled at my reflection before hurrying out.

"*Bonjour*, Mademoiselle Odys," the secretary greeted me. "Citoyen Bolingo is expecting you. I'll let him know you're here." I wondered to myself if this was the secretary who had "lost" my phone messages, though it didn't sound like the same woman and she didn't show any hostility toward me.

I heard him tell the secretary over the intercom, "Send her in."

Meeting me at the door, he shook my hand and invited me to a sitting area on the other side of his large office. "I've asked you here because I'd like to get to know you better."

I wanted to ask him why but decided it might be too bold.

Almost before I could finish that thought he continued, "I admire a determined woman with a sense of adventure. Let's have a glass of champagne to celebrate your arrival in Kinshasa." Without giving me a chance to decline or to accept, he pushed a button on his phone. "Please bring a bottle of champagne, two glasses, and some hors d'oeuvres."

The intensity of his eyes made me lower mine. The fact that he admired *a determined woman with a sense of adventure* didn't really explain his desire to get to know me better. I focused on the ceremonial masks and a built-in bookshelf that decorated the walls of his office. The telephone's ring was timely, as it relieved me of the discomfort of his gaze.

He picked up the receiver on the desk, and I shot furtive glances at him. I then got up to take a closer look at the masks. As I admired an oval hand-carved mask of a warrior with contemplative slanted eyes, I sensed his presence behind me.

"That mask is used during a leader's initiation to a secret society," he said.

When I turned to face him, I realized how close he was to me. Our eyes met. I looked away and pretended to examine a solid wood mask with carved black and red stripes.

"That one is an ancestor spirit mask."

The secretary brought in a bottle of champagne in a silver ice bucket, two glasses, mini-sausages, and slices of orange. She placed the tray on the coffee table next to a stack of newspapers and magazines, and filled our glasses before leaving.

"Welcome to Kinshasa." Citoyen Bolingo raised his flute, keeping his eyes on me as he sipped his champagne. "How was your stay in Dakar?"

"Very pleasant."

"Did you visit the Slave House?"

"Of course."

"When I was there, years ago, I was ashamed to be reminded of the role we Africans played in that trade," he said, taking another sip.

"It was a moving experience."

"Dakar may be the Paris of Africa," he said, "but you will soon discover the richness of the culture of Zaire." He picked up a sausage with a toothpick. "I would like you to put on a production for the *maréchal* and the diplomatic community. I like the idea of a fusion of modern and traditional techniques. I also think it would be good to give visibility to your work."

"I need a few months to train the dancers and work on the choreography."

"Let me know when you think you'll be ready." He bit into the sausage and chewed. "The director told me you were born in Haiti. What's that country like?"

"It's like Africa in a lot of ways. I guess one could say the black man is atavistic."

"Man only?"

"You know what I mean."

"Just teasing," he said, leaning back in his chair. "You sound so academic. I like that."

The phone rang again. He walked to his desk to answer it. "Tell the *maréchal* I'll be there in less than an hour."

I took that as a cue to leave.

On the following day, I went to the institute an hour before my class to speak to the music instructor about composing the music for the production. I found him in front of an instrument made of different-sized wooden bars on a horizontal rack. Hitting the keys with a stick, he created melodies and harmonies. I stood at the threshold of the open door and listened.

"*Mbote*," I said when he looked up.

He smiled, rested the sticks next to the instrument. "What can I do for you?"

I sat on a chair across from him, asked if he would like to work on a project with me, then discussed my idea for the performance. "I thought it would be nice if you could compose the music. I like your work."

"*Kitoko*, that sounds beautiful." He picked up the sticks again, hit on the instrument enthusiastically. "My *malimbe* thinks so too."

"Your what?"

"Some people call it a xylophone," he said. "When do we start?"

"I'm not coming to the institute tomorrow. But if you don't mind, you can stop by my house in the afternoon."

* * *

When the doorbell rang, I expected to find the music instructor but instead of his frail figure, Citoyen Bolingo stood before me.

"You look surprised," he said. "Are you expecting someone?"

"The music instructor is supposed to come by so we can talk about the performance."

"You didn't waste any time."

I smiled awkwardly, leaving him standing there, holding a brown shopping bag.

"May I come in?" he said, reminding me of my manners.

"I'm sorry. Please, do." I led him into the living room.

"This is for you." He handed me the shopping bag and looked around. "Your place is cozy."

I took a seat across from him, stared at the bag, wondering what it might contain.

"Open it," he suggested. I found a mask of three pointed heads. "That's a chief mask of the Pende tribe. I noticed you liked African art when you were in my office."

"This is beautiful!" I placed the mask next to me, and removed a book on the history of Zaire that was in the bag.

"Maybe we can talk about it sometime. How about dinner the day after tomorrow?"

"Sure," I said, as casually as I could.

"I'll pick you up at eight o'clock."

I thought he was a little forward, but didn't mind. In fact, I liked his direct style.

"Eight thirty is better," I responded to hide my eagerness.

"I look forward to sharing dinner with you," he said, walking toward the door.

I had been ready for more than fifteen minutes and had been waiting in a frenzy of anticipation when Citoyen Bolingo picked me up at eight thirty. "Ready to go?" he asked, as soon as I opened the door.

"I'm taking you to my favorite Belgian restaurant," he said, opening the door to the passenger seat of his Mercedes-Benz. "You mind if I listen to the news?"

I didn't mind, though I would have preferred to talk. I wasn't the least interested in the local news that I knew was censored and that had no other purpose than to spread the *maréchal*'s propaganda. He, however, listened attentively as he drove down Boulevard du 30 Juin, Kinshasa's main avenue, named for the date the country had gained its independence from Belgium.

"Allow me," he said when I reached for the door's handle. He got out of the car, walked around to the other side.

The Belgian hostess greeted him with a smile, and he shook her hand. "Your table is ready," she said, leading us toward the back.

The numerous plants and the grotto made me think of pictures I had seen of the Pygmy jungle. I studied the menu in awe, thinking a meal for two represented the average Zairian's monthly wage.

"I've never had Belgian food before," I said, unsure of what to order.

"The Belgians are known for their culinary art. Let me order for you."

"Have you been to Belgium?"

"I studied at the Université catholique de Louvain," he said, looking up from the menu. "The buttermilk soup with apples is a good appetizer. That's what I'm having."

"I'll try it."

"I recommend the beef stewed in red wine with pearl onions and mushrooms. You'll like it."

"Whatever you say. You're the expert."

"I'm having the sautéed rabbit with cherry beer and dried cherries."

The waitress took our order and returned with a bottle of Saint-Émilion that he tasted, expressing his approval with a nod. She poured the wine and said she would return soon with our first course.

Citoyen Bolingo gazed at me, and I wished the waitress had left a menu so I could hide behind it. I was relieved when she returned with the soup. I realized that I had eaten too quickly; he was only halfway through. I listened to the sound of water from the grotto and finally began to relax.

"What convinced you to come to Africa?" He refilled my glass after the waitress took our bowls away.

"My great-grandmother told me that this is where my soul belongs."

He raised his eyebrows in disbelief. "Is that so?" He seemed amused. "I see you're also a storyteller."

I smiled faintly, disappointed that he didn't believe me.

The waitress placed the main course on the table. "You should try the rabbit," he said, placing a piece on my plate. "What did your boyfriend think about your coming to Africa?"

"How did you know I had a boyfriend?"

"I would be surprised if you didn't."

I guessed he would have been more than surprised to hear I didn't have a boyfriend until after I graduated college. "I broke up with him before I left New York."

"Why?"

"All he's interested in is making money."

His laugh surprised me. "Making money is not always a bad thing."

"There's more to life than that."

"Like what?" He watched me think, and when he realized I couldn't come up with an answer, he went on asking what I wanted out of life.

"I haven't decided."

He tilted his head to one side. "Are you sure?"

"What about you? What do you want out of life?"

"To change the destiny of my people."

"How do you intend to do that?" I held his stare for the first time, wishing to penetrate the world behind his eyes.

"You'll find out when we get to know each other better. What would you like for dessert?" he asked in a dismissive voice, making me think my question had been indiscreet.

CHAPTER 6

Love's fire heats water, water cools not love.
—Shakespeare

What have you been up to?" asked Amba, who had stopped by to visit.

"I had dinner with Citoyen Bolingo the other night."

"I ran into his wife at the supermarket yesterday," she said, looking into her pocket-sized mirror.

"He's married?" I should have known a man in his position had to be, especially an African. "Why didn't he say so?"

"Maybe it's because you didn't ask. Anyway, what difference does it make?" She stretched out her legs as she spoke.

"I can't date a married man."

A broad, open smile flashed on her face. "That's not unusual in our culture—"

"Never mind!" A wave of annoyance covered me, a taste of disappointment lingering in my mouth. I didn't want to talk about Citoyen Bolingo anymore. "What would you like to drink?"

"Do you have a beer?" Amba asked, then followed me to the kitchen.

I took two bottles of Primus from the refrigerator. "Had I known he was married, I wouldn't have gone out with him," I said, suddenly willing to discuss him again.

"There's nothing wrong with dating a married man," Amba insisted. She took a seat at the kitchen table and poured her beer into a chilled glass. "Many African men have more than one wife."

After Amba was gone, I continued to think about Citoyen Bolingo, even though I was aware it was not a good idea to allow him to invade my thoughts as much as he did. When the telephone rang, I didn't feel like answering it, but its insistent sound prompted me to pick up the receiver.

"How are you?" said the immediately recognizable deep voice.

"Fine."

"Am I interrupting something?"

"No."

"I wanted to know if you're free this evening."

"I'm afraid I'm not."

"Tomorrow evening?"

"I'm sorry, I can't."

"Give me a call when you have time," he said and hung up.

Unable to reconcile my desire to see Citoyen Bolingo with my scruples, I spent more and more time at the dance studio to keep my mind occupied. One afternoon, I noticed his car in front of the institute. My heart skipping a beat, I considered rushing back inside to avoid him.

"Mademoiselle Odys, Citoyen Bolingo would like to see you. His driver is waiting for you." I hadn't noticed that Ngwendu was standing right behind me. "Come with me," he went on, and I followed him to the black Mercedes-Benz. "This is Miss Odys," he told the driver, who was leaning on the vehicle.

Grateful for the silence in the car, I closed my eyes and thought about what Citoyen Bolingo could possibly want to tell me. I didn't realize that the car had actually arrived at his office building until the driver opened the door.

"Citoyen Bolingo is waiting for you," the secretary said. "Please go right ahead."

I knocked at the door and waited to be invited in.

As soon as I sat across from him, he asked, "Why are you avoiding me?"

I shrugged. "What do you mean?"

"I like to be direct with people and expect the same courtesy. If I have said or done anything inappropriate, you should tell me."

Turning away from his stare, I said, "I found out that you are married."

He peered at me with amusement. "Is that what it is?" he asked, quickly changing to a look of innocence and admiration.

I avoided his eyes. "You're talking about adultery."

"You're assuming I want to take you to bed?" he asked with a smile that seemed ironic or maybe sarcastic. I wasn't sure. "The word *adultery* doesn't exist in my language."

"It does in mine and has a definite meaning to me," I said, aware of the level of discomfort the conversation had caused.

He held my glare and, after a moment of challenging silence, said that he would drive me back to the institute.

I quickly noticed that he was driving in the opposite direction. "This is not the way to the institute," I said.

"I know. I want to show you something."

He drove deep into one of the most deprived areas of Kinshasa. People emerged from muddy alleys. In front of dark cinder-block hovels, women pounded cassava or plantains with mortars. Piles of rotten garbage accumulated on street corners and in vacant lots. Music blasted in the air.

"Do you remember asking me what my purpose in life is? Well, it is to fight poverty and, as you can see, there's a lot of it here." He turned the car around, drove back the way we had come, away from the festering shantytown. "I like you," he said out of the blue.

I cast a curious glance at him. "You don't even know me."

"More than you think."

"What do you know about me?"

He turned onto the street where my car was parked. "I know you're a tree about to be rooted."

The following day Citoyen Bolingo rang my bell. It was still hard for me to get used to the way people just dropped by without calling, even when they had access to a phone.

"What's this *malimbe* doing here?" he asked, frowning.

"The music instructor and I are working on the production."

"Why don't you work at the institute?"

"Because there's no interruption here," I said, walking toward the instrument. "I've been teaching myself to play."

"Why would you want to do that? Women don't play the *malimbe*."

"Don't be so traditional!" I picked up the two sticks, hesitantly hit some chords. Pleased with the timid sound that came out, I set my eyes on him invitingly. "Try it."

He sat on my chair's armrest, and a streak of sun shone on his forehead, glistening over his dark skin. I became nervous when he covered my hand with his and brought it close to his eyes. My hand grew moist and I removed it.

"How would you like to go dancing tomorrow night?"

I didn't answer.

"Come on. Tomorrow's Friday. I'll pick you up around eleven."

I followed him inside the nightclub, comfortable in the white ankle-length embroidered linen dress that contrasted well with my complexion. Most of the patrons were expatriates, with the exception of a few members of the elite class, since the average Zairian couldn't afford to frequent this kind of place.

The music ranged from rhythm-and-blues to disco, salsa,

reggae, and *soukous*. We watched couples dance while we sipped champagne. When the slow *zouk* of Martinique and Guadeloupe filled the room, he took me by the hand and led me to the floor. As our bodies moved closer together, I felt his strong yet gentle grip around my waist, and I rested my head on his shoulder. Then suddenly I imagined the Zairian women looking at me with disapproval and a surge of guilt came over me.

Bolingo stared at me with a puzzled expression. "What's wrong?"

"I shouldn't be dancing so close to you," I said, smiling hesitantly.

He pulled me close to him again, a triumphant smile on his face. "Don't be silly."

I offered no resistance and was willing to let myself go, at least until the music was over. A feeling of oblivion allowed me to let down my guard.

When we reached the villa, he kept the motor running and offered me his hand. "How about lunch in the countryside tomorrow? I'll pick you up at eleven thirty."

Lying in bed that night, I thought about his intriguing eyes and his confident stride and realized there was a forceful calm about him that I found very attractive. In my dream that night, an oversized face of an already big Mambo Lolotte appeared. I heard her say, "Your godmother's prayers have been heard. It's up to you now." When I woke up I felt her presence in the room, and recalled the icon of Ezili Fréda holding her bleeding heart, pierced with an arrow. I turned on the radio and fell back to sleep. I dreamed no more that night.

The next day as we headed to the countryside, I admired the imposing mountains and lush greenery. "It's a shame that people here are so poor when the land is so rich," I commented.

"The problem is that people are allowing the *maréchal* to

get away with too much." He took his eyes off the road to glance at me. "In the two decades he's been president, he has done nothing for the population. You probably think I'm a hypocrite because I represent the government that I criticize. But I can do more for my people in the position that I'm in."

Music came from a large hut in the middle of nowhere. The car slowed and came to a complete stop in front of a white and red billboard advertising *Restaurant Papa Dyabanza.* The owner smiled broadly when he saw Bolingo and beckoned the waitress to take our order. Slowly, she walked away swaying her hips.

"She looks Haitian," I said. "In fact, a lot of people here remind me of Haitians."

"I'm not surprised," Bolingo replied. "Many Bantus were taken to the New World. My paternal ancestor was a Kiswali broker who made a fortune in the slave trade. He brought people in from the interior to sell to Portuguese buyers."

"Really?" I exclaimed, stunned that he carried the blood of a slave trader.

"It was such a shameful commerce. But I don't think he knew he was committing a crime against humanity. At least that's what I like to believe."

"Were you born in Kinshasa?" I asked, relieved that he thought the trade was an abomination.

"I was born on the Angola border. My father was also a merchant, whose business suffered after the government closed the Benguela railroad to keep the communists out of Zaire."

"I'm surprised you're not a businessman like your Kiswali ancestor and your father."

"Funny you should say that. I'm the head of a fruit-exporting business managed by one of my uncles."

"How did you become interested in politics?"

"*Mon Dieu,* you sound like a journalist!"

"Am I prying?"

"Not at all. It's no secret. When I was growing up, I watched my father collaborate with Patrice Lumumba to help form regional organizations to secure our freedom from Belgium. Now that you know everything about me, how would you like to see my private retreat? It's only a few kilometers away."

"Everything?"

"Everything you need to know for now." Bolingo handed a bill to the waitress, told her to keep the change. He smiled at me, and I returned his smile. "Is that a yes?"

"Why not?" I said, surprised by my decision.

We left the main street and turned onto a rutted road where a burgundy cottage stood, hidden behind trees that I couldn't identify. From a nearby bush garden I could smell wild flowers.

"I come here to rest and be alone. An old couple from my native village keeps an eye on it for me," Bolingo said, opening a window. "They live down the road."

We sat in an open hut in the backyard. "Does your wife come here?"

He avoided a direct answer. "You're my first guest."

I held his stare, then looked away.

"Come here."

I moved to the bamboo seat next to him, and he rested his head on my lap.

I patted his hair, hesitantly at first. "You need a haircut."

"I was supposed to have one this morning but didn't get around to it. Want to do it? I have my trimmer in the car," he said, sitting up.

He came back with a black leather kit and a towel. Threatening clouds covered the sun, and it suddenly grew darker. "What would happen if I mess up your hair?"

"You would cause me shame."

Unable to control my unsteady fingers, I put down the

trimmer and combed his hair instead, thinking about the job I'd agreed to do, fully aware that I didn't know anything about cutting hair.

"How about giving me that haircut?" he said in a serious voice.

I imagined putting an irreparable dent in the middle of his head. Still, I picked up the trimmer in a decisive gesture, then changed my mind. "I think you should let your barber do it," I said, removing the towel and putting the trimmer down.

"Mama Nzari," he said, turning to look at me with a mischievous smile, "I was only kidding. Did you actually believe I was going to let you mess up my hair? He pulled me close to him, wrapped his arms around my waist, and looked into my eyes. His lips touched mine. I kissed him back with a force that shamelessly drew my desire out of its scrupulous nest. I closed my eyes, savored the chills that traveled through my veins, and responded to the galvanized sensation with passion and abandon.

He carried me to the master bedroom, kissed me again. His hands slowly explored my body. As he undressed me, his touch made me quiver. Our bodies intertwined. Chills and warmth filled me. I welcomed him, moved to his rhythm, letting out moans of delight until the slow pleasure escalated into the sublime explosion of sexual gratification.

Resting on top of him, I listened to the thudding of his heart.

"Why did you call me Mama Nzari?"

"*Nzari* means river. When I was a young child," he said, "I used to fear being swallowed by the river, yet another part of me was insanely drawn to it. I was like a doomed sailor who had heard a mermaid's song." He stroked my back as he spoke. "Whenever people wanted to find me they would go to the river. My mother used to tell me that one day Mama Nzari would take me away from this life to an unknown world under the river."

CHAPTER 7

A man's Conscience, and his Judgement is the same thing;
and as the Judgement, so also the Conscience may be erroneous.
—Thomas Hobbes

Rather than bringing the pleasure I'd anticipated, the content of the letter from Pépé tied a knot in the pit of my stomach and made me reconsider the precarious nature of my relationship with Bolingo. Exhausted and demoralized, I was restless for hours until I finally came to terms with the fact that Pépé's feelings were the product of values that I didn't want to be reminded of. The words from a single sentence repeated over and over in my head: *What can you expect from a married man?*

I tried to write her back and, after drafting several versions that I tore up for being too abrupt, I finally came up with one that I thought was appropriate, though still quite brief.

Dear Pépé,

You asked me what I expect from a married man. I'll try to answer you as honestly as I can. I'm sure it will sound as ambiguous to you as it does to me: I don't care if he's married. I'm letting life take its course, and I'm ready to accept the consequences, even if that makes me immoral.

Take care,
Iris

Having shared my thoughts on paper, I felt relieved. But as the sun set that day, I felt tormented again and decided to visit Amba. On that overcast, humid, and heavy evening, we sat on her porch, discussing my relationship with Bolingo.

"The point is, you two are not dancing to the same tune," she said, putting ice cubes in two glasses. "As far as you're concerned, you should have him to yourself." She poured whiskey into one of the glasses. The bottle was probably a gift from the general because only the wealthy could afford expensive imported drinks.

"I don't want to be a mistress," I said, fanning myself with a newspaper while hoping for rain.

"You may not want to be, but you are."

"What will my family think?"

Amba sucked her teeth. "How are they going to know if they're not here? You think my family in Bandacar knows what I'm up to? Just keep Bolingo at bay when they come to visit." It suddenly began to pour. "A woman like you can scare men away," she told me, then went inside for a moment to close the windows. "You may be in love, but you don't have the financial dependency that makes men think a woman will always be there."

The phone rang and Amba left to answer it, returning a minute later. "The general's going to give me money. I'll be right back," she said.

"Don't you feel uncomfortable taking money from him?"

"I'm a television journalist. People expect me to look good. You think I can do that on my lousy salary?"

She made up her face, changed her wrapper for a dressier one, replaced her T-shirt with a matching top, put on dressy shoes, and picked up an umbrella from behind the door.

"I'll be back in less than an hour," she said, walking out into the rain.

Watching the stillness of the night, I dozed off until Amba's footsteps woke me from a light sleep.

"*Nsango nini?* What's happening?" she asked.

"*Nsango té.*"

She changed back into the same wrapper and T-shirt she had on before she left. As she counted a handful of new bills, her face became increasingly devoid of expression.

"Don't you want a family?" I asked.

"Of course I do. But until I meet the man who will take me for his wife, life must go on." She lit a cigarette. "There are two types of women," she said, and blew smoke in the air. "The independent one wants freedom and is concerned with building a career; she's the mistress type. The life of the other is built around her husband and her children. She accepts whatever her husband does as long as he comes back and pays the bills. I can play each role separately. But *you* want to be both at once." Amba shrugged and opened the bottle of whiskey.

"Is there something wrong with that?"

"Absolutely not. It just makes you frustrated," she said as she sipped from her glass.

I wanted to believe Amba's argument made sense, but I knew I was in a relationship that would be condemned at home. "I don't think I will renew my contract with the institute."

"What are you running from?"

I didn't answer. I was absorbed by that feeling that kept coming back. A feeling that I felt, for the very first time, that day of the fight in the school cafeteria. I felt it in Dr. Connelly's office and again when Wanda attacked me for having white parents. When I returned to Haiti for Hagathe's funeral, it would sometimes grab hold of me. I was determined not to dwell on it this time, but to try to understand and even give it a name. I think it was a combination of fear, rejection, anger, sorrow, callousness, and pity. It was also the need to find a sense of self and belonging.

"I hate being different," I said.

"Your difference is your charm, *ma chère*."

She went inside and returned with a can of sardines and a loaf of bread that she placed on the table. As we ate in silence, I continued to think about Bolingo and my attraction to him and decided that it was the self-confidence and pride that his presence exuded. Something about him commanded respect and enveloped him in a mystery that stimulated my curiosity. He also possessed the traits that in the past had attracted me to other men; leadership qualities: dedication and determination. Yet, I was annoyed with myself that I found him irresistible. Drunk with whiskey and thoughts of Bolingo, I finally fell asleep on the mattress Amba had placed on the floor for me.

On my way home the next morning, I drove by the imposing SOZACOM building on Boulevard du 30 Juin. Floating high above was the yellow, green, and red flag, with a black hand holding a torch. In front of the building, musicians and dancers performed their daily celebration to give thanks to God for their leader, whose voice rang out from loudspeakers throughout the country, as he launched a daily reminder to those who considered opposition.

"*Mama bo?*"

"*Moko!*"

"*Papa bo?*"

"*Moko!*"

"*Molikili bo?*"

"*Moko!*"

"*Parti bo?*"

"*Moko!*"

How many mothers? How many fathers? How many nations? How many political parties? To those questions, Zairians enthusiastically answered, "Only one!" Blinded with fanaticism and fatalism, they confirmed the slogan, even though they lacked the means to feed, clothe, educate, and shelter their families. Intoxicated with daily propaganda, they were oblivious to the corruption, brutality, greed, illiteracy, and fear that imprisoned their lives.

CHAPTER 8

Oh, that the tongue would quiet stay,
And let the hand its power display.
A boaster and a liar are much about the same thing.
Little bantams are great at crowing.
—Charles Haddon Spurgeon

I read the note from Bolingo urging me to call. After staring at the phone for a moment, I picked up the receiver and dialed his number slowly in order to give myself time to change my mind. As soon as he recognized my voice, he said he wanted to take me to his country home that afternoon. Lying in the bathtub, I envisioned our naked bodies exploring, discovering. The anticipation of being in my lover's arms translated into longing, eagerness, and fear.

The sounds of crickets filled the cottage. Their shrill chirping sounds reminded me of the joyous cries piercing through the dancers' throats in front of the SOZACOM building, as they executed movements with the same vitality their ancestors did centuries ago.

"What's behind the *maréchal*'s authenticity?"

"It represents his eccentricity," Bolingo said, stretching out his arms above his head. A white sheet covered him from the waist down.

"Some of my students go a full day with nothing in their stomachs, but they still dance and smile."

He moved closer to me and rested his head on a hand. "Hopefully, one day they'll be hungry enough to conquer their fear of the *maréchal*."

"I can't stand the thought of you working for this corrupt government."

He wrapped his arms around my naked body. "What are your plans for the Easter vacation?"

"Why?"

"I'd like you to come with me to Paris."

"I would love to," I said, recalling my last trip there, when Mom lectured at the Sorbonne about her book on Haiti. The prospect of spending time with Bolingo became increasingly exciting, and I looked forward to spending entire nights in his arms.

The taxi stopped in front of the Georges V. Located in the 8th *arrondissement*, close to the Champs-Élysées, it was nothing like the three-star hotel in the Latin Quarter where I had stayed with my family. Seventeenth-century tapestries and sculptures decorated the lobby; long-stemmed flowers filled Oriental vases. My feet sank into the plush carpet as we made our way to our suite on the sixth floor. I pulled a cord, and the pastel blue drapes uncovered a view of the Eiffel Tower under a misty sky.

Bolingo took off his *abacost*. Lying in bed in his underwear, he made phone calls while I unpacked and hung up our clothes. "What do you want to do this afternoon?" he asked.

"I'm going to meet Antoine, Pépé's friend," I replied.

"I have a meeting with members of my party."

"What party?"

"Come here." He patted a place next to him on the bed, inviting me to sit down. "I once told you I wanted to change the destiny of my people."

"You never told me how."

"I'm an opposition leader," he said, then took a deep breath. "I'm going to meet with members of the party I represent. To avoid suspicion, we meet on neutral ground."

I stared at him, at a loss for words.

"My people deserve a better future," he added, folding his hands under his head.

Political parties, other than the *maréchal*'s, were banned in Zaire. But stronger than the fear I felt for his life was my desire to know how I compared to his wife. "Does she know about it?" I asked and immediately realized I was being irrational.

"You mean my wife?"

"Why do you have to call her 'my wife'? Doesn't she have a name?" I said, expecting an explosion.

"Okay. I won't call her my wife."

The calm in his voice annoyed me. "You just did," I said as I crossed my arms over my chest. "Sometimes I would rather pretend she doesn't exist."

He curled his upper lip. "Why would you want to do that?" he asked, holding my stare. "You might as well get used to the idea. She does exist. Neither you nor I can ignore it."

There was a gnawing feeling in my heart. I sucked in my breath, slowly letting out the air. I suddenly felt as though the room was suffocating me. "I'm going for a walk," I announced, heading out of the suite. Turning toward him I said, "I may not want to get used to the idea."

He ignored my comment. "How long are you going to be gone?"

"No idea."

He reached for the remote control on the night table. "I'll meet you here at about eight o'clock for dinner."

I walked aimlessly on the Champs-Élysées, obsessed with the notion of changing my own destiny. Trying not to dwell on the life that was mine, I admired clothes draped on smiling mannequins. I picked up a copy of *Jeune Afrique* magazine from a newsstand and ordered mint tea at a sidewalk café. Tourists strolled by, many of whom were American teenagers on school trips who rushed into stores to buy souvenirs. Others posed for pictures.

The elevator door in Antoine's apartment building, with its diamond shapes that opened and closed like an accordion, reminded me of the window gate over the fire escape in my Manhattan apartment. Inside the tiny elevator that could only fit three, I focused on the moving metal ropes.

The apartment was spacious and tastefully decorated with antique furniture. Antoine was wearing a navy-blue cardigan and gray cotton pants. His light brown eyes projected kindness, and his square jaw suggested a determined character. Pleased with the wooden Bantu sculpture I brought as a gift, he immediately found a place for it on a bookshelf.

"So, Monsieur Lemont, my sister told me you're a journalist."

"Yes, I work for a television station. But please, call me Antoine," he answered and settled on the sofa.

"How did you meet Pépé?" I asked, just for the sake of conversation.

"I was a guest speaker at Northwestern University, and I met her through a mutual friend who teaches journalism there. Do you miss Haiti? Your sister constantly talks about her country."

"I grew up in Westchester, in New York."

He raised his eyebrows but said nothing.

"Actually, we're half sisters."

"Would you be my guest for dinner tonight? Your sister wouldn't forgive me if I didn't invite you."

"I'd love to, but I'm here with someone."

"No problem. I'm inviting the two of you to my favorite African restaurant."

"I have to check with him. But it couldn't be tonight."

"Tomorrow then?"

"I'll call to confirm."

Six o'clock. I didn't want to go back to the hotel yet, so I took the *métro* to the Latin Quarter and browsed in bookstores. A man's angry voice shrieked on the platform of the Maubert-Mutualité station. His dirty hair was dreaded unfashionably, and his unkempt beard looked like black pepper grains on his charcoal skin.

"We're not welcome here," he ranted in accented French. "When you come to our country, we let you have the best of everything, even the best of our women. But when we come here, you treat us like dirt!" The man, who sounded African, roared and scratched his filthy head.

He and the Haitian woman in the New York subway, victims of loneliness and hostility, had crossed the line of reason in their quest for a better life. New soil could indeed be detrimental to the survival of a transplanted tree, but would life have been better at home?

I returned to our hotel room and looked through the issue of *Jeune Afrique* and thought about my earlier conversation with Bolingo. I didn't understand how he hoped to reconcile his official position with his aspiration to change Zairian society.

A soft knock interrupted the silence. "Delivery for madame," Bolingo said, handing me a dozen red roses. I hugged and thanked him for the beautiful bouquet and quickly requested some plausible explanation of how he planned to achieve his political objectives.

"It's a simple plan," he said. "I'm here to negotiate funds for students and will do the same in other European countries and in the United States." He sat on the sofa, legs stretched out. "My goal is to educate abroad as many students as possible. Hopefully, the exposure to democracy will rub off. Once they've learned about democracy, they will want to challenge the *maréchal*'s hegemony."

"You actually think those students will return home, considering how bad things are there?" I asked.

"Of course some of them will stay abroad. But no matter how bad things are at home, many will miss their country and will want to go back."

I wrapped my arms around his neck and whispered as if making a love confession: "Enlighten the people generally, and tyranny and oppression of body and mind will vanish like evil spirits at the dawn of day."

"You're brilliant!"

"Thank you, but it's not original, and I can't remember who said it."

"You're still brilliant."

"I'm trying to remember who I quoted," I said a little while later, as we stepped inside the elevator on our way to dinner. "I remember now! It was Thomas Jefferson."

Decorated in gray and gold, the restaurant in the hotel's lobby had a view of the courtyard and garden. The tables were covered with exquisite tablecloths and set with fine silverware. I studied the menu and looked forward to another extraordinary dining experience.

"We belong together," Bolingo said, patting my hand soothingly. "I need you by my side."

A driver from the Zaire Embassy drove us to Quai André Citroën to meet the head of Le Haut Conseil de la Francophonie, whose mission was to integrate France into the cultural, economic, scientific, and technical development of French-speaking countries. We left the office after a discussion on professional training and funding higher education for Zairians. Bolingo had asked the driver not to wait for us, so we caught a taxi on Quai de Grenelle that took us to a café on avenue de Montparnasse. We walked to the back

where members of the MDZ, Movement Démocratique Za-
ïrois, his underground party, waited. They stood to greet
Bolingo, who introduced me as a good friend of the party.

"Citoyen Bolingo," greeted Ngandu, who was a history
professor at a Belgian university, "these are the two men I've
told you about."

"Gentlemen, thank you for your hard work," Bolingo
said, adding too much sugar to his tea, as usual. "Ngandu
has told me about your enthusiasm and dedication."

"It is a pleasure for us to finally meet you," said one of
the men, who was an accountant. "We will do our best to
contribute to MDZ. Do you think it would help to recruit
journalists to write about the *maréchal*'s policies and practices?"

"Good idea," Bolingo responded. "France, Belgium, and
the United States think his dictatorial rule means stability
for commerce." He paused and sipped his tea. "We need to
exercise caution with the foreign authorities. The *maréchal*
has corrupted many of them with his wealth."

"The negative publicity about the *maréchal* will help us
gain international support," Ngandu added.

"We also need to think of a national strategy to demys-
tify the *maréchal* and elaborate on our program for social and
economic development. This must be done thoughtfully. It
will take time. We shouldn't be too eager."

Ngandu spoke again after a pause: "I gave them the party's charter."

"We're happy with your leadership," said the accountant, "but we think you can operate better in exile."

The other man, a lab technician, spoke for the first time.
"Being so close to the *maréchal* would make you an easy tar-
get if he finds out about the party."

Up until then, all I felt was admiration for Bolingo's
courage to achieve a greater mission in life. But fear seized
me as I envisioned the leopard's claws attacking him.

"I appreciate your concerns," Bolingo said, and looked at me for the first time since we sat down. "I've thought about that. Working close to the *maréchal* makes me better equipped to fight him. Besides, when you enter politics at this level in a country like ours, you must expect your life to be in danger." Bolingo smiled courageously and took a pad and a pen from his briefcase. "Let's work on a plan to get our message to student organizations and to other compatriots living in Europe. Our immediate goal is to implant the party throughout Europe, then in the major provinces in Zaire, and finally in Kinshasa. We will eventually fight for an elected government, a free press, and a fair system of justice. I'm looking at each of you here, each putting your expertise to the service of foreign nations, and I'm thinking that men of your caliber should be helping at home."

He picked up his pen, and they continued with their plan to destabilize the *maréchal*'s government. It was difficult for me to concentrate on what they were saying because I couldn't stop thinking about what might happen to Bolingo.

The next evening in the restaurant we waited for Antoine while listening to African musicians. A European man in a blue African robe stood out. The sounds coming from his saxophone were as passionate as Manu Dibango's. It seemed that many of the patrons had lived in Africa. I overheard some of them revel in nostalgia as they exhibited their knowledge of its "exotic" culture.

Leaning close to him, I asked Bolingo, "Why did you tell me about your underground party?"

"If you're going to share my life, you need to know who I am." He reached for my hand and brought it to his lips.

Antoine soon arrived and Bolingo stood to introduce himself. As the evening progressed, they talked about the general state of African politics. Antoine predicted that democracy would eventually prevail, even though some leaders were too attached to power.

I listened to them absentmindedly, watching the dancers on the floor and moving my shoulders to the beat of the music.

"Dance with her," Bolingo encouraged Antoine, who had now stopped talking and was bobbing his head as well.

Heated by the music, the liquor, and the spicy food, we joined the couples on the dance floor. When we came back to the table, Bolingo said to Antoine, "Iris talks about Pépé a lot."

"I'll be sure to tell her that when I see her tomorrow. I'm catching an early flight to Chicago."

It was two o'clock in the morning when we returned to the hotel. Bolingo stood at the door as I looked up from the bathtub. Smiling at me, he got on his knees, stroked between my thighs, and fondled my breasts. He parted my lips with his, before leading my wet body to the king-size bed.

"*Je t'adore*," I whispered, head resting on his chest, wishing to capture the moment. But memory often fades in clouds. Then again, it can emerge unexpectedly in idle moments, making one prisoner of the past.

On the following day, alone in the hotel suite while Bolingo was at a business lunch, I enjoyed the smoked salmon I ordered from room service while listening to Edith Piaf on the radio sing, "*Non, je ne regrette rien*," encouraging me to sink into the melancholy. By the time I got to the shrimp and *haricots vert* with crushed almonds, the lyrics had another effect on me. I realized that I needed to balance the values between the two cultures.

That evening we went to la Comédie-Française. After laughing at Harpagon's scheme to make money and keep people away from it in Molière's *L'Avare*, Bolingo and I took a taxi to rue Mouffetard. As we strolled among the crowd in the narrow medieval streets, enjoying the cool breeze of the night, a light drizzle suddenly turned into heavy rain.

Back in the hotel, Bolingo took off his wet clothes and dried his hair. When I came out of the shower, he was on the phone.

"How's Michelle? Give her my love . . . Yes, I'm tired . . . We'll discuss it when I get home . . ."

I slipped under the covers.

"I wonder if it's going to rain again tomorrow," Bolingo said after hanging up minutes later.

I pretended to be asleep.

"You're sleeping already?"

He turned a switch, and darkness flooded the room.

CHAPTER 9

Let every bird sing its own note.
It is hard to get two heads under one hat.
All bread is not baked in one oven.
All feet cannot wear one shoe.
—Proverbs

I hadn't heard from Bolingo since his driver had picked us up at the airport a week ago and taken me back to my villa. A pervasive anxiety took hold of me while I struggled with my desire to dial his number. I remembered Mom used to tell me to read the Bible to find strength in moments of distress. Even though we didn't live a religious life, the Holy Book was respected in our home. However, in this moment of uncertainty, this is the prayer that emerged in my mind.

Forgive me, Lord.
I want to call, see, smell, and feel him.
Pardon me, Lord.
I want to sin, ignore, forget, and forgive him.
Thank you, Lord.
I will not call, see, smell, and feel him.
Please, Lord, stay near and comfort me.

My anxiety escalated as I imagined someone had found out about Bolingo's party and had turned him in to the *maréchal*, who conveniently arranged his disappearance. I watched the news on television, listened to the radio, and read the newspapers. Nothing about Bolingo. Then it occurred to me that if the *maréchal* had done something to him, it would never be breaking news. He would just disappear, and no one would ever know what happened. I stared at the lawn. Its thirst for rain reminded me of Bolingo's absence from my life. Caught in the maze of moments we had shared, I felt like a fish on shore, waiting for the waves of a rising tide. I hoped for the healing that would bring me salvation and take away the sadness engulfing my heart. The times we spent together continued to occupy my mind. The memories of each instance seemed greater and more sublime than the actual moments themselves. I feared the time when those memories would become a figment of my imagination, too distant to resemble reality. My distress turned into restlessness. To avoid the cloister of my thoughts, I walked around the residential streets of Limété. The flaming color of flamboyant trees and the sight of children playing in front of their villas brought life to my heart.

"*Mundele! Mundele!*" cried a boy no more than six years old, pointing at me. He was calling me a white woman, probably because I had on jeans, a T-shirt, and sneakers. The *maréchal*'s brainwashing process was at work.

Someone shouted my name, waved an arm, and a taxi came to a stop. A tall, slender woman stepped out.

"Marie Madeleine!"

"*Eh! Mama!* I thought I'd never see you again." She kissed me on the cheeks. "Where are you off to?"

"Just taking a walk. I don't live far from here. Would you like to come over?"

"Why not? I was going to visit my uncle. But I don't even know if he's home," Marie Madeleine said, adjusting her wrapper.

I opened the door to my villa and invited her in.

"*Mama nangai!*" Marie Madeleine cried out. "This is a very nice place."

"Let's sit on the veranda. It's warm inside."

She ran her fingers through her loose braids. "Things worked out with this dancing job?"

I told her about Bolingo's secretary "losing" my messages and delaying the start of the dance job.

"*Mama-é-é!*" she cried when I finished my story.

"Would you like something to eat?"

"In a little while."

"Would you like a drink?"

"How about some palm wine?" she asked, kicking off her shoes.

"I don't know what that is."

"You can't be in Africa and not know what palm wine is. I'm sure your servant knows where to find some." She put her shoes back on, followed me to the kitchen where the servant was washing vegetables and humming a tune from a top ten album.

Mama siba ngai
sinon je vais
rater mon avion . . .

Marie Madeleine cleared her throat. "*Mbote, papa. Ozali malamu?*"

He returned her greeting, and she asked him to get us some palm wine.

"I went to your house after I moved here," I said, sitting back down on the veranda. "I saw your mother at the gate. She started yelling at me in Lingala. I was too scared to go back."

"I'm sorry. I should have told you she's sick."

"What's wrong with her?"

"I was born when she was fourteen, and my sister Huguette five years later. She eventually married the man who is now her husband." Marie Madeleine lit a cigarette. "My mother found out the same day she gave birth to their first child together that only a day earlier he had a child by another wife. The worst thing is that she didn't even know there was another woman." She puffed on the cigarette. "My mother jumped out of bed in a fit, wailing. She tore her nightgown to shreds, threw herself to the ground. From that day on, her husband makes sure she gets pregnant every year. She goes crazy for two or three months after giving birth and is aggressive to any woman who isn't immediate family."

The servant returned with the palm wine and poured two glasses. Marie Madeleine raised her glass. "Chin-chin. It's good to see you again." We drank in silence for a while. "When she gets crazy like that, he spends extra time making love to her to keep her calm, or maybe it's because people of his tribe believe sleeping with crazy women brings good luck and good fortune to a man." Marie Madeleine sighed, then went on with her story: "He hardly gives her money. As the oldest, I have to support her, her children, and my own. Now you know why I sleep with men for money." She smashed the cigarette butt in an ashtray.

I looked at her with feelings of both condemnation and understanding. "Maybe your mother should be on medication," I suggested for lack of anything better to say.

Marie Madeleine waved a hand, dropped her shoulders. "The first time she lost her mind was around the time my children's father left me."

"What's the story with him?"

"He was a medical student when we were together. As soon as he finished his studies and started making money, he married a woman from a better family and forgot about us."

"Where is he now?"

"Last thing I heard, he was in the Shaba region. But luckily I have Ana," she said and smiled.

"Ana?"

"My friend who came to the Intercontinental Hotel with me."

The palm wine gourd was now empty. The servant served us white rice and chicken cooked in a peanut butter sauce. Marie Madeleine was in a better mood after she ate, and she asked me if I wanted to go dancing.

"Tonight?"

"Now."

"It's only four thirty in the afternoon."

"Here in Kinshasa we dance twenty-four hours a day."

The owner of the *nganda*, a hefty woman with beady eyes, was good at manipulating men to buy jewelry and the other goods she sold. Her older sister was the cook; her two daughters were waitresses; her son was in charge of the music. Lower-class diamond traffickers, men who bought and sold foreign currencies on the black market, met at the *nganda*, alongside poor women looking for men with some money to spare to help feed their children. They gathered in a room decorated with pictures of the *maréchal* holding a chief's cane. Glued to their destiny, the leader of the nation hovered over their heads with the treacherous eyes of a leopard, watching them get drunk with local beer, palm wine, and the sounds of *soukous*.

Proud to have an American in her "home," the owner sat with us. She had a beer with us while keeping a close watch on the shoe box that served as cash register. "Do you know Muhammad Ali?" she wanted to know.

I shook my head.

"What about George Foreman?"

She seemed disappointed that I didn't and went to sit at another table. Marie Madeleine and I soon joined in with the dancing crowd.

"*Ep-a-a!*" She rhythmically clapped her hands, encouraging me to move to the beat of a frantic *soukous.* "*Miri, miri, miri, miri! Asanga té! Asanga té!*" she exclaimed as I executed Kinshasa's latest dance. Feet firm on the ground, my hips moved in a circular motion, going down as far as I could, then back up again.

I left the *nganda* happy to have gotten out of my house for a bit, to have had some fun, and to have seen Marie Madeleine again.

An early-morning storm woke me from deep sleep. My body yearned for Bolingo's touch, craved the inner bliss he provided. I listened to the screeches of passing cars, tried not to succumb to the desire to call him. I finally put the words that floated in my mind on paper.

> *Dearest Darling,*
>
> *I watch crystal raindrops beat against my bedroom window. I close my eyes to better listen to the murmur of rain and the splashing sound of cars. I long to lie next to you, to feel your protective arms around me. I watch the rain and hope the sun is on its way.*
>
> *I miss you,*
> *Iris*

I asked the servant to take the note to Bolingo, insisting that he deliver it to him personally. "If he's in a meeting, just wait for him. Here's the cab fare," I said, even though he never took cabs. He didn't mind riding crowded buses and preferred to pocket the difference. Soon after I returned to my bedroom, I changed my mind about sending the note. But the servant was already gone.

About an hour later, the phone rang. "*Allô, oui.*"

"*Bonjour,* Iris. I tried calling you last night. I finally gave up a little before nine. Were you with Amba?"

Hearing his voice again made my heart jump, but I tried to contain my happiness. "I went dancing with my friend Marie Madeleine."

"I wish you would be more careful with the friends you make here."

"I'm a big girl, remember?"

"Whatever you say. Can we have dinner tonight?"

A ray of sun penetrated through the window, bringing warmth to the bedroom and to my heart. "I'll be ready," I said, showing more eagerness than I intended, forgetting to ask him why he hadn't called in so many days.

"Why do you always reserve the same table?" I asked Bolingo, looking for something on the menu I hadn't tried.

"I like the sound of water from the grotto. It reminds me of your voice, Mama Nzari."

"You haven't called me Mama Nzari in a while."

He raised his eyes from the menu. "Because you keep slipping through my fingers."

"What have you been doing since we came back from Paris?"

"Following up on my plan to send students to France. I'm serious about having them learn about the French Revolution," he said, smiling. "But I have something important to discuss with you."

The waiter approached the table and the conversation stopped. Two members of the government stopped at our table, and Bolingo invited them to join us.

"So, this is our sister from America," one of them said.

"I hope you're enjoying being in our country," said the other.

As I wondered how they knew about me, the waiter returned to take their orders. They spoke to Bolingo about the last cabinet meeting in a coded language. I gave up trying to figure out what they were saying. But the conversation became interesting when the man in black said the *maréchal*'s two wives weren't getting along these days and that he had heard them fight.

"He has two wives?" I asked, raising my eyebrows.

"Twin sisters," said Bolingo.

"Twin sisters!"

"The Ngbandis believe a man with means must marry the widow of a close relative, to make sure she's cared for. Bobbi is the official wife. Her twin sister was first married to the *maréchal*'s uncle."

"What's unusual," said the man in beige, "is that she was the *maréchal*'s lover while married to the uncle."

"He loves Bobbi so much he can't resist anybody who looks like her," the man in black said, bringing laughter to the table.

"The *maréchal* was married to Marie-Antoinette when Bobbi became his *deuxième bureau*," Bolingo said. "They had four kids together before Marie-Antoinette died."

"How did she die?" I asked, increasingly interested in this family.

"He literally killed her," the man in beige said. "When Marie-Antoinette heard Bobbi had lost a child, she and her friends celebrated with champagne and music. The *maréchal* got angry and beat her so hard that she started spitting blood. He rushed her to a hospital in Switzerland, but she didn't survive."

My fascination with the *maréchal* and his women turned into horror. "How long did he wait before he officially married Bobbi?"

"I'm not sure," the man in black said. "His family had someone else in mind for him, but he wanted Bobbi."

"Why didn't the family want her?" My curiosity was on the rise again.

"They were afraid of her strong character," the man in beige explained.

"I think they were mostly afraid of her because she's a twin. Twins are supposedly natural sorcerers," Bolingo added. "Anyway, people say the woman his family chose suddenly went blind. They took her to Europe to be treated. She regained her sight, but when she returned home, the *maréchal* was officially married to Bobbi."

Changing the subject, the man in black asked Bolingo if he was ready for his trip to China.

"What difference does it make?" Bolingo said. "Ready or not, I have to go."

I thought that must have been what he wanted to tell me.

"Where did the *maréchal* get the idea of taking the whole cabinet with him every time he leaves the country?" the man in black asked, burying a spoon in crème brûlée.

"I really don't know," the other said, "but it's probably to make sure no one stages a coup d'état in his absence."

The three men laughed. But I didn't find the situation amusing. I watched Bolingo laugh with them, awed that he could so easily live the double life of a government official and an underground opposition leader. An inflamed awareness of the dangerous life that was his seized me. In order not to betray the emotions that rose inside me, I decided to join in the conversation again.

"Is this your first trip to China?" I asked Bolingo.

"I was there in 1980 when the two countries signed a cultural agreement," he said. "I was new at my post then."

As we enjoyed a cognac after the meal, one of the two men lit a pipe. The smell of the smoke, though different from Lamercie's, took me back to Monn Nèg, and I wished I knew the name of the village where Nlunda a Kinkulu came from. But all I knew was that she spoke Kikongo.

"Where is the Kikongo language spoken?" I asked.

"In the western part of the country, the Bakongo," Bolingo replied. "That's where my mother's family is from."

"It is also spoken in Congo-Brazzaville and in Angola," the man smoking the pipe commented.

Their answers made it clear that there was no hope of finding my ancestral roots. The waitress brought the check and we left. As Bolingo drove away from Gombé to the suburb of Limété, I asked him why he had stayed away from me.

"I thought you wanted space."

"Why do you say that?"

"That was how I interpreted your behavior."

"It's just my way of dealing with pain."

"You mean a lot to me. Don't ever forget that."

Back in my villa, I rubbed away the tension in Bolingo's shoulders, happy to smell, see, touch, and hear him again. A burgeoning hope infused me with a burst of anticipation for better days.

CHAPTER 10

Hang your hat where you can reach for it.
—Haitian proverb

I sat in the backseat of Ana's burgundy Renault, whose engine spewed smoke. She and Marie Madeleine were on their way to collect money from clients, and I went along for the ride. We visited the homes of women who bought on credit fancy cloth, shoes, and eau de toilette that they couldn't afford. Each one had an excuse for not paying her debt, and each one promised to come up with the money by the following month. When we reached the fifth house, a petite woman, whose generous smile revealed a gap between her upper front teeth, welcomed us. Her name was Solange, and just like the other women, she could not pay her debt. Her husband, she said, didn't give her the money he had promised her.

Moments after Solange left to buy drinks, an older, sturdier woman came into the living room holding a toddler. She was an imposing presence and not only because of her height. There was something about her that commanded respect. It was her erect posture, her raised chin, and her piercing eyes.

Marie Madeleine's face lit up when she saw her. "Auntie! What are you doing here?"

"I came to see my nephew," the older woman said, smiling at the child she was holding. "This is your brother, your stepfather's child. And she is the mother," she added, pointing to Solange, who had returned to the living room, carrying a tray of beer and soft drinks.

As she stood up, Marie Madeleine's eyes widened. Her hands clasped on her hips, she spoke in an angry voice: "So you're the bitch who's making my mother's life miserable. I'm the one who's got to support her and her children, you know."

"How dare you insult me in my own house?" Solange exclaimed. "*Mama e-e-e-e-e!*" she screamed, raising her arms. "Since earth became earth, no one has heard such a thing."

"My mother can't even feed her children," Marie Madeleine went on, speaking as loudly as Solange, who looked at her defiantly.

"Do you think I have an easy time with mine, huh?" Solange said.

Moving quickly to stand between the two women, Ana quietly beseeched, "Calm down. Yelling at each other isn't going to solve the problem."

I slouched in my chair, wondering how far the argument would go. The woman Marie Madeleine called Auntie rocked the baby as she watched and listened, then slowly undid the cloth on her head and used it to tie the toddler to her back. "Sit down, both of you," she ordered. "You're making fools of yourselves." Catching her breath, she continued, "Let's face it. Most of our men will never have just one woman." She wiped her forehead with a bare hand. "I don't understand all the talk about authenticity when you're not willing to live the way our ancestors did."

"You spoke very well, Auntie," said a woman standing at the threshold of the door, leaning on its frame. Her bleached skin left reddish spots on her face that was three shades lighter than the rest of her body.

Solange introduced her as her younger sister.

"You're the dance teacher from America!" she exclaimed when she heard my name. "I'm sorry I was transferred out of Citoyen Bolingo's office before we had a chance to meet."

Marie Madeleine cast a knowing look at me, while So-

lange played a cassette on a boom box. As she served us
drinks, the sounds of electric guitars and bouncing bass
lines vibrated in the room. Marie Madeleine's auntie started
dancing with the toddler on her back. She pulled Marie Madeleine up from her chair, inviting her to join in. Their upper
bodies bounced as they repeatedly moved one foot to the
side then brought the other close to it.

L'argent appelle l'argent.
Mbongo esengi mbongo.

Money draws money. They sang the French and Lingala
lines from the song that told the story of a man who needed
to borrow money, but the bank told him they couldn't give
him a loan because he had no money.

Usually I drove to the institute, but that morning I had
taken my car to get a tune-up. While I waited for a taxi,
two men dressed in olive-green army uniforms stood a few
feet away. One of them was short and stout, the other tall
and skinny. Their uniforms had holes and looked like they
couldn't stand another washing.

"*Citoyenne, yaka wa*," the tall one said.

I knew enough Lingala to understand he had asked me
to come here. They looked me up and down with stern faces
as I approached them; the foul smell of stale perspiration
made me want to step back.

"Don't you know women aren't supposed to wear pants
in this country? Are you defying authenticity?" The short
man moved closer to me as he spoke.

I realized only then that I had on jeans and that I had
forgotten I was going to take a cab when I got dressed. Otherwise, I would have worn a dress or a skirt to avoid this
kind of complication.

"I'm not Zairian," I told them in French. "I'm American."

"Your papers!" the tall one cried out.

I happily took out the navy-blue booklet from the bottom of my bag, handed it over. I smiled when I saw they were holding it upside down. The smile, however, disappeared from my face when the short one asked me how much money I was going to give them.

"Money for what?"

"For beer," the same one answered.

"I'm not giving you a cent."

"Come with us then!" the other one ordered.

"No problem. But you're going to regret this," I managed to say in a neutral voice, recalling Marie Madeleine's *kaponaj* the night we arrived at the airport.

They spoke to each other in Lingala, but I couldn't understand most of what they were saying because they talked too fast. As their voices grew louder, I gathered they were arguing over what to do with me. Arms crossed over my chest, I waited for them to come to a consensus and tried to collect enough nerve to tell them I was Citoyen Bolingo's wife. But I didn't have Marie Madeleine's guts.

"Mademoiselle Odys!" called a voice.

Three of my students walked up to the scene. Once I told them what was going on, they confirmed that I wasn't Zairian. Still, the soldiers wanted beer money.

"Give them ten zaires," one of the students pleaded.

"I will do no such thing," I said, even though the sum was only the equivalent of two dollars.

"Give them the money," another one insisted. "It's not worth the trouble."

I stubbornly shook my head.

The three young women searched their bags. Together they came up with eight zaires that they gave to the men, who smiled and returned my passport. I paid the students back and told them they shouldn't encourage corruption.

"We're not encouraging anything," one of them explained. "It's better to avoid unnecessary trouble."

Now that I think about it, she was right. After all, it would take a lot more to change the way people thought or acted in a country where the olive-green uniform meant power over civilians, just like the blue denim did for Dieudonné and the other Tonton Macoutes of Haiti.

The humidity was unbearable on that particular morning. The merciless golden sunrays penetrated our skin. We assembled in the auditorium, where there was not even the slightest breeze. Students fanned themselves with newspapers, pieces of cardboard, colorful wicker fans, or whatever else they could use for relief from the heat. Two hours earlier, I had asked Ngwendu if we could postpone the rehearsal until the weather was less humid. "There are only two weeks left until the performance," he had said. "I must make sure that it is appropriate for the *maréchal* to see. If it's not, you will have enough time to make adjustments."

When he showed up in the stuffy auditorium at exactly eleven o'clock, the dancers reluctantly left their seats to assume their positions backstage.

When the music began, the dancers and musicians felt each other's energy and immediately forgot the heat, proving that they were dedicated artists. The director sat next to me, motionless, totally absorbed in the magic of the music and the dancers' movements.

"*Mon Dieu!*" he exclaimed. "I'm so impressed. Imagine how much greater the impact will be with complete décor and lighting."

Concerned that the dancers were dehydrated, I couldn't bask in the glory of his words and excused myself to distribute the water, oranges, and bananas that I had bought to replenish the carbohydrates and electrolytes they had lost while performing in the punishing heat.

* * *

When I recognized Amba's voice on the other line, I tried to hide my disappointment. I was hoping the call would be from Bolingo, who had traveled to China the week before.

"Oh, you're home. That's good," she said, ignoring my greeting. "I've been delegated to fulfill an important duty."

"What is it?"

"I can't tell you right now. I'm coming over in about an hour with two important guests."

"The general and your fiancé?" I joked.

Amba had told me some time ago that her aunt had arranged a marriage for her with someone from her hometown. A medical student in Rome, her fiancé planned to return home in a year to start a practice and marry her. But that had not stopped her from seeing the general.

"Don't be silly," she said in an authoritative voice I didn't recognize. "Be on your best behavior," she added, and hung up before I could say anything more.

The sun had set, and a cool breeze had chased the heat away. Amba arrived with Ngwendu and a man in his sixties who reminded me of Bolingo, though a few inches shorter. He turned out to be his uncle.

Confused by his presence in my home, I led them to the living room and invited them to sit. "Can I offer you something to drink?" I asked, after a moment of silence and smiles. The director held up a hand. As for Bolingo's uncle, I wasn't sure that he had heard my question since he didn't react.

After small talk about the weather, Bolingo's uncle spoke. "I'm sorry to have to talk to you directly and not to a member of your family, as I should. Since you're not from here, we have to do things differently." He studied me as he spoke, and I wondered where his words were leading.

He took three kola nuts and a bottle of palm wine out of a brown bag. Amba returned from the kitchen with four glasses. The uncle ceremoniously broke a kola nut, gave a piece to the director, one to Amba, one to me. He kept the last for himself. We chewed on the bitter nut and sipped palm wine without talking. Then he suddenly turned to Ngwendu. "Citoyen, since you represent Mademoiselle Odys's family here, I'm here to tell you one of my roosters saw a chicken with the most beautiful feathers in your yard. He has asked me to talk to you so you can close the gate and keep other roosters away." Amba and the director nodded as he spoke. "My rooster needs your chicken; such is the law of nature and of our ancestors."

Then it was Ngwendu's turn to speak. "Mademoiselle Odys, Citoyen Bolingo has asked me and your friend to represent your family," he explained. "The woman is not usually present at this kind of meeting, but Citoyen Bolingo said you had to be, given that you're not from here and everything."

"My nephew is a man of honor. He will fulfill his duties toward you and your family, I assure you. If he fails to be correct, he will shame the whole clan. We won't let that happen."

"Citoyen," Ngwendu said. "As you know, the chicken belongs to a family in a faraway place. We have to wait until your nephew can personally go to them to make the commitment final."

"I understand that," Bolingo's uncle said. "We also need to know Mademoiselle Odys's customs so we can conform." He stood up, formally bowed before me. "We will leave you with your friend now."

"I knew Citoyen Bolingo had good intentions," Amba said, watching the car drive off. "You're happy now?"

"I don't know," I replied. "This is so sudden. I need to let it sink in before I can say anything."

"What do you have to eat?"

I took a bowl of tuna salad from the refrigerator and

placed it on the coffee table, along with some crackers. "Why didn't the man just tell me what he had to say, instead of all the talk about a rooster and a chicken?"

"We speak like that." Amba put some of the tuna salad on a plate. "Now, if you agree to become Bolingo's wife, you'll have to invite his family over for dinner. That's the second step."

I handed a glass of beer to Amba. "What happens next?"

"The family comes back with the dowry and there is a reception." She took a sip from her glass. "They'll bring money, a goat, jewelry, and palm wine. Some rich men nowadays may even buy a house for the woman's family."

"I thought the woman's family is supposed to give a dowry."

"Not in our culture," Amba said. "When a woman is married, she belongs to her husband's family. The dowry is to say thank you for the good daughter they raised."

"How come Bolingo never said anything about any of this?"

"He told me he was going to talk to you about it the night before he left for China. But I guess he changed his mind."

CHAPTER 11

When you do dance, I wish you
A wave o' the sea, that you might ever do
Nothing but that; move still, still so,
And own no other function.
—William Shakespeare

Mama Nzari!" Bolingo held me in his arms, kissed my cheeks. He had been gone for over a week, and I was happy to feel his magnetic energy.

"This is for you," he said, handing me a package that contained the finest white raw silk. "I thought you might get a dress made for the wedding." He sat next to me, wrapped an arm around my shoulders. "I know a fine designer who will make you something lovely."

"It is beautiful," I said, without enthusiasm.

"What's the matter?"

"You never even asked me if I would marry you. You just assumed I would."

He stood up, took my hands into his, and helped me to my feet. "Mama Nzari, would you do me the honor of becoming my wife?"

I probably would have jumped with joy had the circumstances been different. But the thought of becoming a *deuxième bureau*, a second wife, tightened my heart. "I don't know," I said. "Polygamy is foreign to me."

He touched my chin, turned my head toward his, forcing me to look into his eyes. "I want our relationship to be official."

I accepted his kiss, though I remained aware of the confusion in my head.

The big day of the dance performance finally arrived. Moments prior to the start, I coached the dancers backstage in breathing exercises to relieve their anxiety of appearing before the *maréchal*. The upper parts of their bodies rolled toward the floor in eight counts and returned to their upright positions by rolling their spines back up, while breathing in and out. As they began to repeat the movement for the third time, Ngwendu informed me that the *maréchal* was in the theater.

Now the performance could begin. On signal, the house lights gradually dimmed. Stage lights came on. Curtains slowly rose to present *Mowuta*, the story of a girl lost in the forest, who is found by travelers from another tribe. When she becomes old enough to marry, her surrogate family can't find a suitor for her because she is of unknown ancestry. One day she sets out to find her tribe, only to be rejected because she doesn't know their ways. In the final scene, Mowuta returns to the forest, leaving the audience to guess her fate.

The energetic clapping at the end of the performance confirmed that the dancers had captivated and dazzled the audience. Ngwendu called me to the stage and handed me a bouquet of white roses. Elated by the standing ovation, I couldn't stop smiling. But my smile turned into a frown when Bolingo came backstage to tell me the *maréchal* wanted to meet me.

"Be cordial, but don't linger," he whispered. "Excuse yourself as soon as you find it appropriate." I thought his advice was a question of protocol, but I later realized it was a warning.

The *maréchal* sat on the leopard-skin chair that had been installed specially for him. A leopard-skin cap crowned his head. Later, Bolingo told me about special initiation rites that a leader had to go through to be able to sit on a leopard skin and carry the sculpted cane, both of which were symbols of power. His cunning eyes shone behind his dark-framed eyeglasses. His left hand rested on the crafted chief cane. He broke into a seductive smile and extended his free hand to me.

"Congratulations! I look forward to seeing more of your work. It is modern yet authentic."

"Thank you, Excellency," I said, reminding myself I was standing before *the all-powerful warrior who goes from conquest to conquest, leaving fire in his wake,* as he liked to refer to himself.

"Keep up the good work," he said, then turned to speak with one of the men standing next to him, leaving me wondering what was next.

"Please excuse me," I said as soon as there was a break in their conversation. Walking past bodyguards and government officials, I returned backstage for an interview with a journalist from *Elima*, a national newspaper.

Later that night, as soon as he could get away, Bolingo came to congratulate me again. "I'm proud of you. Imagine what we would have missed if you hadn't come to Zaire."

"I'm happy to have had that opportunity."

"The *maréchal* kept asking me questions about you. I'm not too happy about that."

"Why not?"

"He's a leopard who attacks without warning."

Coming down from the euphoria of the performance, I was feeling the usual withdrawal symptoms when Amba rang the doorbell the next morning.

"Great job!" she said, walking into the living room. "Your show is the talk of the town. Sorry I missed it. I couldn't get someone to work in my place." She unfolded the newspaper she had taken out of her bag. "There's an article about the performance on the front page and an interview inside."

She opened the paper to the center page, read out loud in a clear voice:

—*Mademoiselle Odys, what motivated you to come work in Zaire?*

—*I saw the opportunity to realize my artistic vision and to discover a new culture. And who knows? This is perhaps the very same place where my African ancestors came from.*

—*What does dance mean to you?*

—*Dance is like poetry. It is a medium to express feelings in a creative way. Body movements replace words, but the same fluidity and rhythm are there.*

—*What is the role of music in dance?*

—*It is the fuel that lights the fire. By the way, I wish to thank Citoyen Mbwaka for his musical talent and fine collaboration.*

—*How did Mowuta originate?*

—*I wanted to tell a story that would reflect the level of acceptance of those who are different in a society.*

—*What does our authenticity mean to you, an American?*

—*From an artistic point of view, authenticity means embracing a form that embodies the collective values of a nation, to reveal the essence of its culture.*

—*How about authenticity from a political point of view?*

—*I can only speak about art. I don't know much about politics and I don't think about it.*

"Have you had breakfast yet?"

"Yes. But I'd love another cup of coffee, if you have any."

"I have something to tell you," she said when I returned from the kitchen with the coffee.

"What?"

"I saw Citoyenne Bolingo's best friend at a dinner party

last week. I wanted to tell you sooner but you were busy with your show."

"What happened?"

"The couple hasn't been getting along since way before you came into the picture." Amba stirred sugar in her black coffee as she spoke.

"Why does he stay with her then?"

"Their marriage was arranged by the two families. Actually, they're both putting on a show for the public eye."

"What do you mean?"

"I heard she has a lover in Brazzaville."

"Are you kidding?"

"That's what I've heard."

I wasn't sure of what to make of Amba's words after she was gone. What I did know was that I was disappointed Bolingo would be such a hypocrite. I thought it would have been easier to bear if I'd known he was bonded to her by emotions and not for the sake of society. In a moment of whimsical blindness, I picked up the phone and called his direct line.

"I can't take the agony of this relationship," I said, without any word of greeting.

"Excuse me?"

"It's hard for me to cope with this relationship."

"We should stop seeing each other then," he simply said.

I wanted to hear him tell me he couldn't live without me. But what dignified Bantu man would speak that way? Minutes after I hung up the phone, Bolingo's driver delivered a bouquet of flowers and a copy of the newspaper. I guessed he had sent them before I'd called.

CHAPTER 12

What time to tard consummation brings,
Calamity, most like a frosty night
That ripeneth the grain, completes at once.
—Sir Henry Taylor

I felt light-headed and tired and moved about painstakingly as I got ready to teach my morning class. After nearly an hour of deliberation, I decided I couldn't go to work. I thought that I might have come down with malaria, even though I had taken the vaccines and the weekly doses of Nivaquine the doctor had recommended before I left New York. I could still hear Mom and Dad's recommendations about contaminated food and water and recalled how I conveniently "forgot" the supply of insect repellent they had bought me because I had more important things to pack, like clothing and shoes. "Diseases can be transmitted through insect bites," Mom had said.

The dinner I had eaten the night before suddenly rolled inside my stomach before erupting like a volcano. I couldn't think of what would make me feel this ill and wondered if it really was malaria, even though I didn't have the chills or fever that usually accompanied the ailment.

I stayed in bed the whole morning. By mid-afternoon the heat and humidity were on the rise. I thought a shower would make me feel better. When I reached into the closet for deodorant, I saw the box of tampons and realized my period was two weeks late. I went back to bed, thinking that the stress of the performance was the reason while continuously checking my panties, hoping to see a stain. I never imagined that I would look forward to that monthly occurrence. How could I have been so careless? I had stopped taking birth control pills when I returned from Paris, thinking my relationship with Bolingo was over. But there was the night before he left for China, when we fell into each other's arms, oblivious to any precautionary measures.

Tired of speculating, I went to Dr. Blanchard's office without making an appointment. When he called the following day to confirm my suspicions, I wasn't sure if my head began to spin and ache because of my condition or because of the thoughts swirling inside. The pain rolled in a whipping acrobatic motion. I took a couple of aspirins and dropped my tired body on the bed, still hoping blood would soon drench my panties.

The following Saturday afternoon Amba dropped by for a visit on her way home from work. As she sat in an armchair in the living room, she picked up an envelope from the coffee table to fan herself. The traditional wrapper she wore and the embroidered top that left her shoulders bare distinguished her from other women who could not afford such intricate needlework. She also wore a pair of four-inch sandals that buckled around the ankles with an opening that allowed her painted toes to breathe freely. A designer bag and expensive cologne were additional touches. I had no idea how much her salary was, but she certainly needed the general's help to dress the way she did. She was the *mwasi kitoko*, the beautiful woman, of her time.

She put the envelope back on the table, cracked her knuckles, and shifted her weight. "I had a dream about you last night," she said.

"What was it about?"

"You have a beer? It's so hot and humid today."

I went into the kitchen and returned with a bottle of Primus and a chilled glass.

"Just what the doctor recommended," she said.

"What was the dream about?"

She took a pack of cigarettes from her pocketbook. "You and I were on a boat in the middle of the ocean. It became windy and the peaceful water was suddenly troubled. A woman appeared from under. She rocked the boat and made it fall in the water. I made it ashore, but your body disappeared. I don't mean to scare you, but I think there's a message for you in the dream."

"What do you think the message is?"

"Probably that you'll go through some hard times," she said and paused. "Look, I'm no expert. We should visit someone who understands these things."

"You're talking about a reading?"

"Yup."

"I don't believe in those things."

"Why do you say that?"

"I saw a reader in Senegal who told me I'll have some problems, but everything will be resolved. Think about it, life is about ups and downs. Nothing good or bad lasts forever. I don't need to pay someone to tell me that. How can you believe in those things when your father is a Baptist minister?"

"One thing has nothing to do with the other. There are ancestral forces that influence our lives," Amba lectured. "I also know there are a lot of crooks out there, but there are also sincere medicine men and women who believe in their mission to help."

"I don't know—"

"You have nothing to lose."

"True," I said, thinking I had nothing better to do either.

I picked her up the next day and drove to a compound with

crowded sun-beaten houses made of cinder blocks. Women cooked *saca saca*, *fufu*, and dried fish on small portable stoves fueled by charcoal. Children ran around. The elders sat with eyes focused on a world only known to them.

The *nganga* wore nothing but torn pants. His bare ribs showed under his wrinkled skin. He snapped out of a daze, flashed a toothless smile when he noticed Amba. He invited us inside, and I watched him pour a libation from a cup and wash his eyes with the rest of the water. He then reached for a mirror from under his bed and asked for my name.

"Do you often dream of water?" he asked, staring into the mirror.

I told him yes.

He started singing a song that sounded vaguely familiar. It was only when he repeated the song a second time that I realized it was the same one Lamercie had learned from Nlunda a Kinkulu, except for the fact that he was singing in Lingala:

Mama ha eeeeeeee
Nakweyaki na maiyi eeee
Elima Ngando oooooooo
Ayei kokamata ngai aaaaaa

"Your soul is engaged in a spiritual world but you don't know it." He studied me for a moment that seemed too long. "You're a lucky person." It seemed that his squinting eyes tried to see through me. "You ended a relationship with a man not long ago."

Amba raised her eyebrows. "You didn't tell me that!"

"We'll talk later," I whispered with tight lips.

"You don't want to share him," he said, looking into my eyes. "You must cleanse yourself, sacrifice a goat, and wear protection."

Amba nodded in approval.

"But it's not over between you and that man," he continued. "You're going to have his child." He looked away from the mirror, turned to Amba. "You're worried about your friend. She will be okay if she does what she's supposed to do. If she wants the medicine, I need a minimum to buy the ingredients and the goat. After that, it will be up to her to decide what she wants to give me."

"I'll be back," I said, convinced that he only wanted to get money out of me.

"This is no game," he cautioned. "I'm afraid of what might happen if you don't protect yourself."

His words didn't faze me then. But now I wonder if sacrificing a goat would have changed my destiny.

"I have something to tell you," I said to Amba as we waited for the food we ordered.

"What?"

"I'm pregnant."

"Does Bolingo know?"

"No."

"Why haven't you told him?"

"What difference does it make?" I blurted out.

"You should appreciate the fact that Bolingo defied tradition by loving a foreigner from another continent! There's a tale about Nkenge falling in love with a foreigner whose ancestors no one in the village knew—"

I put a hand up. "Please, Amba! This is no time for folktales."

"I'm just telling you how we think here. You're going to do what the old man asked, aren't you?"

"That's like living in the dark ages."

"My father used to say this . . . He studied medicine for two years before he became a Baptist minister . . ."

I tried to hide my impatience. "What did he used to say?"

"Science without religion is lame. Religion without science is blind."

"That's a quote from Einstein."

Amba rolled her eyes. "Our African science may not be recognized by the Western world, but it has its place in our society. That woman *can* and probably *will* hurt you."

"The man saw sorrow in my eyes, the kind of sorrow only love can cause, and he exploited that. Does that mean he has mystical powers?"

"Why are you shutting your mind?"

"Probably because I am being myself. I'm fascinated with the cultural aspect of these practices, but they can be the cause of paranoia and psychosis. If he has the power to do so much, why does he look like he himself needs help?"

"You're talking about material help. I'm talking about something entirely different." She took a long, deep breath. "I could sacrifice the goat for you, but I don't see how I can get you to cleanse yourself and wear protection."

After a long, uncomfortable silence, I asked, "What are you thinking about?"

"That you won't let people help you."

I was grateful for her concern, but I saw no point in doing something I didn't believe in.

"What more do you want? Bolingo does love you," she said.

"Not enough for him to get a divorce," I replied brusquely.

"You're complicating things."

"I'm not ready to live in a harem."

"You won't have to. You will have your own home." Her voice was callous. She winked and cracked a smile.

"*Nokei*," I said to her, having run out of arguments.

"*Malamu*." She agreed that we should leave.

CHAPTER 13

It's too late to shut the stable door after the horse has bolted.
—Proverb

H ow are you?" he said when I answered the phone.
"Very well, thank you. Who is this?" I asked, pretending not to recognize his voice.

"You know who it is."

"Ah, *bonjour*," I said in a flat, casual voice.

He cleared his throat. "Your friend Amba just left my office. We need to talk."

He took me to Le Flamand, the Belgian restaurant where we often ate. The smell of food suddenly made me nauseous and prompted me to run to the restroom. Just as I leaned over, the last meal I had eaten violently gushed into the toilet bowl, weakening and dizzying me.

Bolingo was behind the door when I left the ladies' room. When our eyes met, his stare pleaded for an explanation. "Are you okay?"

"I'll be all right."

He held me by the elbow, leading me to the car. In complete silence we drove to the villa.

"Are you pregnant?" he asked, handing me a steaming cup of mint tea, a look of concern on his face.

I tried to swallow the lump in my throat. "You stayed away for a month and out of the blue you ask me to dinner, as if your absence didn't matter."

"You didn't want to see me again, remember?" He spoke in a soft voice. "You didn't answer my question."

"Yes, I am."

"Were you planning on telling me about it?"

"It wouldn't have changed anything," I huffed.

He set dubious eyes on me. "What do you mean?"

Eager to provoke a surge of guilt, I told him he already had a child.

"What does that have to do with you?"

Annoyed at my failure to make him feel remorseful, I waved a hand. "There's always going to be a part of your life that will be closed to me."

"You too can be my wife," he said and smiled.

"I'm honored," I countered, unable to contain my sarcasm.

"I can't take any more of this melodrama," he said, a stern look on his face. "I'll call you in the morning."

I sat on the veranda the next morning, enjoying the quietness of the street. I observed a young woman entering the gates of a villa across the street where she worked as a maid. Her hair, parted in a checkerboard pattern, was wrapped with black thread and each square pointed up like an antenna. Her wrapper had pictures of the *maréchal* and words that read, *Our leader for life.* I watched her, puzzled that some people so willingly accepted a dictator.

I eagerly opened a letter from Pépé; she wrote that Baby Doc's chief of police had arrested Pierre, who had publicly accused the Haitian government of human rights violations. It may seem odd that someone I knew so little could have an impact on me, but there was something about Pierre's gentle and honest nature that made me consider him a dear friend.

I settled on the couch next to Bolingo later that evening. "I don't think you love me the way I love you," I told him.

"No two people love the same way," he said in an imperious tone.

"Maybe I should love you with more detachment."

"The problem, *ma chérie*," he said, tossing his jacket on the armchair, "is that I don't know how I want you to love me and I don't know how to love you." He sighed deeply and wrapped his arm around me. "Sometimes I feel threatened when I think someone can take you from me."

Elated that he was capable of such a petty emotion as jealousy, I told him I loved him so much that sometimes I felt pathetic.

He rose from the sofa, thrust his hands in his pants pockets, and said, "I think that you have too much pride to love pathetically. You probably mean that you love intensely." He held my stare. "Anyway, even poets find it hard to put love into words."

"Sometimes I wonder if I would love you with the same intensity if I were the only woman in your life."

Lines formed on his forehead as he smirked and asked, "Is your love based on a desire to conquer?"

"You know me better than that."

"I can never be too sure." The lines on his forehead vanished and gave way to a boyish smile.

"You know what?" I said.

"No. Tell me."

"It annoys me that you're so rational."

"It would be irresponsible of me to love irrationally. So much depends on the choices I make—"

"So the solution is not to choose," I interrupted.

"That's one way to look at it."

My throat tightened with sudden sadness. "I hope to be around when you decide to choose."

"I hope so too, Mama Nzari." His face relaxed. "Stop analyzing so much. It's not good for a woman."

"Do you realize how chauvinistic you sound?"

He went on laughing until he noticed my stern face. "Only kidding!" he said, putting up a hand. "I'm particularly attracted to your analytical mind."

"So it's my mind and not my body, huh?"

"I'll ignore that comment."

"I'm thinking about going home for the summer vacation. I miss my family," I said, watching him lean forward and rest his elbows on his knees.

"I was going to ask you to come to New York with me. Le Haut Conseil de la Francophonie has agreed to fund ten students a year for the next five years. My plan now is to speak with the president of the African American Institute in New York. I also must meet your family to ask for your hand," he said, leaning back in his seat. "I'm going to arrange for you to have my family over when we come back. That would be our formal engagement."

The seriousness of the situation suddenly dawned on me. A lamenting voice echoed as the sun suddenly set. "*Marta, Marta, Marta,*" the voice cried out at intervals.

"It's six o'clock."

Bolingo peeped at his watch. "So you have ESP."

"I know the time because the crazy man passes by at the same time every day. A neighbor told me he got his sweetheart pregnant. And a month after she gave birth to twins, he married another woman. The heartbroken woman went to a medicine man to make him crazy."

Bolingo laughed. "The story itself is crazy."

"Listen to this. The couple used to meet on this street at six o'clock. And now he comes here to look for her every day, doomed to calling out her name at the time they used to meet."

"Interesting story. But I won't abandon you, even if you have twins."

"Do you believe the medicine man has that kind of power?"

"Mama Nzari, the mind can be powerful."

Thoughts of Pierre suddenly surfaced. I recalled the dinner at L'Auberge de Grand-Mère, the New Year's party at his home, and the afternoon at the beach. Dieudonné's face then emerged and an idea came to mind, like lighting in a dark sky. I would write a letter that Marie Ange could hand-deliver to him.

"What are you thinking about?"

"That the political pattern of Haiti is the same as here," I said. But I was really thinking that Pierre's fate could become Bolingo's.

"Africa and Haiti need leaders who seek power because they have the country's best interest in mind." Bolingo's baritone voice sounded as passionate as Pierre's had been when we talked about Haiti. Thoughts of Bolingo's subversive activity intensified, and the fact that he was somewhat oblivious to the potential danger became worrisome. I stared at my lover, the tireless one who was willing to sacrifice his life to free his country from mediocrity and oppression.

"Don't you worry about your security?"

"Why should I? I'm doing what I have to do." He slapped his knees, emphasizing his words were final.

There was no hope that he would change his mind about politics. I feared harassment, incarceration, or even death. Under his watchful eyes, I sat with my feet up on the sofa, arms wrapped around my knees. His gaze made me feel like a grain of salt in a bucket of water.

"Come here," he whispered, reaching for me.

CHAPTER 14

Yes, I have doubted. I have wandered off the path, but I always return.
It is intuitive, an intrinsic, built-in sense of direction.
—Helen Hayes

As I began to pack my suitcase, thoughts of New York inundated my mind, making me realize I missed the streets of Manhattan with their yellow cabs; the multitude of people moving at a fast pace; the would-be artists who made it to the city of infinite dreams from faraway places; the magnetized energy of the theater district; the myriad activities the city had to offer. I also missed the elegant calm of our Westchester suburb.

Bolingo sat in the armchair in my bedroom, watching. "I have a favor to ask you," he suddenly said.

"What would you like me to do?" I asked, folding a blouse.

"I'm going to give you an envelope with some party documents. You remember Ngandu? One of the men you met in the café in Paris."

I nodded yes.

"He'll be at the airport to meet you during the stop-over in Belgium."

"No problem."

"I'll walk you inside the plane to make sure no one goes through your carry-on luggage."

"Can I get in trouble for carrying these documents?"

He leaned back on his chair, stretched out his legs. "I would never put you or my baby in any danger. That's why I'm accompanying you inside the plane."

The envelope was in my carry-on bag when I boarded Sabena Airlines. Escorted by Bolingo, I took my seat in the first-class section, and he said goodbye. I was in my second trimester, and he had insisted that I not travel in coach. "It's a long trip, and you need to be comfortable," he had said.

A husky, brown-skinned man with a square face, who had tried to make eye contact from across the aisle, approached me when we reached Zaventem Airport in Belgium. His intense stare made me self-conscious about the documents in my carry-on luggage and my stomach begun to churn.

"Madame *ou* Mademoiselle?" he asked, staring at my pregnant stomach with a smirk. "I'm Citoyen Mbolivu, chief of protocol. I met you the night your dancers performed for the *maréchal*. How are you?"

I wiped my sweaty palms on my pants, noticed his broad neck and the hair inside his ears. I accepted the hand he offered and held on tightly to my carry-on bag with my free hand.

"Citoyen Bolingo accompanied you inside the plane," he went on, in a soft but disturbing voice. "You must be special to him."

I looked away, annoyed by the indiscretion.

"I stopped by to see you at the institute last week, but you were home sick. I was going to look for you again after this trip."

I shifted my weight that suddenly felt too heavy for my swollen feet. "What is this in reference to?"

"The *maréchal* instructed me to bring you to his private quarters. He was pleased with the interview you gave." Citoyen Mbolivu touched his chin as he spoke. "Our leader likes a woman of challenge, a warrior woman." He lowered his hand and continued, "When he heard you were home sick, he told me to wait until you were better. He wants you in your best condition when he sees you. Maybe he can help you understand the politics of authenticity." He smiled again, winked in a manner that suggested complicity. "I guess he'll have to wait some long months. When are you coming back to Kinshasa?"

"At the end of the summer vacation." My leg muscles felt limp, and I yearned to sit down. "Please excuse me." As I rushed out of his sight, he said something I didn't hear.

I breathed freely again when I came out of the restroom and saw that he was gone. I had heard of the *maréchal*'s voracious appetite for women, but I didn't imagine the extent of his audacity. It occurred to me then that it wasn't just because of protocol that Bolingo had asked me not to linger the night of the performance.

I joined a line, waiting to go through customs. "Nothing to declare," I said to the clerk and walked out. Passengers received greetings from loved ones, and I waited to the side until a man in a brown cardigan sweater approached me. "I hope you had a good flight," he said.

"It's nice to see you again."

"How about a snack?" Citoyen Ngandu asked, relieving me of my carry-on bag.

I followed him to a corner in an airport coffee shop. Once we sat down he said, "I spoke with Citoyen Bolingo this morning. I'm going to call him again when I get home to tell him that we met."

"Could you please hand me the bag?"

I removed the envelope and passed it to him.

"Thank you for your help."

Someone hugged me from behind.

"Cynthia!" I cried, hugging her back.

"My God, aren't we fat!"

"You look good though," Pépé said, waiting for her turn to hug me.

Heading out of the airport to the parking area, I asked Pépé about Antoine.

"He's going to work as a New York correspondent," she informed me. "I just found him an apartment."

Cynthia, looking into the rearview mirror, asked why I had kept my pregnancy a secret.

Pépé followed suit: "Yes, how come you never told us?"

"I'm not comfortable talking about it."

"Why not?" asked Cynthia, a dubious expression on her face.

"It's a complicated situation."

Cynthia glanced at me as she drove toward the Whitestone Bridge. "Why is that?"

"I told you he already has a wife."

"I thought you didn't mind being a second wife," Pépé commented from the back.

"I never said that." I turned on the radio, hoping they would understand I didn't feel like talking anymore. Leaning my head on the headrest, I closed my eyes and pretended to fall asleep, thinking about what I was going to say to Mom and Dad. It was clear to me that they wouldn't take it as smoothly as Cynthia and Pépé did. The soft sound of Ella Fizgerald's voice coupled with fatigue helped me doze off in the middle of my thoughts.

I opened my eyes when Cynthia beeped the horn. Mom and Dad rushed out as the car reached the driveway. I had looked forward to the comfort and security their open arms always provided, but their look of disapproval and the tension in their eyes intimidated me as I dutifully hugged them. Mom's lower lip trembled and the lines on Dad's forehead did not go unnoticed. Other than Mom's thinning hair and Dad's slightly larger frame, they both looked exactly the same.

"Can you girls excuse us?" Dad said to Cynthia and Pépé. "Margaret and I would like to have a word with Iris."

"How are you feeling?" Dad asked.

"Fine." I wanted the small talk to stop so we could get to the heart of the matter. "I'm sorry. I didn't plan the pregnancy," I told them, turning away from their stares.

"I'm assuming you've seen a doctor," Mom said in an even tone.

I nodded yes, but avoided eye contact.

Dad cleared his throat. "You didn't even have the decency to inform us."

A knot tied my stomach. "I thought it would be better to tell you in person."

Dad crossed his legs, peered at me. "What do you mean?"

I shrugged and wiped my tears with a bare hand.

Mom handed me a tissue then folded her hands in front of her. "Is the father the man you told me about when I asked you if you were seeing someone?"

"Yes. But I didn't tell you he's married," I said in a voice that was probably too casual.

"Jesus Christ!" Dad exclaimed.

"You didn't think getting pregnant by a married man was something worth mentioning?" Mom shouted, which was unusual for her to do.

Unable to think of anything better to say, I told them I didn't remember to mention it. I lifted my chin from my chest and saw anger in their eyes.

"What were you thinking then?" Mom asked in a lower voice.

Dad shook his head. "I thought we did a better job raising you."

At that point, I decided it might help to tell them Bolingo was coming in a few weeks to ask for my hand.

Dad raised his eyebrows and clucked his tongue. "Am I missing something here?"

"Didn't you say he was married?" Mom's voice had recovered its calm.

"I'm going to be his second wife," I said, and paused to detect the effect of my words, but they were too dumbfounded to react. "I'm in love with Bolingo—"

"I need to talk to your mother alone," Dad interrupted, his voice coated with controlled anger.

I decided to take a long shower. I stared at my naked body in the full-length mirror and realized my breasts were tender and swollen; the veins were visible and the nipples darker. A gush of crystal liquid sprinkled on my head, tears of frustration flowed like the water from above, relieving some of the stress the long trip and the conversation with my adopted parents had caused.

A soft knock at the door woke me up the next morning. Mom stood in front of my bed. "Your dad and I feel that now that it's a *fait accompli*, we have no choice but to support you." She sighed, sat on the edge of the bed. "Tell me about this man."

"He's a good man."

"Have you thought about what it would be like to live in a triangle?"

I didn't answer.

"Do you realize *you* will be the intruder and not the first wife?"

Frustration brought tears to my eyes again. "I know I'll be second-rate. But I'm prepared to live with that."

"Are you sure?"

I nodded yes.

"How far along are you in this pregnancy?"

"Six months."

Mom stood up, started to walk out. "Tell me his name again."

"Bolingo."

"Nice name," she said and left the room.

When I finally came out of my room an hour later, I noticed the changes in the living room for the first time. A Palmer Hayden still life of a Fang mask from Gabon and a Bakuba raffia cloth from Zaire hung over the fireplace, replacing a painting by the same artist of young dancers doing the Lindy Hop. I wondered what happened to it. Other than the new curtains, nothing else had changed. The familiar steady ticking of the grandfather clock made me realize I was happy to be home.

CHAPTER 15

When you get into a tight place, and everything goes against you
till it seems as if you couldn't hold on a minute longer,
never give up then, for that's just the place
and time that the tide'll turn.
—Harriet Beecher Stowe

What happened the evening before Bolingo's arrival set the stage for what was to come. Even though I was glad no one mentioned my pregnancy or my second-wife status, my family behaved in a way that made me wonder if they would say anything that might offend him. But reflecting back, I think I was just being overly sensitive and defensive.

I sat on a barstool next to Mom, who was writing a grocery list and planning the next day's dinner, while Cynthia took dishes out of the dishwasher.

"I'm not sure what an African would eat," Mom said, looking at me.

I thought she was talking about him in a condescending manner, as though he were coming straight from the bush. "Bolingo is a wordly man," I said, trying to stay calm.

"No one is doubting that," Cynthia butted in. "But what does he like to eat?"

"Good food," I said with a hint of annoyance.

"How about a leg of lamb, garlic potato, string beans, and a salad?" Mom suggested.

"That sounds good," I answered in a neutral voice.

Mom peered at me with a worried look on her face. "Would it be all right to serve wine?"

"He likes good wine," I replied dismissively.

I pulled into the driveway in Cynthia's car and noticed a head behind the living room curtain. It had to be Cynthia's. The door opened before I could use my key or ring the bell, and there she was, smiling. Mom, Dad, and Latham showed up behind her.

"Welcome to our home," Dad said to Bolingo in French, and introduced himself.

The others did the same.

"Please, come this way," said Mom, leading us to the living room, where a tray of hors d'oeuvres sat on the coffee table. About half an hour later, we moved to the dining room for dinner. The conversation, a mixture of French and English, varied from African art to the United States policies toward Africa. Bolingo had an excellent command of English and I was pleased that everyone seemed relaxed and comfortable.

But that didn't last. Looking into darkness through the window and holding a cappuccino in one hand, Latham announced, in English, that he was concerned with the demographic problem polygamy has created in Africa. "It's important to hold onto traditions, but it's even more important to live within the realm of a modern world," he concluded, placing his cup back in its saucer.

"True," Bolingo argued in French, "but Africans are aware of the problem. They're not having as many children now, whether they live in polygamy or monogamy. One woman used to have ten or twelve children, but that's changing. Everyone knows about birth control now."

"What's wrong with having one woman at a time?" Latham challenged.

Instead of saying something in Bolingo's defense, I

agreed with Latham, who I knew must have been thinking about my living thousands of miles away from home and being the object of another woman's contempt. Although I had been told the wives often became friends and lived in harmony, I couldn't imagine it. The conversation continued with each one speaking in the language he felt most comfortable with.

"Africa has her own traditions," Bolingo's voice interrupted my thoughts. "Why should we allow the West to dictate our way of life? Polygamy is a long-standing tradition and wasn't considered a problem until the missionaries arrived. I have opted to live the life of my ancestors because I am the product of my culture. Since women outnumber men, it is unfair that only some should have the privilege of having a family of her own."

I sensed Bolingo's humiliation behind his calm appearance and wished for the conversation to stop and for people to leave that one aspect of my life alone. I imagined having to sit through many more conversations of this sort, when Bolingo would have to defend his culture and I would feel a judgmental finger pointing at me.

"If you think about it," Mom said, "a lot of men in developing countries have mistresses, who sometimes have their children. From a social point of view, I think it's better to be a second wife than a mistress, if the culture allows it."

"The anthropologist has spoken," Dad said in a light tone that contrasted with the rising tension in the room.

Encouraged by Mom's comment, I finally decided to speak, but Latham intervened first. "I'm trying to be understanding. But some of these African brothers have more than two wives!" he said. "Don't they think about the emotional and physical needs of women?"

No one answered. They all avoided looking at me, but I was sure they had me in mind, which made me want to scream, to tell everyone to butt out of my life. A lump in my throat, however, now prevented me from uttering a word. I also knew if I tried to speak I wouldn't be able to hold back my tears.

Latham leaned toward Bolingo. "I hope my comments didn't offend you," he said. "I was only playing devil's advocate."

"It was an interesting discussion," Bolingo replied, and I wondered what exactly he meant.

"How about going to the Yellow Bird in Greenwich Village?" Latham was obviously trying to relieve the tension he had created.

Just as I expected, Bolingo declined. "I appreciate the invitation," he said, "but I'm tired from the trip."

"We don't have to stay long," Latham insisted, determined to make peace with Bolingo. "It would be a good way to end the evening."

"If you're still tired when we get there, we can go back to the apartment," I suggested.

Cynthia tucked her hair behind an ear. "I promise it will be fun," she encouraged.

Bolingo hesitated, but finally agreed to go.

The phone rang. Cynthia jumped to answer it in Mom's study and returned to the living room minutes later. "Sorry, guys, I can't go with you," she said. "I need to be at the hospital in the morning."

I was thinking about the way that young man made the violin cry desperately or laugh jubilantly, when I realized I needed to break the silence that persisted during intermission. But before I could think of something to say, Latham spoke: "There was nothing personal in what I said earlier. I was expressing my opinion so we can understand each other. Iris is like a daughter to me, you know."

"Does that mean you don't approve of our relationship?"

I covered Bolingo's hand with mine, broke into a sad

smile. "There's nothing my godfather likes more than a controversial discussion."

Latham raised his shoulders. "Hey, it's really none of my business," he said, and dropped his shoulders. "It's between the two of you."

"I respect your honesty," Bolingo said, then leaned toward Latham. "I was wondering if you could help me out. I'm not sure how I'm supposed to ask for Iris's hand."

"Do it the way it's done in your culture," Latham suggested. "What do you think?" he added, turning to me.

"Of course," I answered, overwhelmed with the prospect of the unusual life that lay ahead of me. I was happy the two men were communicating in a friendlier tone. I sipped ginger ale and listened.

"In my culture," Bolingo explained, "it's a close friend or a family member who approaches the woman's family."

"Let me be that family member or that close friend."

"Would you really do that?"

Latham reached across the table, patted my hand. "I want to see Iris happy."

"I don't know how to thank you, especially since I know how you feel." Bolingo paused. "How do I offer the family the goats my culture calls for?"

"Forget the goats. Just take everybody out to dinner."

The two men laughed, and I thought of the irony of an ancient tradition caught in a modern world.

"I don't think your family will accept me," Bolingo said, as soon as we returned to the apartment and were alone.

"They're just not sure I will be able to cope with being a second wife."

"I see," Bolingo said, tightening his lips.

I sat next to him on the sofa, thinking about the baby in my womb. I then stared at Bolingo with an intensity that drew his attention toward me. He pulled me close to him, and I rested my head on his chest. Rain streaked down the living room window and I listened to its murmurs and to Bolingo's heartbeat.

The next morning we walked around the neighborhood, caught up in the rush of New Yorkers heading to work. Some men and women, seemingly homeless or dependent on drugs and alcohol, moved like zombies in an open field. A few desperate souls pushed carts of empty cans and bottles, looking for more in trash cans. Each morning, joggers separated themselves from others, plugged into their Walkman.

"So this is life in the world's most talked-about city," Bolingo said. "It's scandalous to see how some people live in this land of opportunity. How can this happen in a country like this?" We turned on Columbus Avenue. "These Western countries are supposed to be an example for us. What am I to believe?"

I sat in the family room, trying to block out the sound of cicadas in the background and thinking about Bolingo, who earlier that day had flown down to Washington to meet with the ambassador.

Cynthia turned on the television set, surfed channels with the remote control. "What's up?" she asked. "Is something bothering you?"

"Why do you ask?"

"You look sad."

"I'm confused."

"About what?"

"I'm not comfortable with being a second wife. I'm not saying I want to leave him, but . . ."

Cynthia's clever eyes gazed at me as she brushed her copper-colored hair that smelled of Granny Smith apple shampoo and coiled it into a bun. A soft ray of light bathed her chestnut skin, and I noticed lines of maturity on her face that I hadn't seen before.

"It's a difficult decision to make," she said and shrugged. "But if it's okay over there, what's the big deal? That's where you'll be living, right?"

A patch of clouds suddenly covered the sun.

"Would you do it if you were me?"

"Are you kidding me?" she said and laughed. "I wouldn't be caught dead living in Africa. I will visit though."

The clouds disappeared and the sun brightened the afternoon again.

Hunger pangs woke me the next morning and the fetus kicked. I touched my swollen belly and smiled at the thought of a life growing inside me. My pregnancy was a journey of fear, and my anxiety was like that of an artist during the creative process. It was a period of apprehension that would last until the day the baby discovered life and breathed on its own.

"Good morning," I said to Mom as I entered the kitchen.

She looked up from Margaret Mead's book on relativity of customs and returned my greeting.

I reached for the refrigerator door. "Dad's already gone?"

"He left early this morning."

I placed a bowl of Raisin Bran and a banana on the table. "The baby kicked this morning, and a thought came to me," I told her. "Bolingo won't always be around to share those important moments."

"Is it the fact that he might not be around that's bothering you?" She took her glasses off as she spoke.

"What do you mean?"

She twirled her glasses. "Could it be the thought that he might be with his other wife that you're worried about?"

"I'm expecting his child!"

She frowned. "Is that the only reason you're staying in the relationship?"

"I want to be his wife, but I don't know if I can cope in the long run."

"What are you going to do?" she finally asked, still staring at me intensely.

I shrugged and peeled the banana. I lowered my eyelids to avoid Mom's gaze. My doubts covered me like a blanket of fear and prompted me to understand that I couldn't continue to pretend to be happy with the life that lay ahead of me.

"I can't go through with this marriage," I said matter-of-factly.

"You're welcome to stay home." Mom put her glasses back on and looked for her gynecologist's phone number.

I sifted through my conversation with Mom and finally realized that my willingness to accept polygamy had been illusory.

"How's Pierre?" I asked Pépé, who took a seat across from me in the Manhattan apartment. She looked ravishing with a new haircut; her eyes radiated happiness.

Before she could answer me, the phone rang. It was Brahami, who I had called days after I arrived to New York.

"Iris! Good news!" he said as soon as I picked up the phone. "Dieudonné received your letter. He said he'll make sure Pierre is treated well until he can get him out."

A silence followed. I imagined Pierre smiling at me the way he had at his parents' beach house. I also remembered the bouquet of anthuriums he had left for me the morning before I returned from Monn Nèg, and the sadness in my heart on the plane that took me back to New York.

"Are you there?" Brahami asked.

"I'm too happy for words."

CHAPTER 16

The river can stop you from crossing
but can't prevent you from turning around.
—Haitian proverb

My heart somersaulted when Bolingo turned the key in the lock. I greeted him at the door, eager to tell him what I had to say, afraid that seeing him might make me reconsider.

"How are you feeling?" he asked, kissing my forehead.

"I'm fine," I said and followed him to the bedroom.

The smell of his cologne and the sight of his broad shoulders made my decision even more difficult. After a moment of deliberation, I told him we had to talk.

"We don't have much time," he said, glancing at his watch. "Don't we have to meet Pépé and Antoine soon?"

I composed a stern look on my face to let him know I meant business. "I won't be long." I crossed my arms over my chest. "I've thought about my life as a second wife and decided I can't do it," I blurted out.

Hurt registered on his face. He slipped his arms into a polo shirt, and gazed at me with a tightened jaw as impatience shone in his eyes. "Why is it so difficult for you to make a decision and stick to it?"

"This time my mind is made up."

We walked out of the apartment and waited for the elevator in total silence. I watched him from the corner of my eye as the elevator descended. He stared straight ahead at the red light illuminating each floor number as if it were an object of great interest.

At the restaurant I tried to focus on the conversation around the table, but the words were like a distracting noise to me. Bolingo, Antoine, and Pépé talked about the new influx of African immigrants to New York City, and I thought of what Bolingo and I had said to each other and what remained to be said.

"Isn't that true, Iris?" I heard Pépé say.

"Yes, of course," I answered in a distant voice. A forced smile flashed across my face.

"What's the matter?" Pépé asked, and the two men turned to look at me.

"I'm fine, really. Just a bit tired."

I held back the tears that frequently came to my eyes lately. The others went on with their conversation. Though furious that Bolingo looked relaxed, I had to admit I found his calm and his ability not to display emotions admirable.

Exhausted from the strain of emotions, I went to bed as soon as we returned to the apartment. When I awoke, Bolingo was in the living room, talking on the phone. The puffiness underneath his eyes suggested he had slept little.

"How are you?" he asked, putting the phone back in its cradle. The ticket on top of the open Yellow Pages made me realize he had been talking to an airline agent. "Let me have your parents' phone number again. I want to say goodbye and thank them for their hospitality." There was no trace of anger in his voice. As he wrote down the number, the door buzzed from downstairs. "It's the driver," he said. "Tell him I'm coming down."

The ambassador of the mission usually put his driver at Bolingo's disposal, so I thought he was going to a meeting or to run an errand. But as I reached for the intercom, I saw his suitcase in front of the door.

"You're leaving now?"

His skin glowed under the patch of soft sunlight coming through the window. He looked at me hard with eyes filled with hurt and disappointment. "I'm leaving for Brussels late this afternoon. I want to go shopping before my flight."

My knees weakened when he hugged me at the door. I watched him walk away in his confident stride, listening to his footsteps down the hall. Feeling empty after his sudden departure, I looked in the closets and drawers to find something he might have left behind, something that belonged to him that I could feel or smell. I finally came to terms with the fact that the only thing left behind was the life growing inside me. A bird landed on the windowsill. Our eyes met, and it flew away.

I agreed to meet Paul for lunch. It is true that we didn't agree on the issue of Africa, but I still thought of him as a friend. I remembered the movies, the plays, the concerts, the conversations, and the walks in Central Park.

He waved at me from a table in the back of the restaurant, decorated with paintings of boats and fishing scenes. He turned red and his mouth dropped when I got closer to him. He stood up to greet me, looking like he was waking up from a nightmare.

"Look at you!" he said, hugging me lightly.

"How are you doing?" I asked, taking the seat across from him.

"I'm up for a big promotion soon, so I'm working my butt off."

"Good for you!"

"How about a lobster?" he proposed when the waiter came to the table.

I welcomed the suggestion and ordered a garden salad as well.

Paul stared at my bare ring finger. "So, are you married?" he asked with a sarcastic smile.

I shook my head.

"Then how come you're in the family way?"

The waiter approached and momentarily saved me from the awkward question. I smiled politely, dipped a chunk of lobster tail in melted butter. "You don't need me to tell you about the birds and the bees," I said, feeling uncomfortable.

He took a sip of bottled water and peered at me. "If this is what you went to Africa for, I could have managed." There was resentment in his voice. "Is the father some wild African who got you back to your roots?" he asked after a brief silence, his deep blue eyes still set on me.

"There's no need for name calling," I replied, wiping my fingers with a napkin.

"I didn't mean to offend you," he apologized. "I picked up a copy of Joseph Conrad's *Heart of Darkness* after you left for Zaire. I wanted to have an idea of the place where you were living."

"And?"

"It's hard for me to imagine you among those savages."

"Kinshasa is a city," I said, piqued. "Besides, Africa is stereotyped in that book."

"Perhaps. But the character named Kurtz makes it clear that one can become a savage living among them."

"You're missing the point. According to that book, Africans are irrational and violent," I said, clearly annoyed, "which is not at all true, not from my experience anyway."

He raised his shoulders. "I'm sure there are exceptions."

"Is that book your only reference?"

He offered no answer.

"What do you have against Africa?" I asked, looking at him with fiery eyes.

"Nothing." He reached for my hand across the table. "I've thought about you often and always hoped that you would one day admit leaving was a mistake." Leaning closer to me, he continued, "It's not too late, you know. I will take you back even with someone else's child."

"Thanks for your generous offer. But it *is* too late. I'm in love with the baby's father."

He arched his eyebrows. "Why didn't he marry you?"

I imagined Paul's reaction if I were to tell him about Bolingo's proposal to become a second wife. "We *are* getting married," I said, then felt guilty for lying.

"Then there's nothing left for me to say." He signaled for the check.

Days later, I sat in Latham's loft, watching him set the table for dinner. "Margaret says you're going to have the baby here," he said.

"I've changed my mind."

"Is that so?"

"I miss Kinshasa."

"You miss Bolingo!"

"Tell me something I don't know."

"I usually tell people I never married because being a *vieux garçon* helps me keep the exciting freedom of youth," he said, serving coq au vin over noodles. "But the reason is because of a disappointment. I was in love with a woman who married someone else." He filled his glass with red Bordeaux. "The worst part is that I had no idea there was someone else in her life." He ate a mouthful of noodles. "She just sent me a letter one day, saying she was getting married in a month and that we should stop seeing each other."

"Who was she?"

"An African girl I met in Paris."

"From what country?"

"Gabon." He sipped from his glass. "Sometimes love hurts more than it brings happiness," he concluded.

"I couldn't agree more."

"I haven't been in a serious relationship since." His confession was a surprise, and I wanted to hear more about it. But he said nothing else.

I was drawn toward a nearly completed portrait of a woman, whose features suggested a quiet strength of character. Her ebony eyes were a sea of unspoken miseries; her smile, though timid, accentuated her high cheekbones. I looked at the painting with growing intensity and thought of the photograph on my night table back in Kinshasa.

"She looks divine," I said to Latham, who had come to stand next to me.

"I've wanted to paint Hagathe that way since the day I heard she passed away. That's going to be my gift to you when you become a mother."

CHAPTER 17

I wish you could invent some means to make me
at all happy without you.
Every hour I am more and more concentrated in you;
everything else tastes like chaff in my mouth.
—John Keats

When the plane landed I unfastened my seat belt immediately, longing to see Kinshasa again, to smell and taste local spices, to see the bright colors of clothing, and to hear the popular music blasting in the streets. As I stepped off the plane, the sun welcomed me. Bolingo was not at the airport but had sent his driver. I looked through my mail when I reached the villa and found an envelope with Felicia's handwriting. She wrote that she and Ousmane planned to marry and reminded me that I could get a job in Dakar if I ever wanted to leave Kinshasa.

Bolingo came over every day, but the distance between us had settled in. The pain it imposed was so familiar that it became bearable. He showed no more than responsible concern, making sure I always knew where to find him. He even insisted that I call his house if I needed him. But we were no longer lovers.

One evening as we sat on the couch watching a soccer game, the baby kicked within the cocoon of my stomach and stretched a leg. Amused, I watched the distorted shape of my stomach. "Look," I said to Bolingo, who impulsively placed his hand over my stomach. I covered his hand with mine, guiding it to the lower part of my stomach. He glanced at me evasively and quickly removed his hand.

When the soccer game was over, the *maréchal* appeared on the screen, coming out of clouds. I stared at him and he stared back. The news that followed was the usual propaganda. I dozed off in front of the television set and was vaguely aware of Bolingo covering me with a blanket before leaving.

The next morning I read an article in *Jeune Afrique* on prostitution which prompted thoughts of Marie Madeleine. When I called her uncle's number to leave a message, her sister Huguette was there. She told me that Marie Madeleine was very sick and agreed to take me to the hospital.

Named after the *maréchal*'s mother, Mama Yemo Hospital was shockingly unsanitary. Trash was piled at the gate in plastic bags, not sturdy enough or large enough to hold it all. Drawn by the foul smell of blood, pus, and rubbish, flies buzzed in the air. Employees, from doctors to cleaning personnel, looked discontented.

The room was crowded with beds, where women with rampant diseases awaited death, looking like skeletons with remorseful eyes. Two of them had visitors standing by their beds which were covered with soiled sheets. When Marie Madeleine noticed me, her face broke into a genuine smile that soon turned into a frown. She looked feeble and pained from bedsores, but she managed to wave a weak hand to chase away a fly that landed on her nose.

"*Mama nangai!* It's you. I can't believe it." She tried to sit up but couldn't. "Go . . . home," she managed to say. "This . . . country . . . no . . . good." The little strength in her subsided, and she shut her eyes.

"Are you all right?"

She didn't answer. I stood there feeling helpless, with a

lump in my throat. "Should we get a nurse?" I finally asked Huguette.

"That won't do any good. We should just let her rest."

Marie Madeleine turned her back to us, and I followed Huguette out of the hospital.

"Someone jealous of her wants to kill her," she said when we reached the gate.

It struck me as odd that a law student should be so irrational when it was clear that Marie Madeleine suffered from the disease of the time, the one people were afraid to call by its name. "Your sister shouldn't be in that hospital," I told Huguette. "They're not doing anything for her. Her health is deteriorating quicker there. She needs to be home."

"She can't walk anymore, and we don't have anyone to look after her. I have to go to school." Huguette looked away, uncomfortable with the choice she had made. "I was at my uncle's today to see about the wheelchair he promised to buy her, but he doesn't have the money yet."

"I'll get her a wheelchair and pay someone to take care of her at home. That way she can be with family. Come see me tomorrow."

When Bolingo heard about my visit to Mama Yemo Hospital that evening, he was beside himself. "You've become suicidal," he said, annoyed.

"What do you mean?"

"If you don't care about yourself, you should at least think about the baby. Didn't you realize you could catch some virus in that filthy place? I've been tolerant about your friendship with that woman, but you're really taking it too far."

I couldn't remember seeing him so angry before. "That was a humane gesture," I said, instead of an apology. "I didn't touch anything. I even made sure I showered and changed my clothes as soon as I got home."

"You do know what your friend has, don't you?"

"Of course I know. But you don't catch that disease from someone just by breathing the same air."

"Promise me you won't go back," he said in a calmer tone.

"No problem. She's not going to be there much longer anyway."

I had stopped working two weeks before, now that I was in my last trimester. My students were to continue training without me until after the baby's birth. It had since become a routine for me to sit on the veranda, enjoying the street and the bright flowers on the flamboyant tree, waiting for news from loved ones.

Today there was a letter from Pépé.

February 1, 1986

Dearest Iris,

I gave up trying to get you on the phone. It is impossible to get through to Kinshasa. I don't have all the details, but it seems that there's hope for Haiti and for Pierre. His family is not saying much, except that they're optimistic.

The State Department announced that Baby Doc and his government fled Haiti earlier today. But it turned out to be an early April Fools' joke. The president told the nation he is as firm as a monkey's tail. But we all think it's a matter of time before he loses power, which hopefully means political prisoners will be freed.

I spoke with Papa today. I shouldn't be the one to tell you, but he's going to Kinshasa ahead of us for the baby's birth to bond with you.

Antoine is leaving for Port-au-Prince with a crew of French journalists tomorrow. Too bad I can't take time off from work to go with him. He's going to do a documentary on Pierre.

I'll be in touch real soon, hopefully with good news.

Kisses,
Pépé

Thrilled with the cataclysmic moment in modern Haitian history, I began to yearn for the day the baby and I would visit Lamercie so she could tell me more about Nlunda a Kinkulu.

When Bolingo let himself in, I looked up from the book on pregnancy that Cynthia had bought me. "I had the wheelchair delivered to your friend today," he announced, sitting down.

But I already knew, because Huguette had called earlier to thank me. "That was very kind of you to do that, especially since I know how you feel about her."

"You would be surprised how much I would do for you," he said, setting loving eyes on me. He then turned his attention to the book in my hand. "When you're done with this pregnancy, you'll be able to teach a course on the subject. Did you do your exercises today?"

"First thing this morning." The taped production of *The Trial in Makala* ended. I pressed the stop button on the remote control.

"I saw the chief of protocol today," Bolingo said. "He wants to know if you can put together a performance for a special event in Gbabolite."

"Where's that?"

"In the middle of the equatorial forest. A spectacular place. People say the *maréchal* had Versailles in mind when he had it built."

Evening was setting in. "*Marta, Marta!*" cried the crazy man in his droning voice.

Bolingo looked at me and smiled. I guess he remembered the story I had told him. But my mind was focused on the encounter I'd had with the chief of protocol at Zaventem Airport. The thought of the leopard claws on me made me shiver. I had to find a way to get out of the Gbabolite performance.

CHAPTER 18

There are times in politics when
you must be on the right side and lose.
—J.K. Galbraith

I was not prepared for what came next. Now that I think about it, I should have known that anyone who puts himself in the *maréchal*'s path is likely to be attacked. I think up until then I had it in my mind that Bolingo was practically invulnerable, beyond the reach of the leopard's claws.

"Something has come up," he said, taking a seat next to me on the sofa. "The *maréchal* has heard about an underground political party from one of his spies in Belgium and he's getting nervous."

The words rang heavily in my head, tightened a knot in my stomach. I studied the lines of worry on Bolingo's face and the intensity in his eyes. "Are you in danger?"

"Could be. I just need to act quickly and smoothly," he said without a trace of urgency.

"What are you going to do?" I asked, unable to disguise the worry in my own voice.

"They think the leader is in Belgium. The party members are spreading false information, and that gives me time to get you, my daughter, and her mother out of the country. We talked about a divorce last week," he added matter-of-factly.

Under other circumstances, I would have been relieved to hear the news that he casually slipped in the conversation. But now, the pressing political situation made it seem banal.

"First," he continued, "you're going to have to move out of here. You cannot stay with Amba. In fact, she shouldn't even know where you are." Silence filled the room, except for the humming of the ceiling fan. "I thought of taking you to the cottage," he said after a pause. "But in your condition you should be close to a doctor."

"I don't understand why I have to go into hiding," I finally said.

He paced the floor. "A lot of people know about our relationship. The Secret Service might come looking for you if they can't find me."

Silence again. Immersed in thoughts of what to do, it came to mind that my friend Barbara and her family had gone on their annual leave a week earlier and they wouldn't be back for another three weeks. She had left me the keys to their home to water her plants since her servant was also on vacation. Her place would be ideal. I had met Barbara at a reception at the American ambassador's residence months earlier. She was from Atlanta and married to a Jewish diplomat from Long Island. We had gotten together a few times, but didn't see each other frequently because she was kept busy driving her two boys to their activities and socializing with the other American wives from the embassy.

"I can stay at Barbara's place," I told Bolingo. "I'm sure she and her husband wouldn't mind."

The lines on his forehead softened. "You should call to let them know you're staying there. Do you have a number for them?"

I told him yes. Thank God Barbara's husband, at the last minute, had remembered to give me the telephone number at the house they rented in Maine.

"It will only be for a few days, long enough for me to get you on a flight to New York. Now, let's take care of details.

When your servant comes in the morning, tell him you're going home for a month and that he doesn't have to show up for work. Give him a month's pay. You don't have to say anything to the guards. Let them come to work as usual. I'll take care of them before I leave the country."

"When will that be?"

"Michelle and her mother are leaving for Brazzaville in two days. I'm going to Brussels after you leave. As soon as I get there I will see a lawyer about the divorce. Michelle will attend a boarding school there. Her mother wants to stay in Brazzaville. She apparently has some ties there."

I then remembered Amba had said his wife had a lover in Brazzaville, though at that time I had thought it was unfounded gossip.

"Why do you look worried?" he said. "Everything will be fine. I will meet you in New York for the baby's birth. As soon as the divorce is final, I want us to get married. We'll start all over. This time it will be done on your terms."

"What about your business?" I asked, suddenly concerned about how we would live.

"I'm going to sell it to a Belgian who has been trying to go in with me as a partner. I'll start another business in Brussels."

"So you're giving up politics?"

"I didn't say that. I'm going to operate from overseas for a while. It's only going to be a temporary exile," he said. "I'll be back here as soon as the party is firmly implanted."

We talked about how I was going to get to Barbara's place without raising any suspicions. After Bolingo left and after I had thought of what I was going to say, I dialed the number Barbara's husband had given me and told them I was getting some work done on the villa and that I preferred to be away from all the dust and paint.

As I drove to Marie Madeleine's house the next morning,

the vibrant sounds and the acrid smells had no effect on me. My mind was set on the plan I needed to execute. I parked the car in front of the gate, hoping her mother would be well and that she wouldn't chase me away.

Marie Madeleine's sister Huguette opened the gate. Marie Madeleine was in her wheelchair; even though it was hot, she had on a sweater. The sound of Franco's gentle and melodic voice came out of an old boom box that stood on a stool next to her. She didn't seem to mind the static. I remembered, at that moment, that I never did go with her and Ana to ladies' night, as she had proposed that afternoon at the Intercontinental Hotel bar. Hair braided neatly in cornrows, she looked much better than she had when I visited her in the hospital.

"*Mama nangai*," she said, "I was just thinking about you."

"How are you?"

She shrugged. "I'm here."

"How's your mother?"

"Her mental state got so bad she had to be hospitalized."

The children came running into the living room, and Marie Madeleine told them to go play outside. She lowered the music and smiled faintly.

"*Ozali malamu?*" she asked in a soft voice.

I told her I was fine and moved to the edge of my seat, closer to her. "I need your help. I have to find a way to leave the villa with my luggage without stirring the guard's suspicion. I can't give any details now."

She pushed the stop button on the boom box and seemed to go into deep thought. "Huguette's probably in the kitchen. Can you get her?" she finally said.

I drove with Huguette to Ana's house, also in the Matongué district, famous for its nightclubs. It hadn't rained in a few days so the roads were dusty, and the humidity high.

"Hey!" Ana cried when she noticed me walking behind Huguette.

This was the first time I had gone to her house, and also the first time I saw her without makeup. Huguette told her that Marie Madeleine wanted to see her and that it was important. She didn't bother to change the old wrapper and stained T-shirt she was wearing. "Let's go," she said, dragging her slippers to the backseat of my car.

Once Marie Madeleine explained the situation, Ana agreed to help. "I need to go home and change," she said. "I can't go to Iris's neighborhood looking like this."

"Don't bother," Marie Madeleine told her. "Huguette, show her where my clothes are." She turned to Ana again. "We don't have the same shoe size, but you can fit into my sister's."

Minutes later, Ana showed up in the living room with her face made up with too much eye shadow. Ironically, the outfit she had chosen was the same one Marie Madeleine had worn on the day I'd met her on the plane. Marie Madeleine then told her sister to bring the two suitcases she used when she traveled to Lomé to buy merchandise. We agreed that I would go home and that Ana and Huguette would follow minutes later with the empty suitcases.

"Did anybody come looking for me?" I asked the guard, who was dozing off under the almond tree.

"No one came," he said, opening his sleepy eyes.

"I'm expecting two *citoyennes* who want to show me the merchandise they brought back from Lomé."

"They probably stopped at a *nganda* for a beer or two before coming over," he snickered.

I glanced at the empty beer bottles under his chair, wondering how much help he would be if someone tried to break in. I sat on the veranda and waited.

Twenty minutes later, Ana's beat-up Renault stopped in front of the villa. The guard didn't offer to help. Both women pretended to struggle under the weight of suitcases that were in fact empty.

"Hey, papa!" I heard Ana say. "You just go on and sleep off the beer you've been drinking. We'll manage."

The guard just sat there in silence. While Huguette and Ana ate the noodle casserole I had made the night before, I packed some of my most valuable belongings—among them, Hagathe's picture. I also took a few pieces of the baby's layette.

Huguette and Ana didn't have to pretend this time. The suitcases were quite full and heavy. When the guard noticed me with the women, he hurried to carry the loads to Ana's car.

"Citoyen," I said, looking into his reddish eyes, "if Citoyen Bolingo comes by, tell him to let himself in. I'll be back in a few hours."

I sat in the driver's seat, looking into the rearview mirror to make sure Ana's car was behind mine. The sun peeped through clouds with a false promise. I turned onto a street perpendicular to mine, stopped the car so Ana and Huguette could transfer the two suitcases to my car. Fifteen minutes later, Bolingo met me in front of Barbara's place. He took the suitcases inside the high-rise apartment building the American Embassy owned on Boulevard du 30 Juin.

CHAPTER 19

What is that wall that always rises up between human beings?
—Françoise Sagan

Bolingo left the bag of groceries he had brought on the kitchen counter and looked around the apartment. "I'll bring two suitcases tomorrow. You can't travel with those," he said, setting his eyes on the stained and overused suitcases in the middle of the living room.

"How long do you think I'll have to stay here?"

"Not long. I called the head of Sabena Airlines, but I didn't get him. I'm going to try again first thing tomorrow morning." He sank his hands into his pants pockets. Leaning on the doorframe, he watched me take the food out of the grocery bag. "Be prepared to leave within the next two days. What are you having for dinner?"

"I can't think about food right now."

"But you have to eat."

I glanced through the glass doors. Gray clouds rolled across the sky, and the roaring menace of thunder filled the room. "I'll eat something when I get hungry," I promised.

"I have to go before it starts pouring. Call if you need me. *Tikala malamu.*"

"*Quendé malamu,*" I replied, thinking about the day we would start a new life in Belgium.

The three-bedroom suite could have been an apartment in the United States. It was furnished with a beige couch and two armchairs; there was a glass coffee table in the center of the living room with an Impressionist art book on top. The beige lace curtains blended with the wall-to-wall carpet. Abstract paintings from unknown artists completed the décor. There was nothing to remind me I was in Zaire, except the two majestic elephant tusks on a malachite table.

The rain washed away the stuffiness in the air, and I thought about the day's events. The past was shifting; the future was uncertain. Driven by a feeling of restlessness, I sat in front of the television with a glass of milk and chocolate chip cookies, imported from apartheid-ruled South Africa. Amba's face appeared on the screen. She looked even prettier than she did in person. I listened to her introduce the evening's movie on Zaire National Television, the only station in the country. I grew hungrier and couldn't stop eating. The baby suddenly rolled over in my womb, kicked sharply.

I propped the pillows on the couch, settled in to watch *Black Orpheus*, my favorite movie. A growing discomfort in my stomach and heartburn made me think I had eaten too much. While Eurydice and her cousin got ready to join the carnival float, the tension in my lower abdomen grew. When a gush of warm liquid ran from my upper thighs, I rushed to the bathroom in a panic. Staring at the blood I was so eager to see eight months ago, I let out a gasp, hoped it was only a trick of my imagination. I wrapped my arms around my stomach to protect the life inside. "You're going to be all right. Mama will make sure of that," I whispered.

The discomfort soon turned into sharp pain. Unlike the pains of labor that come at intervals, these were uninterrupted. I wobbled back to the living room, picked up the phone, and dialed Bolingo's number.

A female voice greeted me.

"*Allô, oui.* I would like to speak with Citoyen Bolingo, please. This is Iris Odys."

"Please stay on the line. Citoyen Bolingo will be right

with you." The voice was detached, flat, impersonal.

"Iris! I was watching *The Cosby Show* on satellite. His daughter Denise wants to work in Zaire and that made me think of you!" Bolingo quickly realized it wasn't a social call. The pain and I were one. "I'll be right there," he said and hung up the phone.

Death was pursuing Eurydice at the railroad station. She looked frightened, hopeless. I turned away from the screen. Head hanging, I kept protective arms around my stomach, begging the baby to stay still, rocking my upper body back and forth, hoping to overcome the pain that made me dizzy. My eyes returned to the screen. Eurydice was hanging from a power line, trying to get away from Death, but Orpheus accidently electrocuted her when he turned on the power. Death was victorious.

The doorbell finally rang. I wanted to run to the door, but I was only able to take small, cautious steps.

Bolingo examined me with incredulous eyes. "What happened?"

"I'm bleeding, and I can't get Dr. Blanchard on the phone."

"We have to get to his house then," he said, taking me by the arm.

I leaned on him for support. Sheltered under the umbrella he carried, we braved the rain and the raging wind that accompanied the thunder.

Bolingo sat upright in the car, held the wheel with both hands, and struggled to drive to Dr. Blanchard's through the heavy rain. "Please hang on," he said several times.

Driving around a curb on the mountain of Binza, the car hit a patch of water and skidded sideways. The back end swerved out, pulling the rest of the vehicle with it. The level of pain suddenly escalated, and I let out a cry. Panicked, Bolingo took his eyes off the road to check on me. The car then did a couple of turns on the slippery road. Bolingo kept a firm grip on the wheel and stirred in the direction of the skid. Managing to regain control, he put the car in neutral and brought it to a stop. When the moment of panic was finally over, he wrapped an arm around me, repeatedly asked if I was okay. Even though I felt his fast heartbeat under his polo shirt, there was a miraculous calm on his face when he resumed driving.

I was relieved when the car stopped in front of the doctor's home. The three of us hurried into his clinic so he could examine me. Even though the pain made it difficult for me to speak, I could hear the conversation between the two men.

"Her blood pressure is up, and there is albumin in her urine." The doctor paused. "The placental abruption is due to cervical incompetence."

"How did that happen?"

"When the placenta is not high enough and has been separated from the womb, it causes a hemorrhage. But this is highly unusual for a woman carrying her first child." Another pause. "She's going to need a blood transfusion."

Because the AIDS scare was ravaging the country, Bolingo panicked when he heard the words *blood transfusion*. Dr. Blanchard proposed finding an analyst to process Bolingo's blood, to make sure we had compatible types. The shot the doctor gave me before he left the clinic had an immediate effect and I woke up to Bolingo's whisper, about an hour later.

"Mama Nzari." Hearing him call me by that name brought a faint smile to my face. "The doctor said he will have to perform a C-section," he said, holding my hand.

I almost immediately drifted back into sleep, and he was still at my side when I woke up again.

"How are you feeling?" he asked, stroking my hair.

"I'm drowsy."

He continued to hold my hand while I considered the

dream I'd just had about chasing a woman. When she'd turned around, I realized the woman was no one else but me.

"I need to talk to you."

"What's the matter?" Bolingo asked, tightening his grip.

"If anything happens to me, I want Pépé to raise my baby."

"Nothing's going to happen to you," he said in a firm, reassuring voice that didn't succeed in convincing me.

Dr. Blanchard, who was delayed by the dangerous road conditions, finally returned to the clinic with a nurse. Bolingo's blood type was compatible with mine, so the doctor could administer the transfusion. The nurse then came with a stretcher to take me to the operating room for the operation. A white cotton cloth hung above my chest, leaving Bolingo on one side, the doctor and the nurse on the other. Even though the epidural soothed the pain, my nerves were sensitive to the cold betadine and the instruments in the doctor's hands. A pulling sensation in my womb made me squeeze Bolingo's hand, then a cry from a newborn's throat suddenly pierced the silence.

"It's a girl!" the doctor exclaimed, handing the baby to the nurse, who cleaned the blood and the amniotic fluid.

"Her name's Zati Nlunda Bolingo."

His face beamed, and he kissed my forehead. "Beautiful name."

The nurse handed me the baby wrapped in a towel. "You can hold her for only a minute. She has to go in the incubator."

Zati weighed just four pounds. She had no hair and kept her eyes shut in a frown.

"She's beautiful," Bolingo said, reaching for her.

I fell asleep again and dreamed of a conversation with Hagathe. Even though her voice was filled with suffering, it projected strength.

"Did you love Brahami?"

"I only wish he could have seen me like a woman, not just as a maid. But, regardless, you need to let go of your anger."

"That's done. I stopped judging him once I began to understand the complexities of Haitian society."

"I'm happy to hear you say that because he has enough regrets as it is."

When I woke up from the dream, Bolingo was still at my side. And in spite of the air-conditioned room, sweat glistened on his forehead.

"How's Zati?" I asked in a feeble voice.

"She'll be in the incubator for a few days," he said, studying me. "You look like you're in pain. Should I get the doctor?"

I nodded yes.

The pains that were pulling and tearing me inside responded to the shot the doctor administered. Baron Samedi, the Haitian spirit of death, appeared in a long black tailcoat, a top hat, and dark glasses. His face was covered with white powder. He held his cane with one hand, a cigar in the other. He stared at me with mocking eyes, then burst into laughter as his image gradually faded away.

People dressed in white with indistinct features emerged. I could see them up close at times; other times they seemed distant. The room suddenly grew misty. The morning breeze whispered secrets while I reflected on my life. I was, once again, a young girl running with my cousins in Monn Nèg; Cynthia was smiling at me as she handed me my first doll; Mom and Dad were taking me to Dr. Connelly. I then saw Pépé like I did for the first time at Wayberry College; Brahami was greeting me at the airport. I saw Hagathe lying in her coffin and Lamercie telling me my soul belonged in Africa, and I was holding a trimmer, trying to cut Bolingo's hair.

In the midst of those visions, Aïda Wedo, the *vaudou* spirit, appeared in a fine, translucent sea-blue silk robe, flowing in a light breeze.

Hopes for a future with Zati and Bolingo swirled in my head. Wary of what was to come next, my body was engaged in a battle. But my soul left it behind in its human frailty. Before the doctor could come back with Bolingo, I was choking. I coughed and gasped for air. Bells tolled in my head to celebrate a soul liberated from a body, marking the end of a life. I hovered above my body, and an elated feeling of tranquility filled my soul as it traveled toward infinity. I reached a wooden door, hesitated briefly, and knocked. Engulfed in thoughts of Zati's life in a motherless world, I prayed she would find solace, love, and guidance.

EPILOGUE

Other world! There is no other world!
God is one and omnipresent;
here or nowhere is the whole fact.
—Ralph Waldo Emerson

W atching the flow of clear water from the cascade, I listen to its clinking sound, engulfed in myriad memories. I look into the water to be connected with the world I left behind. I have yet to understand the passage of time in this place. It seems that I have been gone for a while, yet what I see and hear when I look into the water is what happened immediately after my death.

The sun rises along with the heat and humidity. Bereft by my death, Bolingo seems to have aged as he faces the finality that impedes a future he took too long to decide upon. He is still in the clinic, in a room adjacent to the one where I stayed. A glass of water, half full, and two empty packets of sleeping pill samples lie on the night table next to the bed. Tears glitter in his eyes as he stands behind the glass, looking at Zati in the incubator. The doctor walks him outside. With the movements of a robot, he gets into his car and puts on his sunglasses. He drives by Catholics, Protestants, and Kimbanguists on their way to church. He doesn't even see the chief of protocol wave at him as he heads to his office to call my family.

Dad is still in bed, watching the morning news. He listens to Bolingo then lets the phone drop to the floor. He sits up, buries his head in his hands. He then picks up the phone from the floor, brings the receiver back to his ear. There is a dial tone. He wants to call Bolingo back but doesn't have a number for him. Jaw tightened, he goes to Mom's office. She's busy researching a new book on polygamy. She looks up, sees Dad leaning against the doorframe. She knows something is wrong.

"What's the matter?"

He does not answer. He takes her by the hand, leads her to the sofa in the living room. "Prepare yourself. Something terrible has just happened," he says. "God has called Iris to his Kingdom."

"What are you saying? She's dead?"

He reaches up for her, takes her into his arms. Her body convulses. She sobs, head buried in Dad's chest, and he holds her. Uncontrollable, silent tears pour out of his eyes. The phone rings again. It's Bolingo calling back.

Latham is proudly holding a paintbrush, happy with the completion of his work, anticipating my joy when he gives it to me as he has promised after the birth of my child. Cynthia is sitting with an opened book but thinking about me. She wonders if she is going to be my baby's godmother, even though she realizes the magnitude of such responsibility.

I think of Haiti. The pictures in the clear water show a turbulent world. The end of the Duvalier dynasty has come, and it is a time of jubilation. The streets of the city are filled with joyful people. The rich and the poor celebrate the coming of a democracy and a glorious renaissance. *Dechoukaj*, the uprooting of the Duvaliers and the Tonton Macoute regime, is the order of the day. But the sturdy oak tree, with memories deeply rooted in the mysterious water that nourishes it, sighs deeply and knowingly.

News of the end of Baby Doc's presidency reaches the

most remote villages, like Monn Nèg. The younger people dance and jump while the older ones brandish their canes with youthful optimism. People improvise songs, beat on drums. Lamercie silently puffs on her pipe, watching the festivities. She knows, though she doesn't say it, that death is on her doorstep. She glances at the mango tree, notices a blossoming new branch. She picks up two dried branches from the ground, throws them into the sugarcane field.

Jésula is working in the banana fields. She hears the creaky sound of a *corneille*, the black bird that announces death. She looks at the sky to determine the time of day by the slant of the sun. She straightens up, wipes the sweat off her forehead. Hands on hips, she glances around anxiously then heads home. Tired from dancing with the young ones, she leans against a tree, stuffs a pinch of tobacco powder into her nostrils for quick energy. She hears the *corneille* again, looks up, and watches it fly away, flapping menacing wings.

Later that evening, Marie Ange enters the room where they sleep, lights a *tèt gridap*. The lamp brings a dim light to the room. A black butterfly lies on Lamercie's bed.

It is now early morning. Life seems calm in Monn Nèg again. Marie Ange places a cup of coffee for the spirit of the dead under the tree where the family's umbilical cords are buried.

Lamercie and the other women are listening to a transistor radio. They hear that Dieudonné has been killed in a *dechoukaj* on his way back from freeing Pierre from Fort Dimanche. "He was not afraid to do what he thought was right," his mother Jésula proudly says between sobs. According to the radio report, he died with a rubber collar set on fire around his neck. His burned body was tied to a rod and paraded throughout the city streets.

For the first time in years, Haitians boldly wave the original blue-and-red flag that Duvalier had changed to black and red. They also wave branches of green leaves to clean the air for democracy. Brahami circulates through the streets with his friend Georges, who has come to witness the end of the Duvalier dynasty. They join thousands of others under the royal-blue Caribbean sky. A woman shouts the word *freedom* over and over with hands up in the air, as she walks by Brahami's jeep. He thinks of the young *restavèk* he saw decades ago when he roamed the streets of Bel Air, hoping for a better understanding of life for less fortunate Haitians. The thought reminds him that it was around that same time the incident with Hagathe in the kitchen occurred. *I have to call Iris tonight*, he tells himself.

After hours of observing the open-air celebration, the two friends return to Brahami's house to share a bottle of champagne.

"To the future of Haiti," Brahami says, lifting his glass. "Now that the Duvaliers are gone, what do you think is next? I have mixed feelings about the interim government."

"The question is, can we separate the army from the Tonton Macoute?" Georges says.

"But the army collaborated with the people to get Baby Doc out!"

"That's because they want to fulfill their own ambitions." Georges keeps his eyes on his friend. "Why would you want to be a pope if you can be a god?"

Brahami turns on the television, hears the head of the junta's address to the nation. "*Haïtiens, mes frères . . .*" His hoarse voice reeks of rum and hypocrisy.

I'm still not sure how long I've been here. The notion of time continues to puzzle me. It is always daylight; the soft sun reminds me of manufactured stage light. I am never tired, hungry, or thirsty. The only time anything happens is when I look into the water; this new life of voyeurism connects me to those I love. How impressive it is to watch people when they don't know you're watching, and to be able to hear them thinking!

I take another glance at the water to see what Bolingo is doing. He knocks at Amba's door. She lets him in and tells him she was worried because she stopped by to visit me the day before and the watchman said he hadn't seen me.

"What happened?" she wants to know.

"We had a girl. Her name is Zati."

Amba becomes anxious when she notices the lines of pain on Bolingo's face. "Is the baby fine? She wasn't due for another month."

"The baby's fine, but Iris is gone."

"What?"

He shifts his weight. "Iris is gone!"

"*Mama nangai e-e-e-e!*" Amba cries out loud, resting her hands on her head. Bolingo wraps an arm around her shoulder to keep her calm.

Minutes later, when he reaches home and notices his wife's Range Rover is gone, he remembers she was leaving for Brazzaville with their daughter that morning. He drops heavily on his bed, allowing his heart to drown in sorrow. In a kaleidoscopic vision, he sees me as he did the first time, in leotard and tights, teaching a dance class at the National Arts Institute. Eyes closed, he summons the hours that preceded my death.

He was watching a *Cosby Show* episode in the living room with Michelle when his wife said, "Mademoiselle Odys is on the phone—or is it Madame Bolingo?"

He walked past the alley of tropical foliage. Drenched in rain before he even reached his car, he went back inside the house, replaced the wet pajama top with a polo shirt, put on his shoes, and grabbed an umbrella.

Bolingo shakes the past out of his mind. There is a lot to do. First, he has to pick up Pépé at N'djili Airport.

Head resting on the cushioned seat, Pépé pays no attention to the sights of one of Africa's famed cities, already tired from the thought of the sad formalities she will have to complete during her short stay in Kinshasa. Bolingo takes her to the Intercontinental Hotel where, holding back tears, she washes her face in cold water. She meets Bolingo down at the bar, tells him Mom and Dad want me buried next to Hagathe.

He has no objections. "I'm going to Haiti with you for the funeral," he tells her.

I still don't know what my fate will be. But it seems that nothing will happen in this new life until I have completed this writing task. Hopefully, Aïda Wedo will comply and get my story into the hands of my daughter. Then what? Perhaps I will be united with Hagathe and might even meet Nlunda a Kinkulu. I would like to ask her about the Africa she knew.

Bolingo and Pépé are now standing behind the glass window watching Zati sleep peacefully, oblivious to the turmoil of anxieties we're all doomed to experience sooner or later in life. Tears flow down Pépé's cheeks onto her linen dress. He wraps a strong arm around her frail shoulders, hands her a white handkerchief. A throbbing on one side of his head weakens him, and he shifts his weight. Walking at the pace of an aged man, Bolingo goes to the restroom, dabs cold water on his face. As he gazes into a mirror, I smile at him.

Acknowledgments

I would like to gratefully acknowledge my cousin Jessica Augustave Alexander for her unconditional encouragement and support. I also thank my late cousin Danielle Avin and my friends Raymond Blanks, Crispin Grey-Johnson, Patricia Groins, Eric Grossman, John Labonne, Denyse Leslie, Lisa Miller, Guitèle Nicoleau, Donna Peters, and Shelia Rule. My sincere appreciation is extended to each of you.

I would like to especially acknowledge and thank Marva Allen and Regina Brooks of Open Lens for their tireless efforts on behalf of the publication of *The Roving Tree*; Johnny Temple, Ibrahim Ahmad, and the staff at Akashic Books; Ali Mortensen for the book cover design; and Clarence Reynolds for his editorial input. For her guidance and encouragement, I am deeply grateful to Marie D. Brown and am indebted to her for her patience, dedication, thoughtful insights, and mostly for believing in me.

Each of you have been my *lakou*, my support system, in the realization of *The Roving Tree*.

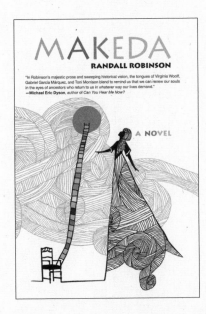